Impossible Fru

A Selection of   Speculative Stories

Gary J. Mack

IMPOSSIBLE FRUIT BY GARY J. MACK

The Magpie's Call, The Dreams of Aeflynn Valkslander and Translation all first appeared in Kyanite Press Volumes 1 Issue 6 (2019), Volume 2 (2020) issue 1 and 2, respectively. Originally edited by BK Bass and Sam Hendricks.

This collection was edited by Catherine Cooke.
Cover by David Collins @CoverCreatorDC (Twitter)

Gary's Twitter @gjm2602

Dedicated to my mother, Mavis Mack who knew I liked books and writing, but never lived to see me published.

AUTHOR'S NOTE

This collection is a melting pot of my ideas - the first year of my short story writing history, encapsulated in a single volume. Some of the ideas are new; others have been around twenty to thirty-odd years and are quite well developed. I have been a writer all my life; the only difference now is that I finish the stories. That has been the key lesson. Finish the story, then go back and edit it. Too often I would fiddle with opening lines until I was bored.

I need to thank my late mother for teaching me to read at an early age, buying me my first book at the age of six: *Doctor Who and the Pyramids of Mars* and my first typewriter for my eleventh birthday. I also must thank my wife Jacey and children Nate, Cam, and Ewan for putting up with a work-away dad. It was those long nights in board and lodgings in Gloucester where most of these tales were finally hatched.

I would also like to thank my readers: Sam and James Alcock, Carol and Jason Saunders, Sam and Mark Baker-Smith, John James Dadd, Stu and Sophie Dunn, and Jacey who took time out to read both this volume and *The Magpie's Collection.* In addition, I would also like to thank Brian (BK) Bass and Sam Hendricks of Kyanite Publishing for releasing three of these tales through their wonderful but short-lived magazine, *Kyanite Press*. Finally, Catherine Cooke who waved her magic wand over my messy manuscript, and David Collins whose artwork has sets this cover alight.

Part One of this collection explores some of my recent ghost story ideas, focussing on the eternal villain that is Isabelle the witch, and her Magpies – her serial killers. *The Magpie's Call* is a prelude to my first novel *The Magpie's Collection*, and is essentially a ghost story. A new story, *The Lure of Magpie Farm* dips further into that ghostly world and explores other evils residing in a place where hope is forgotten. *The Embroidered Handkerchief* features one of the key characters from the forthcoming novel, Inspector Maisie Price, as a young girl.

Part Two is called *Robots and the Future*. I grew up reading Isaac Asimov and Arthur C. Clarke - so I was always going to write about robots and the brave new world. There are many tropes purposefully woven into these early stories; I needed to get them out of my system. I've tried to examine love, hope and loss through the eyes of artificial beings.

Part Three is a collection of longer stories, set in my Skyfliers universe. Characters such as Adam, Bargo, Gus, Van, Fay, and Flynn have been around for many years. *The Dreams of Aeflynn Valkslander*, one of my first published pieces, is the first three chapters of a book I started to write some ten years ago - topped and tailed into a self-contained story.

Parallelapocalypse is set thousands and thousands of years earlier and is an origin story for the Skyfliers universe, where a group of heroes save parallel Earths from danger. *Parallelapocalypse* and *Immortal* feature Large Pockets, the big blue furry alien and Leader of the University of Worlds, a group of scientists who protect our own world across all dimensions. These stories flit between gaslight and high fantasy, two of my favourite reading genres.

Part Four is me experimenting with a female hero (heroine?). I'm a he/him, so it's a push for a writer to try and represent other genders or someone without bias. *Translation* is possibly my personal favourite in this collection. Elli Chambers is a character who features in my forthcoming second novel, the space opera currently called, *Diamond Chamber Memories.* In *Translation,* Elli is a data archaeologist trying to piece together the story of a dying civilisation. *Petal the Assassin,* on the other hand, is a whimsical piece reflecting the ever-changing nature of heroes and anti-heroes; an early exercise in trying to surprise the reader.

I hope you enjoy reading this, my first collection, as much as I did writing the stories. Short stories, to me, are always more of a challenge than longer pieces, so I hope I have done them justice. I want to make you think, make you scared, make you smile and make you cry. If these stories do all those things, then as a writer I'm happy.

Thanks for reading.
Gary, Lichfield, December 2020.

PART ONE: THE MAGPIE CURSE

THE MAGPIE'S CALL

Owain Pleasant stood silently surveying Magpie Farm, like an ancient king cataloguing his lands. He looked across at the beautiful farmhouse, surrounded by acres of fertile land, and thought, *I could do so much with this place. If it were mine.*

The Farm had an attraction - despite its infamy - there was a lure, some imperceptible tie that drew him to the place. He had found himself here many times in the recent past, not really knowing why. He often got in his car and drove the two miles into the countryside just to look around. Every time he imagined a vibrant site, farming, apartments for holidaymakers, animals for breeding. Imagining another life. It felt like an addiction. He needed Magpie Farm and he would have it. It was meant to be.

No wonder the late Terrance Cobden had wanted to keep this for himself. Why had he never moved in? Because Cobden had ended up in prison. What a fool. Magpie Farm was full of potential. It now lay dormant as the courts and the accountants settled Cobden's estate.

Owain strolled up to the farmhouse and looked through one of the windows. The building had not been entered since the late 1990s when George O'Neill had gone missing. They had never found him, even though the investigation had reached as far as Australia, where George's ex-wife Frances had gone to live.

O'Neill, if you listened to the tabloids, had allegedly crossed the world to get away from the farm. According to the investigation, however, the person who ended up in Australia and ultimately deported, was a goon on Cobden's payroll. O'Neill had apparently vanished. Many believed Cobden had been behind the disappearance, but it had never been proven.

It had been surmised that O'Neill had already sold the farm to Cobden by the time he went missing. It had been also alleged, during the investigation, that Magpie Farm had been sold under duress. Cobden had not moved in during the intervening years between the disappearance of O'Neill and his eventual imprisonment, because it would have been such a contentious move. Public opinion was so very easily swayed; Cobden's defence lawyers were at pains to prevent anything impeding a fair trial. Cobden had eventually been convicted on a technicality linked to money laundering, not of killing George. And George had never been found.

So much mystery.

Owain's detective inquisitiveness gripped him like a vice. Would this curiosity consume him when he lived here, he wondered? Despite regular requests, Owain had not been permitted to investigate the farm's crimes as a cold case. He *was* slightly worried there *were* bodies buried on site, however.

Young women had disappeared in the region; local rumour had it that perhaps O'Neill might have been responsible. There were mutterings about O'Neill being a violent pervert and that Cobden might have acted to put an end to O'Neill's murderous ways. Then there was the mystery of the missing twins. Cobden's men, Mark, and Geoff Broad, both with learning difficulties, who had never returned home to their mother after O'Neill had disappeared.

Owain sighed, momentarily forgetting the past. Magpie Farm was stunning. Who would not want to live here? He longed to leave the police force, to start again. Magpie Farm could be the making of him. He just felt it in his bones.

He wanted to be the Magpie of Magpie Farm, treasuring this place like a shiny possession.

After a final longing gaze, he headed for his car, crossing to the other side of the yard past the corrugated barn towards his BMW. He did not want to leave, but duty called; he had things back at the office that could wait no longer.

He shivered; he put it down to anticipation, it was, after all, well over twenty degrees in the shade.

If he had listened more carefully to the leaves rustling in the surrounding trees, he would have heard a long dead voice whisper:

My new Magpie.

Jennie Cobden pulled off her shoes. Exhausted, she threw them across the room. The day had been a strange one: a mixture of stress and relief, with the burial of her estranged father Terrance. She was home now, and all the stress was coming out as tears.

Terrance Cobden had been her Tuesday father.

He'd lived many lives at once. A natural bigamist. He had been betrothed to Sheila her mother and Miranda, although thankfully he did not end up marrying any of the girlfriends who had been named at the trial.

She had grown up with him visiting on Tuesdays. Every week, he brought her chips and a five-pound note. Chips from the same chip bar, with gravy as she liked, and the same amount of money; as far back as she could remember, until three years before he died. That was when he had been imprisoned, and like his Tuesday promises, the fivers had devalued.

For many years Jennie had thought that he was a businessman, that his work kept him away from home. His constant weekend absence should have given it away. As a child, however, you accept things on face value, and if that face was often absent, you tended to not miss it.

Her mother Sheila seemed to be happy with the arrangement. When it came out later that he was a criminal mastermind, Jennie had found that he had bought her mother's silence. Moreover, to buy her silence, her father had given Sheila a regular healthy maintenance payment for Jennie's upkeep, as well to cover the mortgage.

Cobden and his other wife Miranda had no surviving children; Miranda herself had died years before her husband. So, at the funeral, the attendees were sparse, consisting of herself, her mother, one of Terrance's old flames and the odd retired criminal. Jennie was glad to be out of the lies. Her life had been too many false smiles and weak handshakes. *She longed for someone to sweep her off her feet.*

Jennie had been left Magpie Farm in her father's will, along with a small fortune of cash that probate had awarded to her. It was a small but legal slice of the wealth her Tuesday father had amassed. It still added up to nearly a million pounds. That was a lot of fivers.

She would sell the farm of course. It was shrouded in too much mystery.

She closed her eyes. Despite the dark thoughts hanging over her, she soon fell asleep and involuntarily smiled for the first time that day. Tomorrow was the start of the rest of her life. Tomorrow was her birthday, and she had a job interview.

Jennie looked up from behind the front desk and flashed a smile at the man who kept coming into the branch to ask about mortgages. He was cute. Older than her, say by about ten years, so that would put him in his mid-thirties; the tight shirt he wore said he was athletic. He had a mop of unruly tousled hair and stubble: that, she would have to work on.

Jennie had been paying a lot of attention to him over the last few days. His name was Win. A strange little name. Winston? Owen? He was a Detective Chief Inspector, according to Dorothy the cleaner and that made him a catch.

"Morning, Miss ehm?" he said. Why the intoned question? Her mother's maiden name was clearly displayed on her badge. She had dropped the Cobden.

"Morgan," she replied, a slight smile on her lips.

"Do you have any details on that new tracker mortgage?"

He was shuffling like a kid who wanted sweets but was too afraid to ask. She sighed kindly. This was painful. *Put him out of his misery.*

"Meet me for a drink after work tonight if duty allows DCI Win? I'll tell you everything you need to know about mortgages - in return for a large glass of Chardonnay."

His smile lit up the room.

George O'Neill was a simple man, not stupid. But he *was* dead.

Twenty years ago, he had died of thirst and suffocation and for the last twenty years or so, he still found himself reappearing at the scene of his death, down in his underground bunker office.

Twenty years ago, they had tied him to his favourite chair and had poured the concrete into the wooden frame carefully constructed about him. The concrete had eventually come to just below his chin.

The concrete was Blue Circle. He had noticed the bags as he pleaded for his life. whilst they mixed the dusty mixture with water. It had taken hours to harden, and his breathing became more and more difficult as his chest constricted. They had used the least amount of water possible, so it was coarse and dried quickly. They seemed to know what they were doing.

Water. He so needed to drink. He had remained thirsty for days after they had entombed him. He knew now that he would never need to drink again- he was dead.

So why am I so thirsty?

They'd locked the doors to his office behind them, after turning out the lights. Once, it had been his place of safety, built to protect against the Russian nuclear threat. He had heard them talking about mixing more concrete as they slammed shut the bunker entrance, then, sometime after, he had heard something wet being poured over the trap door. Even though the barn cellar was connected to his bunker office via a long corridor, the sound carried easily. George knew they had sealed him in.

It was the Broad twins who had buried him alive. Nasty pieces of work. Cobden chose them well, to force the sale. *The stupid ogres*, Frances' words echoing in his memory. They obviously knew about ways to kill people slowly.

For the last twenty years he'd asked the same question:

"Why do I suddenly regain consciousness for these short periods of contemplation?"

Purgatory was the answer. He had been an evil man. Although he'd never set foot in a church as an adult, his childhood had been ruled by Catholicism. He knew where souls went if they were bad.

You fool. Frances, again.

He still heard her soft Dublin accent, even though she had been gone from him thirty years or more. She spoke to him more often during his contemplation than she ever did during their marriage, particularly after the punch that had broken her jaw. He had been a lonely old man at the end of his life. He now realised he should not have hit Frances so much.

Silly, evil George. I should have never listened to you. This farm was a waste of my parents' money. Mr. Wright should have kept it.

Now he had plenty of time to admit his wicked deeds. His predilection for young girls had led firstly to his fascination, then his habitual abuse of them. He had killed at least four of them, if he remembered rightly, and they lay buried in the woods behind the farm. He had killed other people throughout his life too; he hadn't cared at the time. He once thought he had no conscience.

The police searches couldn't have found the girls he had killed, as their hauntings hadn't gone away. They appeared when the police came, time and time again, during those days when he was slowly dying. He had cried out to the police to find the girls, dig them up, get them away from him; but soon after the concrete had solidified, it had all gone black. For a time.

The office lights flickered, snapping him back to his present - then they went out again. When they stuttered on for the second or third time, four young female figures stood before him. This always happened when there was someone new about.

George looked at the four beautiful young girls, but he couldn't remember their names. Why not?

You buried their names with their bodies, my Magpie.

If he still had breath, it would have caught at that point. The witch's voice always filled him with terror. If warm blood had still coursed through his veins, it would have frozen. Although he was a thing of nightmares himself, he felt horror still.

The girls flickered in time with the lights once more. Then one by one they screamed, just as when he had killed them; but now they screeched in unison. He'd choose an eternity in hell over this reality.

"Don't you go yet, George. The Devil isn't ready for you. One pure of heart approaches. You know the witch wants you to suffer. You can feel Isabelle still pulling your strings."

Frances appeared next to the girls as they began to change from the four beauties they once had been, to the rotting corpses he knew they would be now.

As the girls reached out their bony, skeletal hands to claw at his eyes, George might have screamed, but he couldn't, because he had no breath. His mouth gaped, parched with thirst. He was after all very dead.

My stupid former Magpie.

The day had arrived for Jennie and Win to move to Magpie Farm.

"This place is a wreck, Win. How are we going to get it back into working order?"

Jennie's heart had sunk as soon as she had set foot on Magpie Farm some months before. It was two years after her father's death, and it had taken a lot of persuading from her new husband for her to accept the move.

"The old barns are structurally intact. And the house is lovely. It won't take us long to decorate. The demolition works and second phase can start after we have settled in." Win put a reassuring arm around her shoulder, kissed her head.

They had been together for two years, married for a few months and had lived comfortably up until now. Win was a wonderful husband and loved her immensely it seemed, although he still worked all hours and was rarely at home. She had a privileged life, if not somewhat bizarre. The daughter of a criminal mastermind married to one of the most high-profile policemen in the country.

"Do you think George O'Neill killed them here? The Broad twins, I mean?" She asked nervously, knowing he wasn't one to bring his work home.

Win shrugged. "Forensics never found evidence when they combed this place, so probably not."

"You wanted to re-investigate though, didn't you?"

"The Super said no. And then it was completely blocked because of your father's trial. It's a dead end. Anyway, let's forget about that. We have got a lot to do if we're going to be sleeping in a bed tonight."

They had unpacked the first lot of boxes in no time. The furniture arrived and they arranged it the best they could in the rooms they would be living in. Win wanted to start to decorate one of the rooms, but it was 10 pm and Jennie was tired from a day of moving crates around and building things. He also had to be up for work at six.

A short time later, whilst she was putting their dinner on the table, the phone rang. Someone wanting to wish them well in their new abode, no doubt. Good timing, she had only just plugged their new phone into the lounge socket. Although anyone who knew them would surely call them on their mobile, wouldn't they? Only Granny Reilly ever called on the landline these days.

"Can you get that love?" she shouted to Win.

"Okay," came the muffled reply from two rooms away. Jennie heard him talking on the phone for some time but couldn't make out the conversation. Owain appeared shortly after she had heard the beep of the phone being put back in its cradle.

"Well, I'll be damned," he said. "Someone called Frances O'Neill. I'd spoken with her sometime back. George's wife. She's coming over from Australia to see some of her friends in the village."

"What did she want?" Jennie asked, suspiciously.

"Asked if she could visit the farm. I remember reading in the case file, about the scandal when she left George, sometime in the eighties. He had been knocking her about."

"Seems this place attracts bastards." she said over-dramatically. Then in her best judge's voice, "Are you a good boy Owain Pleasant?"

He was smiling now, as he noticed she had undone the buttons on her blouse. She was sick of the spooky rumours and unpacking of boxes.

"Let's eat later."

Twenty odd years before, as George O'Neill slowly suffocated, Mark Broad smoothed out the concrete he had recently layered over the cellar hatch, sealing George in forever. George deserved it; he had killed Maddie, Mark's sweetheart, there was no supposing about it. Luckily for him and his brother, the police hadn't got to George in time.

Madeline had been a beauty. Tall with curly blonde hair that framed her plump face; she had curves in all the right places. Voluptuous, some had said, whatever that meant.

They were first cousins—not that it mattered in Mark's mind—and they had been very much in love. She was the only girl he had only hit the once. All his subsequent lovers had needed a firmer hand. They had been all clever, argumentative bitches. Nothing like lovely Maddie.

Mark had even had to hit his mother when she had pointed out that he should not have been romantically involved with his cousin Madeline, no matter what the law said. Mark had screamed that it was legal, then he'd hit her again because she would not stop arguing. Paul Stoops, one of his cleverer mates, said one night that his love was lawful. So, mom could just fuck off. Mark wasn't a pervert. Not like George O'Neill, who preyed upon and murdered young girls. He shook away the memories.

Poor Maddie.

O'Neill had never been more than questioned over the disappearances. He had never been charged. Mark's mom had said that the reason Frances had left him was because of George's strange habits. Always trying it on with underage girls, bribing them with sweets, records, and clothes. Mark was amazed Frances had got away and wasn't herself killed.

Maddie had been sixteen when she had gone missing, Mark had been twenty-three and all the sadder, following the battle of wills with his brother Geoff to capture Maddie's heart. Geoff had slept with her first, then Mark had fallen in love.

He got onto his knees with a plasterer's trowel and smoothed over the concrete so that it was level across the whole of the floor, finally using a skimming post to make it totally flat. It was Mr. Cobden's farm now and he liked a good job. Mr. Cobden had killed for less and Mark was determined not to be killed. Not like Maddie.

O'Neill was a stupid bastard; he shouldn't have come back and signed the sale contract. Mr. Cobden had arranged it all to look like he had secured O'Neill's passage out of the country as part of the deal. Old Chappell the postman had pretended to be O'Neill on a one-way trip to Australia.

"Oh, my lovely Mark."

Mark stood quickly, fists up defensively, dropping the trowel. It plopped into the wet cement. He cursed at wrecking the cement finish, then again because he recognized the voice. No. It *couldn't* be. Could it?

"Maddie?"

He looked over to where the voice was coming from. It *was* Maddie, just standing there in the shadow of the barn. He could barely make her out at first; the setting sun touched no part of her, and she seemed formed within an outline of unnatural light - as if from heaven. A nimbus, he recalled – that was what his teacher, Mrs. Butler, had called it, that outline around an angel in a stained-glass window in Lichfield Cathedral.

Then, as if someone had turned the contrast up on the tv, she glowed brighter, more vivid than he had ever seen her. But yet somehow older and skinnier- too skinny. For a while, he just stared, and she stared back.

He became aware that the sun had dropped down behind the barn roof, causing his eyes to cast after-images into his brain; it went cold. He could swear his breath was misting, but it had been twenty-three in the shade earlier.

"He kept me locked in the cellar in his house Mark. He fed me cat food and I drank stagnant water from a dog bowl. All these years he kept me there, Marky. All these years!"

Her words trailed away into silence. Guilt burst through his manly outer shell, tears threatening,

"I didn't know. I'm sorry baby. I would have come for you if I'd known George, had you. But Mr Cobden only just told me. We've killed him for you though, killed him. Or at least – he'll be dead once the concrete sets."

Mark moved over to his lost love. It was a miracle. How strange she should appear just as he was thinking about her. He took her face in his hands and kissed her deeply. Man, she was cold.

She stepped away from him.

"Still an evil bastard then, Mark? Have you learnt nothing in the time I've been away?" Because of her gentle tone he smiled, half laughing, despite her accusatory words. Then caught himself. Evil? He wasn't evil. A bastard maybe, his mother had never known who'd got her pregnant. He went to take Maddie's hand, but she snatched it away with a force that surprised him.

"Let's go and find Geoff." Her voice was playful this time, and she skipped across the shaded barn floor out into the yard, where the sun had fully fallen below the barn roof.

"Once I've had a shower you can have your way with me." Maddie sang her promise, looking at him over one shoulder. Like a sexy movie star. He gave a little growl of pleasure and felt himself stiffen slightly. Yet, before he did anything in life, he always thought about his twin.

"Where's Geoff?"

Maddie smiled. "He's in the woods, Mark. Follow me."

He followed, not noticing that Maddie kept to the shadows. He *was* wondering how she got out of the cellar, though. He would have to ask - once they found Geoff.

Geoffrey Broad couldn't believe he had found Maddie in the shed. She looked as beautiful as ever. She was glowing. He could see her clearly, despite the faint light coming from a small high-level skylight window above their heads.

He could have loved her for forever, but Mark had warned him off with his fists. He was better with the girls than Mark, though. Mark always looked like he would prefer to beat a girl rather than sleep with her.

"I loved you the best. Geoff," she said, as he used a crowbar to release her.

Geoff looked at the bowls on the floor, the only furniture in the cage, as he helped her to stand. The place smelled rank.

"Cat food and water. Was that all he gave you?"

She nodded.

"George is dead, isn't he?"

He took her face in two big, but gentle hands. "He will be soon. Once the concrete dries out." He kissed her gently. Her lips were very cold.

"Geoff, you were always good to me. Shall we get married?" Geoff smiled. "We can move away to America. Leave Mark here," she said.

Geoff frowned.

"Why would I leave Mark here? He's my twin brother. I'd never leave him."

She continued to smile, even though he thought he might have upset her. He loved his brother more than any woman. Always would. Suddenly she skipped away, calling back to him.

"Then we'd better go and find him. Follow me. He's up near the small woods getting rid of the evidence down the old mine-shaft."

Geoff frowned again. "I don't know of any mine-shafts around here!"

He ran to catch her up. His left leg had once been so badly broken it caused his gait to bow. She slowed and he reached her just on the rise at the back of the farm, where scrub became fern.

"What evidence? I've burned the cement bags."

She giggled when he put his arm around her, but her following words had no joy in them.

"George used to threaten to throw me down the shafts when I wouldn't have sex with him."

She was pensive, as if recalling the terror. She grabbed his arm; he froze at her touch; she was so cold. Then she broke away again, running into the trees.

"Magpie Woods, named after the birds."

She chattered like those noisy birds; her impression was particularly good.

"It's nice up here. Lots of magpies. No magpies on the farm. There's only ever one Magpie there."

She was talking nonsense; he had to almost run to keep up with her. She was a lively thing, as she had been all those years ago. *Oh, beautiful Maddie!*

Then he remembered his brother.

"Mark!" he shouted, as they neared the edge of the woods. "Look who I've found. It's Maddie."

He stopped immediately as he got near the edge of the shaft that suddenly appeared in front of him, like the gaping maw of hell.

"Fuck, I nearly fell in."

He hoped Mark was okay, hoped *he* hadn't fallen in. Where was he? Oh, dear God. Wait, what had she said?

He turned and she was a beauty no longer. She looked rotten, like a piece of old fruit mouldering in a forgotten fruit bowl. She was no more than a bloated corpse.

"If you were in the cage, in the shed, how did you know Mark was here?"

She said it for him, mimicking his voice; it sounded like her throat was made of rustling paper. She'd read his mind.

Maddie was smiling now. It was a smile of the dead, misshapen, maggot-cleaned skull, and lipless teeth. He started to shake his head. Tears stung his eyes. He couldn't get away and despite being a giant of a man, he whimpered. He had started to piss himself. She was close, cutting off his escape. The shaft was behind him.

She dashed forward so quickly that he couldn't defend himself. Maddie shoved him with both hands. He tried to grab her, but where hands should have been, there was only image and air.

As he fell to his death, after banging painfully into the shaft wall, her words rang in his ears,

"I hope you like it down there better than your brother."

Owain was late again. Something to do with an accident on the A5 near Tamworth. His tea was cold; it was just past seven and he should have been home at three, after an early shift.

There was a light knock on the door. He'd left his key at work again, no doubt. Jennie moved through the lounge into the hallway and opened the front door. Standing there was a little old lady, who looked to be about eighty or so.

"Hello, can I help you?"

"Hello, Mrs. Pleasant?"

The Irish tone brought back her conversation with Owain.

"Yes, that's me. Would you like to come in, Mrs. O'Neill? I'm Jennie."

"Please call me Frances. But could we have a look around the grounds first, dear? I have lots of good memories of the farm animals. Less so about the house. It's where he used to beat me."

Jennie's breath caught in her throat. Mrs. O'Neill put a hand on Jennie's arm and smiled up at her. She was smaller than Owain's life-size Dalek cutout.

"He practised the Dark Arts, you know."

They moved away from the farmhouse. Frances avoided the small potholes in the yard. "I don't want to chance falling over and breaking a hip."

They continued into the yard. It seemed colder now.

"Witchcraft. With others from the city. He used to make me bathe in sheep's blood. He said it would make me fertile. It just put me in Queen Alexandra Hospital with blood poisoning."

How could Jennie follow that? She didn't need to; Frances O'Neill continued chattering. She looked down at the paper-thin skin of a translucent hand on her arm.

"George's girl, aren't you? Now he was a gentleman. I bet he never laid a finger on your mother. Miranda, wasn't it?"

"No, I was the result of a short second marriage. My mother was Sheila, the daughter of Horace Morgan."

"Ah. Old money in these parts." The elderly woman was silent for the rest of the tour of the grounds. As they reached the barn, Frances O'Neill sighed.

"He is still here then. I wasn't sure if he had come back to sign the house over or was killed elsewhere. I got half the money from your father, but George just disappeared without a trace."

"Sorry?"

"My George. He's not always as dead as he should be. It's taken so awfully long for him to die. He is in the cellar under the barn. The old, converted air-raid shelter."

"There isn't a cellar under the barn. There *is* one under the house."

Frances looked up at her with rheumy eyes, tearful and intense. "There used to be. He had his office under the barn floor," she said, as if it was an afterthought. Then she stopped still, almost insubstantial in the waning light.

"I need to go now, dear. I've seen what I need to see. Do me a favour. Forgive him for me when you see him that is. You are a good girl. Pure of heart, your soul will finally damn him."

Frances patted Jennie's arm.

The tooting sound of Win's car coming up the drive made her turn.

"Ah Mrs. O'Neill, this is my husband coming back. Don't go yet, let's have a cup of tea, I'd love you to meet him." She turned back to the old lady, but Frances was gone.

Jennie's heart leapt as Win's car pulled in front of her. Her mind raced. Her first thought was *don't tell Win*. He would think she was mad.

Owain watched his wife as she painted the walls of a guest bedroom in the farmhouse. She was wearing a crop top and tight leggings. He liked how they accentuated her curves; somehow even sexier all covered in paint. He used to be able to watch her for hours.

If truth be told, his returning to see her at the bank that day she asked him out was not about his interest in mortgages, but to find out more about her father. He was going to ask to buy Magpie Farm from her when she inherited it; little did he realise he would fall in love with her. It had made it complicated, yes, but whilst he deliberated his future, lying in her arms was no bad thing.

My Magpie.

He stiffened, was that a voice talking to him? There were thoughts in his head that hadn't been there until recently. They'd started as soon as he had arrived on the farm. His plans had changed: they now did not involve Jennie forever. She had the taint of a Cobden. Her dad's bloody-mindedness, too. He didn't tell her anything about the visits to the prison, where he discovered that she would be rich once her father died. It had all been part of the plan he had hatched – subconsciously it seemed.

Knowing she was rich in her own right helped his conscience when he was playing away. He felt better, knowing she had lots of money, as he slept with his mistress; Jennie would be financially secure when she eventually found out and left him. Which reminded him, he must pick a fight. He needed to be away for most of the evening. He had a date.

Jennie had been digging up the floor of the barn for upwards of two hours. She was pissed off with Win and bothered about what Frances had said. She had set about the floor with a lump hammer.

Her arms ached from the concussion of lifting the heavy tool and slamming it to the ground.

Jennie had dug out the plans for the farm, which had clearly shown the old air-raid bunker below. She could not believe they had not noticed it was there the first time they had looked together. Had Win overlooked it? Surprising, if so; he was usually more than meticulous. After their row, one of many over recent weeks, she hadn't had the opportunity to discuss it with him before he had stormed out.

She toiled for another hour; the sun was falling behind the farmhouse and the shadows were growing. She felt she was getting nowhere. There was just more and more concrete. Whilst she had never been shy of manual work, her ability to also use the small pickaxe was limited from shoulder height to the floor in each arc, as she wasn't able to lift it above her head.

"Fucking useless," she said to the pick. It didn't respond.

Jennie was about to abandon all hope when she noticed something gleaming, right on the edge of her excavation. She quickly pulled a hand torch from her jeans and focused the beam on the area; it wasn't dark, just very shaded.

Peering closer, she realised it was the chrome-plated edge of a sliding bolt, the bit that screwed onto a door. The little bolt handle was exposed. Quickly, she got on her hands and knees and started to whittle at the concrete with her trowel. Fortunately, it was soft and came away in crumbs. Jennie had soon shifted a pizza slice-shaped chunk of it to reveal the rebated groove around a perfectly square trap door: exactly what she was hoping to find.

Once excavated and wiped clean, she was looking at what she hoped was a lightweight steel panelled door, but damn, there was no handle. She'd pulled the bolt back easily, then tried to lift the trap, but it was not moving, so she retrieved the shovel. If she could fit it into the rim around the trap, she would be able to lift it. It didn't open at first, but was loosening, so she pushed down on the handle of the spade with all her might. With a resonating groaning sound, the trapdoor came free and sprang upwards. She fell backwards.

A waft of stale air hit her at once. Pity Lara Croft, Tomb Raider, if the tombs all smelled this bad. She conjured the image of a mummy in her mind and caught an anxious breath, then at once laughed.

Let's hope the old fellow isn't down there waiting for me.

Ring, ring.

She jumped. It was one of those old-fashioned tones, like the ones you'd hear in old police dramas. Why had the type of ring surprised her? Why was she not more surprised that there was a working phone down there?

Ring, ring.

As the second peal commenced, the lights came on. Were they linked to the trap door? They flickered inconsistently and in the muddled light, Jennie could now see a set of aluminium steps disappearing into the gloom. Was it a clever idea to go down there? Should she wait for Win?

"Let's see, I can always get out and wait for him," she said out loud. Then dismissed it. "No. Sod the bastard."

Gripping her small pocket torch between her teeth to illuminate her steps, she made her way down the rungs slowly; they were shiny and damp and without grip. As she came to the bottom of the ladder, she found a switch, which she flicked. A corridor appeared out of the gloom, illuminated by safety lights cocooned in Bakelite housings, all of them protected by wired mesh. There were half a dozen lights at least on each side.

Ring, ring.

She moved to the end of the corridor and could now see that the large wooden door was covered in the remnants of a War Office poster. The boldly printed block graphics told her to put her gas mask on before she helped others, then listed things she shouldn't do in an air raid: putting lights on, playing loud music, and dancing.

She reached out for the handle and turned it. There was a creak, but not from the door. It came from behind her. The hatch she had just come through was closing; the evening sun switched off, leaving just torch and safety light. The sound of a bolt being drawn back proved that she was most likely trapped.

Oh shit, no!

Jennie screamed. She ran back to the stairs in the low light as best she could. She was doing well until she got onto the ladder, unfortunately missing her footing on the second step. Her feet slipped from under her, and she crashed into the ladder, winding herself and hitting her head, before falling backwards.

The steps at head level must have had sharp, semi-rusted edges; reactively she put a hand to her brow. A trickle of blood ran into her eye, obscuring her view. Jennie wiped the blood away with her forearm, but it was flowing readily. She dabbed her brow again – unable to stem the blood. She determinedly got up, head spinning with the bravery - or possibly stupidity—of one who is trapped and wants to get out. She then slowly ascended the metal steps. At the top, she checked the trap. It *was* shut. Someone had locked her in.

Sorry dear, he's turned out to be the same as mine, a voice whispered; a voice she now recognised, the now familiar tones of Frances O'Neill, the woman she had met earlier.

Jennie pulled her phone from her pocket. Low signal. Enough to make a call, she hoped. She dialled Win's number and waited for him to answer. The voicemail kicked in after his cheery message and a long beep.

"Win, have you shut the trap in the barn floor? I am down here locked in now. I should have told you. Under the concrete in the garage, there was a door. It leads to the cellar. You probably know though." *Beeeeeeep.* "Bollocks."

Ring, ring.

No, Jen. Don't let the situation fuck with you. Be brave. I need to find out.

She swallowed and dabbed at her cut again. Her head hurt immensely. She made it back to the bunker door. Maybe she could use the ringing landline to call emergency services?

She grasped the handle of the door again and pulled it open, with a creak. The room beyond was illuminated in the same half-light. It was sparsely furnished, with a sturdy oak and leather embossed desk and a matching, heavy guest swivel chair. There were all sorts of papers on the desk, curled and dusty: invoices and notes impaled upon a spike. The only other items in the room were a record player and what looked like a large tank.

Her heart was thumping in her chest, like the timpani she used to play in the junior orchestra. Her bladder was full; she would have to wait.

Ring, ring.

Had the phone been on the desk when she had first looked? It was deep red, just like the bat phone.

Answer it, dear. Frances again. Jennie realised that now, she'd accepted Frances's presence – in spirit, at least.

Shaking, she lifted the receiver to her ear.

"Forgive. Me."

"Hello, who is this?" Jennie asked. The tone and timbre of the voice changed. It was Frances again.

"He is cursed." Her voice distorted. *"I didn't realise until recently, that it wasn't my cursing. I cursed him every day he beat me. I cursed him from my own bed or a hospital bed. Australia was never far enough away. When he said he was selling up and coming to find me, I prayed every night for weeks that he would die. Only today, as I died, in the accident your husband got caught in on the A5, did I know for certain. I had to come back to watch him finally be damned."*

"What do you mean you died? You were alive this afternoon?"

Frances appeared, flickering along with the lighting. Jennie screamed. The old lady's image stuttered for a moment, pixelating like a faulty digital picture.

"No one with ill-intent survives a visit to Magpie Farm."

The old lady vanished again. Shit. She realised then that she'd wet herself; a sob came bursting from her, half embarrassment, half fear.

Ring, ring.

Oh, dear, God! The receiver isn't even down. Despite the teeth-chattering fear, Jennie bent down and picked up the phone from the desk.

Turn around.

And so, she did. And there was George, in a box. Just his head showing. Cadaverous, thin-stretched skin. Dead, yet looking almost alive.

"What did you do? Why did Frances say should I forgive you?" Why she asked that question of a corpse, rather than run screaming out of the room, was beyond her.

I killed those girls. I forget their names. I'm so sorry, please forgive me. Then I saw Maddie kill the twins. They were coming to kill me, on your father's orders. Then Maddie killed them, years after she had been killed by me. A vicious loop.

"What do you mean Maddie killed them? How could she kill them if she were dead?"

The harmed must mete out their justice. You will join them. Soon. Turn around.

Compelled, Jennie turned and gasped. In the cellar with her were ten or more ghostly figures. She recognized Frances. The pretty girl at the front had to be Maddie; the hulking great blokes had to be the twins, strangely identical apart from their hair. One was blond, the other red.

Sweetheart.

A man stepped forward out of the crowd. It was her Tuesday daddy. Terrance.

"Daddy." This was fucking weird. Wait. She had hit her head. That would explain it.

Forgive us. Darling, forgive us. We have all sinned and we need your forgiveness.

Tears welled up. For all his history, his criminality, he was still her daddy. The resentment washed away with the tears rolling down her cheeks. She felt so woozy.

Forgive us all and we move on.

She took one step towards them, and she thought how easy her forgiveness would be to give; then as if in answer, they vanished. She turned towards George, but all that was left were his skeletal remains and what she knew was a faint eternal bone-tingling scream.

Then she passed out.

Jennie eventually came to. Her head was pounding. She was also shouting, as if she had woken from a nightmare.

"There are bodies in the house, in the woods, two in the mine shaft. George...in the cellar. Frances O'Neill – I think it was her ghost..."

"Careful love, you've banged your head quite badly. Twice. You've been in an induced coma for nearly a week." He was talking through gritted teeth. He seemed irritated. Why would he be? It was the first time she noticed the beeping of the hospital machines, as she focussed at his bitter-looking face.

My Win. My lovely Owain.

"His wife Frances was in the car crash that delayed you. But she still came to see me?" She could hear that her voice was like that of a puzzled child.

"What do you mean she came to see you? She was dead." She did not like the way he was speaking; it cut through her blinding headache with a pain that was even more intense.

"We moved here. She rings. Then she dies nearby in a crash. Her old man's body discovered in a concrete-filled box, held down by concrete shoes. Your dad had a hand in it all, didn't he? He wanted to buy this farm for so long. He was blackmailing George O' Neill. George liked to beat his wife, George liked abusing girls, and your father knew. Did you know how many young women George killed? I think you did. Why did you not fucking tell me? I could have solved the case! Now I've got other officers crawling all over my farm."

Jennie winced as he shouted those last few words. She looked at her husband through foggy eyes. "The Broad twins."

"What about them? They were never found. Don't tell me you know where they are, too?" He paused as the realisation hit him. "Down the shaft! Did your father confess to you? We moved here so you could protect his secrets. You convinced me to come here. You have obstructed the course of justice and prevented three people from being lawfully buried, if not more. I hope you didn't fuck with the brakes on Frances O'Neill's car too, in order to cover things up. If it weren't for your obvious mental health issues, I wouldn't have known."

"What do you mean, mental health issues?" Her voice was quiet, disbelieving.

"Seeing spirits from the day we arrived. Talking about ghosts when I got you out of the cellar. Banging on about the supernatural. Dear God, Jen. You have messed up here, big time. There is a female officer waiting for you outside. I'll say my goodbyes."

As he retreated, she could not see the smile on his face reflected in the window of her side-room. Her cries of shock flooded her ears, accompanying the music of his orchestrated betrayal.

"Welcome to Midlands Today. It is six o'clock. The remains of George O'Neill, Mark and Geoffrey Broad, Maddie Stark, Gwendoline Shires, Alesha Martin, and Rebecca Charles were recovered from Magpie Woods some six months ago now. Along with two as yet unidentified bodies found under the kitchen floor.

The trial continues of Jennie Pleasant, believed to be the owner of the farm and daughter of one of the West Midlands' most notorious criminals, Terrance Cobden. Ironically, many know her as the wife of DCI Owain Pleasant of the Cold and Complex Case Squad.

The prosecution said today that they believed that Mrs. Pleasant moved to Magpie Farm to conceal criminal activity. During the hearing, the Crown alleged that the cellar where the remains of George O'Neill, former owner of the farm, were found was discovered after Mrs. Pleasant sustained an injury digging there in a near catatonic state. The court then heard that Mrs. Pleasant made a phone call in order to seek help after mistakenly shutting herself in that cellar. It was only then that the mass graves she had concealed were discovered.

The prosecution also alleges that the accused altered the brakes on the car of one Frances O'Neill, estranged wife of the former owner, who had confronted the accused about her father's involvement in her husband's murder. The trial continues.

Owain could not believe his luck at how it had all happened so quickly. Jennie had been put away for a life sentence for killing Frances. Naturally, he had sued for half of her massive estate as part of the divorce proceedings. She had signed the papers, but only at the point where she found herself seriously ill. Today it was sixty-odd years since she had passed. He had inherited the remaining money and property once Jennie had lost her battle to cancer. The bitch had not changed her will, so he ended up having to go through probate, *again.*

Had he ever loved Jennie? Who knows, but in any case, he had settled down and had five children with Chrissie Broad. Chrissie, the youngest niece of the twins, had run into him outside the solicitor's office in Lichfield the day Jennie was arrested. They had loved each other totally and had had a happy marriage. Most of the time.

The Farm and the Bed and Breakfast had prospered, mostly because of the spa facilities they could offer. Thank God. He'd had to leave the police force quickly after his Jennie's arrest. At the ripe old age of 99, the day before his hundredth birthday, he had decided to tour the grounds one last time. He was about to join Chrissie in a care home, as he was too frail to cope alone. His caregiver Lance took him into the lower floor of the barn conversion for the last time, after they had finished his morning routine. The taxi was due to arrive soon.

"Need to phone the wife, Owain. Won't be long."

Owain nodded. He was a man of few words these days. As he drifted towards sleep, he wondered how Chrissie was; she was waiting for him in Moorgreen care home. Dementia had taken her early.

Hello Win. A familiar voice said from nowhere.

Dear God.

"Jen? Is that you?"

He could barely believe his own eyes as she appeared. She looked the same as he remembered her before she was ill.

It's remarkable you remember me after all these years, you cruel little man. You only wanted me for the farm. You cheated on me.

He was too old to be worried about ghosts. He would be one himself before too long.

"Why are you haunting me? I can't have long left. I will be with you soon. We can laugh about it then."

With me? You are not coming here with me, Win. You are destined for eternal damnation, especially if I promise to forgive you. She laughed. *Yes Win, I forgive you. For ruining my life and my world and for committing me to prison, whilst I was carrying our child. Our child who died in me, because of my inability to accept what had happened to me. You bastard.*

"Child?" He said in a faint voice, four beats before his heart gave out, with a final tear tracking down the left side his face.

As his vision failed, a little girl appeared, like a crackling video of old, beside Jennie. Their child that should have been.

The last thing he saw was his daughter's angelic face twisting into a demonic rage as she approached, holding out sharpened talons, ready to rip out his soul.

During the summer of 1485, John De Vere had broken the neck of a magpie by the tattered stable, on the land that would become Magpie Farm. It had taken him a while to catch one and the witch had done nothing but laugh as he ran about fruitlessly with a net. She needed its blood for the "spell".

Rioters had killed his wife and daughters on his former property in York that previous summer, so he had travelled south to find another steading, far away from that tragedy and those memories. The Sheriff of Lichfield had granted the land in agreement that the tithes would be regular and bountiful. De Vere was a wealthy man and friend to the King's Chancellor, Michael de la Pole, so he was not going to be refused. Michael had introduced him to the witch who had come to cast the spell for him.

"No man will kill another on this farm without reproach, no man will hurt his wife or children. No man should use his position to harm those who live here, be it owners, guests or servants." The unusually beautiful witch, who was said to be an experienced crone with exceptional powers, spoke intently. Although he thought she seemed drunk.

"It's a capture spell, my lord." She said, tying a bouquet of herbs together. "When men or women have evil thoughts on this land, then their fate is sealed. Unless one pure of heart forgives them, eternal damnation awaits."

John was not sure whether he believed her. The two pounds of gold he'd paid was daylight robbery.

"The Magpie's blood will seal the spell. Then tomorrow, you may begin building your farmhouse, safe in the knowledge it is protected for all time."

John hoped the witch was right.

Later that evening, after a night in the Hog's Head Tavern, drinking wine paid for with her spell proceeds, the witch Isabelle of Stafford realised she made a terrible mistake in her protection spell; she had mixed up her damned words. Far from preventing or repulsing evil, the spell she had cast on Magpie Farm would end up attracting evil like a honey trap. Forgiveness would damn those evil souls.

Oh well. It seemed a fitting place for a curse rather than a spell. Who was going to live with that insufferable man anyway? No one was going to know.

Nevertheless, guilty thoughts became abundant in her mind and before long, flagon in hand, she stumbled back to the place where she had cast her final spell.

The earth magic welcomed her back.

Our first Magpie awaits your death, Isabelle.

Isabelle laughed. She was drunk and very tired. Soon, her worries were smoothed by more imbibed liquor than her body could cope with.

Isabelle fell asleep on the land that would become Magpie Farm, and died soon after, choking on her own vomit.

Her spirit, however, lived on for centuries, fused with the curse, hoping to trap other Magpies in it's net.

THE LURE OF MAGPIE FARM

Elizabeth looked at me across the room and smiled as she pulled out the knife from the boy's chest. The blood fountained under aortic pressure like a geyser.

I stared back, locking that horrible tableau in my sight. I loved her, yet now hated her at the same time. I had opened the bedroom door; she was atop a young man and smiled, stabbing him repeatedly whilst she rode him. That poor young man. A coital knife through his hairless chest.

Would I ever kill a woman? Kill Elizabeth? I wondered this as I ran towards them, seizing the knife, pulling Elizabeth off him. I was more embarrassed that I couldn't stop the pumping blood, rather than at the young man's post-aroused nakedness.

After he had passed, I turned to her. Elizabeth's eyes were shallow pools in a bloody landscape. I could tell from the way she was looking at me that behind the display of haunted composure, she might one day kill me too; and this might be that day.

She sat there in the farmhouse for a further hour – mute- whilst I had washed the blood from her and rolled *his* body in our bed sheets. I then made us both a cup of tea. I immersed myself in the day's broadsheet, trying to take my mind off things momentarily before I faced up to burying a fellow human. The Hopelessness would not have me.

I heard a click and looked across to see she had my handgun cocked and pointing at my head. I knew the gun contained two bullets.

Elizabeth was backlit by the early morning sun, like an icon - a Madonna. Motes of dust and fibre reflected the light, like planets orbiting a flaming star. She was smiling - a lustful smile, the smile of an angel or a devil, depending upon your perspective.

The ghost of the boy she had just killed stood behind her, but by the nature of ghosts, or most of them anyway, he had no corporeal sway over the proceedings. What played out on Magpie Farm on the 14th of August 1904 was between Elizabeth and I. The lure had brought her here.

"Put the gun down Elizabeth. There's no need for you to point it at me all the time." I *was* nervous, but I thought her love for me was stronger.

"I don't need your forgiveness." She was distant again. Charmed by faeries, as I used to think, but now I knew better. Elizabeth was governed by demons. Or witchcraft.

"I will forgive you, but you need to tell me what I have to forgive."

A tear escaped her left eye, like a sole escapee from Bedlam. Her left gun-hand trembled, but remained fixed in position. The tear tracked down her freckled face, ploughing a deeper, bloody wound, like a blossoming scar.

"I am not ready." Her voice rose in pitch and volume, the determined toss of her head disturbing the motes, causing them to eddy to and fro. It was as if those bright angels now knew her purpose and could not bear to be near her.

We were due to be wed the next morning. A rushed courtship, my parents had said. *To a farming wench?* Well, that had become my mother's favourite phrase.

Elizabeth was much more than that, and far wealthier than my nouveau riche parents believed. They had worked hard, saved hard and forgot their working-class roots hard. She had lived in the farmhouse in recent times to write her book, but before that Elizabeth had resided at Bell Manor.

Her white wedding dress still hung on the parlour door. The guests left uninvited, with cries of "told you so" as subtle in their whispered tones as the thankful prayers of the ghosts around me.

"I'm going to kill you, Robert. If you forgive me."

"I do not think you will." I hoped.

Then I felt a feeling of utmost dread. Those feelings radiated from the dead around me. They were legion. I felt the breath of the bullet coming towards me - I jumped at the percussive sound tearing through the barrier between silence and noise, just before the bullet was about to hit. In a flash of finality, I saw my pathway to Magpie Farm and reflected upon it.

It was rare to have a man in his late thirties unmarried in 1901. Queen Victoria had educated the population of England to live a life in godly marriage, then Edward the VII had led by example by taking every opportunity to rut in secret. I hadn't done either.

I remember my father taking me aside in my late twenties. He had been very awkward and nervous and he had never ever been like that with me before; he was habitually a monster of self-assurance. All he asked me, late one night in a St Paul's gentleman's club, was whether I liked the taste of a different sort of apple.

It wasn't until years later when I met my good friend Arthur - who did like the taste of other apples, particularly the tall handsome African type - that I laughed myself silly, mainly at the thought of my stiff old bastard of a dad squirming to ask me if I was homosexual.

The ghosts had permanently kept me away from long relationships, but I was no virgin. It's difficult to keep a relationship going, however, if you can see their dead ancestors clambering over each other for gossip. It's true, I had occasionally committed the sin of sex outside of wedlock. I am assured that the gods do not see it as sin - according to the ghosts - neither is lying with your own sex. They see sin in other forms: murder, slavery, rape, and abuse.

As my life flashed before my eyes, I admit under God – or gods plural, as the ghosts are quite clear to remind me- that I put too much stall in those dead relatives. I let many a lovely potential Mrs Waterfield go by the wayside due to what they told me, rather than trusting in my own choice and perceptions. And look where that's got me: moments from my brain decorating the Welsh dresser in the farmhouse.

I had also found in my discussions with the ghosts that *they* were not the problem; it was the other thing, which they feared too. The Hopelessness. The almost entity that lived in the place between life and death. What my mother would have called purgatory, but what I know now to be much more horrific than that Biblical waystation.

I'd had my first brush with the Hopelessness shortly after my seventh birthday.

Grandfather lay dead in the main parlour and had been there for two days. A swarm of well-wishers and what Father called carrion crows filed past his open coffin. Edmund Waterfield had been born in a workhouse, but that had been forgotten by the time he was to be buried in his lead and silk-lined oak casket, with gold leaf handles and ornate fittings.

Grandfather had been a violent, miserable man who everyone had hated and he had been vile to all of them – except his wife and his little Bobby.

"Come sit on my knee, Bobby." He would tap his lap and I would trundle over. Daily, he would secret a florin into my hand when no-one was looking and tell me to hide it in a strong box away from prying eyes, before my father gave it all to prospectors in America.

Father said, one day in anger, that grandfather was as tight as a starving man's arsehole and was amazed he had given me anything. I went on to buy my first piano with that money; my secretive, squirreling nature buying some grudging respect from my father - and a puritanical lecture on avarice from my mother.

As Grandfather succumbed to senility, he would slip back into his workhouse ways. His accent would deepen, closer to Black Country than affluent Birmingham. He began to hallucinate enemies all around and once, following an entertaining argument with a myriad of hallucinations, he called those visions "a bunch of cunts". It was a while before I knew what that word meant and I had almost a lifetime of blushes once I found out. I only ever used it once; my nanny fainted when I had called my rocking horse that particular "c" word one day when it rocked over my toe.

Anyway, I'm digressing- and the bullet is coming.

One night, I crept down to the parlour. I wanted to see Grandfather one last time before they nailed the lid shut. What I found surprised me. A little woman, beautiful but petite, standing by his coffin. She looked pregnant; at the point she had died, she was. It was his wife, my grandmother, staring at me. I stared back and smiled. She looked back flabbergasted. How could I see her? It was a rude awakening for her and me. I wonder why the woman, who until now, had only appeared in the photo frame on the living room mantelpiece, was standing in her translucent glory next to my dearly departed beloved grandfather. I suddenly realised why he might have been so angry; he had loved her so and she had gone.

"Beatrice, this is Bobby. Our grandson."

I jumped as Grandfather appeared next to her. I looked from his body to his ghost, puzzled but not scared - as if it were the most natural event in the grieving process.

Then they were gone, and I was in another place. The same place but different. I suddenly felt scared. Ghostly Grandfather and Grandmother were gone. The corporeal coffin and corpse of Grandfather were also not present in this place.

It felt like a dream, but one I would remember forever. The Hopelessness was there, a gaping void of eternity, more evil than the places where curses lay in wait for their call. I was a young boy and yet I understood. That was what terrified me most. It still does.

I ran from the room into the hallway to escape the Hopelessness. Infinity stretched that journey. I thought, at that time; if I set foot on either path, forwards or backwards, I would be lost forever. I did not want to become part of that rank Hopelessness - where the monstrosity laughed and cried equally at a heinous act.

I looked across into the waiting room, where Father kept his working guests before he met with them. I ran to that door as part of my escape from that void of a hallway and turned the handle. The room before me opened like a fusty grave on a frosted night. My breath crystallised and my lungs filled with fog.

I felt it there - the Hopelessness, a personification of uncaring thoughts, a voided optimism. It wasn't strong enough to trap me, however. So, the Hopelessness welcomed me without words. It took my hand without touch and sat me down. My heart thumped, as if it were trying to spend its allocation of beats and be away from this place. This thing was beyond evil. It had evil for breakfast and expelled horror from its faecal end.

"Robert." It didn't speak, I represent it as speech for my own sanity. "Robert. You should not be here. Why are you here?"

The answer was obvious like asking a pious priest why he did not appear regularly on stage in vaudeville alongside a group of tarts.

"I do not know, Sir." Goodness knows why I called it "Sir". Manners, perhaps.

The Hopelessness un-laughed; it was of course without gender, so the absence of laughter was strange neutrality. Within that one were-laugh, it showed me the evil within. No, I am mistaken.

Thinking of the Hopelessness as evil meant there was polarity. This thing was an absence of anything: faithful or faithless.

I saw in it the hatred between the pain of tortured innocents. I saw the feelings sexual depravity gave its victims, without knowing what it was. I saw the way in which men and women used children for their sin and how those children were broken. I saw the bad luck of the unlucky and the horror of the first witness at a murder scene. I saw trees of corpses all rotting, yet laughing at their own plight- and I saw the hope of the un-rescued leach away.

That was the Hopelessness. The gap between good and evil, where the indifference lived. The Hopelessness did not care if you lived or died, killed your victim, or let them live. It wanted the bits between. The victim's knowledge of impending death and the murderer's fleeting regret.

It revelled in the lack of effect it had on me. It was clearly testing me with the images. At that point, I think it feared me too.

Then I was back in my body, waking in the armchair next to grandfather's coffin. The spectres of him and my grandmother were still there, smiling at me.

I would often spend time with them as a child, long after the funeral.

When I was sixteen, I encountered the Hopelessness again.

I had gone on holiday to my uncle's house in Cornwall with my mother, whilst father took care of business in the good old US of A. It was six blessed weeks without Father's constant quips about my aptitude at schooling and my ability to be a man.

By my sixteenth birthday, I was what they called "strapping". I was six feet tall and looked at least three or four years older, because of the dark shadow of whiskers that had come thick and fast after puberty.

Exploring the village on my own, I came across a young woman who had fallen off her bike. She was probably in her early twenties and was holding her leg. She had her petticoats rolled up, which both surprised and aroused me; she was dabbing at one knee with a handkerchief. I noticed quickly that there was a very faint apparition standing over her, a young man. It was her late brother, I just knew it. He glared at me, but was too translucent for me to be bothered with.

"Are you hurt Miss?" I asked politely.

She looked up, her pale drawn face and streaked with tears. She had a crown of jet-black hair and green eyes that blinked a lot, probably because she did not want to be seen to be crying.

"Just my pride." When she smiled, it was like the sun coming up for the second time that day. His Lordship the ghost suddenly became more opaque and rushed at me with his fists up.

Then I was in that place again. The Hopelessness.

The experience was different this time. There was all the nauseating horror of my first visit, but being in the open, the Hopelessness felt even more expansive, even more infinite.

"He is the ghost of her guilt," it un-said. "Holding her back. Not a curse, but worse, a promise. A promise to look after him that was never kept."

Either I must have looked confused, or it was irritated that I wasn't scared, so it continued.

"She promised she would sit by his side as he got over the flu, however, she went out to play and he died. Drowned in his own sputum."

"And she is haunted so? Did you do this to her?" I knew she had been but a girl when her brother had died, responsible for nothing.

"I cannot interact. I only wait. I wait for others not to care. Her brother appears as a ghost in her dreams. She is tormented. She fell from the contraption because she drinks fermented liquids to try to chase away the pain. We then feed upon her drunken apathy. Pain that feeds us, the pain of indifference. "

"She does it to herself, then?"

It didn't answer, but I felt an absence of sound that was an affirmation.

Then the tableau changed. The woman who had come off her bike was now translucent and the man or older boy that had stood behind her was coming for me. He was as solid as I was. He charged me with an expert rugby tackle. Arms about me like a fleeting lover-head tucked into my lower stomach.

I had the bally wind knocked out of me, I'll tell you. We both rolled away and stood. I nodded an acknowledgement, as I would on the field. He had done well, being much smaller than I.

"Lucky I have a lower centre of gravity," he announced.

"Unlucky that you are dead. Stop haunting her. Or the Hopelessness will have you both," I told him, although I didn't know how I knew. He was as handsome as his sister was pretty, with the same dark-haired Irish look.

"I cannot." He crouched, like he was going to come at me again. That was when I saw the shining black rope, a length of polished, malleable coal, out of the corner of my eye. It was an umbilical cord linking him to his sister, but it only appeared once I thought of it. I might have missed it if we hadn't had been in the throes of what was likely a wrestling match, a show of strength. Once I knew it was there, it became more visible. I tried to grab him by that thick vine, but my hand slipped away.

"I need her not to care. Or I will have to go."

"She needs her life. She needs hope." I retorted.

The pustulating black cord stretched from the boy to his sister, pulsing like a swollen varicose vein, undulating like the most venomous of black snakes. It was the link of a broken promise. Normally the cords of promise looked bright, like a cable of sunshine, unless they were unfulfilled: then they were as black as ink. Once more, the Hopelessness had fed me its un-knowledge.

I checked my back pocket. My penknife was there, substantial. I approached the boy.

It was like hitting a low brick wall or a baby rhino. He was strong, this lad. Strong in his attempt to keep his sister in her drunken apathy. He knocked me back and then rabbit-punched me. I staggered. It bloody hurt. I fished the knife from my pocket and flicked it open. Knowing then what I was about to do, he turned and ran.

I took chase, and he ran faster. I could feel the Hopelessness starting to fill him; it wanted our suffering, but it wanted his sister, with her drunken indifference, more. What was I doing? In a moment of inspiration, I stopped and ran back to the woman, who had lived for years with the guilt of her little brother dying whilst she'd played.

I reached her and found where the link buried itself between her breasts. Her brother was a raging, snarling mess behind me by now. He was slashing with his hands and fingers, like the shattered branches of trees, razor-sharp pitchfork prongs.

I asked forgiveness for ripping open her blouse, then I took hold of the link and gasped at its coldness. The man launched at me, taking me down. I felt a claw rake my chest, rippling my shirt; the knife skittered away on the road, knocked loose from my now-frozen grasp.

He came at me again, but I hit him with hope. Hope for this young woman - his sister. All the hope I could muster. I pictured her happy, content, a long life ahead of her. I visualised her chance encounter with a sixteen-year-old boy on a road in Cornwall when she was twenty-two; how she stemmed the blood flow from a terrible injury and probably saved his life. And then I imagined how that grateful boy went back to visit her a year or two later and lay with her, giving them both a start on the hopeful pathway of love.

He screamed as I cut the cord, but I slipped and slashed my hand, then Susan Smart forgot her woes and tore those petticoats to make a bandage and helped me home.

Before he vanished, I saw him whisper, "Thank you." He was as much of a victim as his sister had been, but now he was free.

The Hopelessness un-howled.

The bullet missed me. I had subconsciously retained some of the hope I had for Susan and projected it. I remembered being in her arms once again.

Elizabeth looked at the smoking weapon as it backed up, as if it was the gun's fault. Grimacing, she fired again. I threw myself backwards this time and hoped that bullet would sail over my head.

The pathway to Magpie Farm was writ large again.

Elizabeth Bell had always been an independent woman.

I met her for the first time in London, on Fleet Street. It was the summer of 1901. Elizabeth had caused uproar, turning up at the offices of *The Times*, where she verbally attacked the Editor-in-Chief for not offering her an interview for the position of reporter. I had been in the interview earlier and it was I who had secured the post. She was fundamentally independent and Women's Rights were her bag. She was horrified they wouldn't offer her at least a chance to meet with them. I had sympathy with her for that.

Elizabeth was the daughter of the Bells, a wealthy Lichfield family. Bell Manor stood just outside the small Cathedral city, near the old Roman ruins at Wall. Bell Manor was a product of the age when the nouveau riche had made money out of the Enlightenment and Industrial Revolution.

I hailed from Birmingham, a growing centre of industry itself. I was the urban gentleman; she was the rural duchess-in-waiting.

After the Editor's heavies had manhandled Elizabeth out of *The Times'* offices, I followed and placated her. I turned down the job later that day because of their mistreatment of her. I would never have taken gainful employment with such beasts. Instead, I took on editing work for a local publisher. I had plenty of money, I just wanted to be a writer. Father didn't see it that way, but from beyond the veil, Grandfather approved and showed me the places he had secreted monies for a rainy day - or a Bolshevik invasion.

Both the Waterfields and the Bells had townhouses in London, so after we struck up a friendship, we could meet easily. As our love grew and we started to explore each other further, we had the Waterfield town house in which to carry out our illicit affair. Our property was always empty, as Father was constantly overseas.

Elizabeth showed nothing of the strangeness then. It wasn't apparent until we announced our engagement and I visited Bell Manor. Lord Bell wasn't a nice man. He looked haunted most of the time. He was obsessed with birds, especially magpies, crows, and ravens. Edmund Bell refused to accept our engagement and his simpering wife Agatha just did as she was constantly bidden. No wonder Elizabeth was so fiercely independent.

When Elizabeth and I announced our engagement, I was summarily banished back to the farmhouse, never to set foot in Bell Manor again. I had the money to set us up after marriage, so there would not be any concerns about our financial independence. Lord Bell knew that. In those days, however, if you were female and unmarried, you were your father's chattel, no matter what your thoughts. Elizabeth hated that.

The farmhouse itself was interesting. Elizabeth refused to come to it at first, declaring it "evil." I'd tried to enter the Hopelessness the first night I was there on my own, following my banishment from the mansion. I needed to find out whether I was safe here.

I could always access the Hopelessness, but I found there were parts of the estate I could not explore via that world as if there were a block. Part of me felt an urge to try and break through. One night, one of the first I was there, I tried, and upon transference, I was suddenly filled with an insane lust.

From the shadows, a woman appeared: tall and beautiful. I blush to recall the effect she had upon my body.

"Hello. I am Isabelle and you are a strange one, Robert Waterfield."

"Strange? Interesting opinion from a ghost."

Her laugh was laced with cruelty.

"Too weak to be my Magpie, too strong for the Hopelessness."

What did she mean?

"When your concubine eventually comes to see me, she will be a better Magpie than her father. He has not yet killed for me. So, I remain like this." Isabelle waved her arms about her person, as if to illustrate her insubstantial aspect.

"I will not let you have her."

"Oh, I will. Or what you call the Hopelessness will."

Then Isabelle vanished.

When I came back from the Hopelessness, Elizabeth was there. After that night, she would never leave the estate; not once in the nearly three years that I travelled back and forth from London to Lichfield did she leave the Manor. What she needed from outside, the servants sourced for her; she became nothing more than a recluse.

I loved her for her strength and independence. She had been turned into a wreck by her own choices.

One cold February, mere weeks after she moved into the farmhouse, Elizabeth's father died in mysterious circumstances. Apparently overcome with grief, shortly afterwards, her mother fell down the stairs and broke her neck.

Elizabeth was their sole beneficiary, but not once at that point had I suspected her of foul play. Her father was, as his father before him, an only child. No male heirs lurked, ready to take the Bell estate away from Elizabeth.

The day before Elizabeth shot at me, I knew there was something wrong as soon as I entered my home. Someone else's accoutrements lay scattered about the place: male clothing, shoes. I climbed the stairs and found her in bed with a local man. Charlie Spent, the nineteen-year-old son of the Bell estate gardener.

Spent, I remembered, was a handsome young man; because Elizabeth had been so lonely, I almost understood as I confronted her. But almost before I could process the image of her and Spent together, she had driven the knife through his chest.

After the bullet sailed over me and the next empty barrel clicked, Elizabeth declared that she had previously killed six young men, as well as both her parents. Spent had been her ninth victim. She had lured all the men to the farm from far and wide.

In a rage, I took us to the Hopelessness.

As soon as we arrived, Elizabeth broke down. I stepped away from her; knowing that I would never hold her ever again.

"Bobby, those terrible things. She made me do them."

"Isabelle?"

Elizabeth looked at me horrified.

"You know of her? Then you can't forgive me."

I thought about it for a while. "Now why would I not?"

"You are my fiancé. You are meant to be my protector. I will be damned if you forgive me"

"You are evil. Yet you are not beyond god's mercy" I had loved her so, but the hope of a future with her, of a loving marriage, was fast draining away. The Hopelessness un-laughed.

"Forgive her. Forgive her, then hell shall have her for eternity. She is of no more use. Her killing days are over." Isabelle appeared halfway through that speech. My lovely Elizabeth froze, as if captured in a photograph. Still beautiful. How had I not noticed her flickering around the edges before?

"You already have her, don't you?"

Isabelle giggled. "Such a clever Bobby."

"When did you kill her?"

"I didn't - not fully. I have this trick of suspending my people between life and death. That's how *we* were able to rut. I can transfer myself into Elizabeth's body at whim. When she first came to you in this farmhouse, we were linked. When she first put you in her mouth, I had taught her that act."

That had been a surprise and it rocked me to my very foundations, mainly out of embarrassment. One did not discuss sexual acts with others.

I looked closely at Isabelle and imagined the lines of power that had joined Susan and her brother. There were thousands joined to the witch. And then thousands stretching to the Hopelessness in turn. She was equally a servant of the Hopelessness, caught in its thrall. It had realised Magpie Farm was a good source of food.

A single cord joined Isabelle and Elizabeth. I held my thoughts, wrapped them in secrecy. Walking to the far end of the room in a pretence to look at my Elizabeth. I picked up the gun Elizabeth had been pointing at me.

I knew what all the ropes meant in the Hopelessness. I could feel the Hopelessness did not like Isabelle. She kept a lot of false hope for herself.

I whipped around, firing at the link between Isabelle and Elizabeth. Knowing there was one chamber stuck in the gun, I had pocketed a bullet or two earlier that day and had quickly reloaded. The bullet that did emerge under percussion ripped through the link and Isabelle screamed.

"You could have been a beautiful Magpie, Robert. Had you killed for me I should have lived again. Death magic and your love would have healed me."

Then the ghost-witch dissipated. I would see Isabelle once more, but it wouldn't be for another hundred years.

I moved across to Elizabeth; she looked like all her troubles had been washed away. Hell-bound, I supposed. Was I right to let her go, or should I save her? No, Elizabeth had taken so many lives. Something else could have her.

I opened myself up to the Hopelessness; I had reeled it in, purposefully lowering my optimism, so it would think it had me. Elizabeth couldn't see the insubstantial cord that linked her to the Hopelessness itself -now it was growing thicker.

"You can't have her. I forgive her." I announced to the Hopelessness. With that, the blackened thread fully materialised between her and the void.

"I didn't know what I was doing, Bobby." She was crying, yet fading.

"Go to Isabelle, Elizabeth, you are too evil for the Hopelessness."

She screamed as she slowly faded. I never saw Elizabeth again.

It's the year twenty-twenty two. I am over one hundred and sixty years old. I have never aged, nor have I grown ill. I am standing on the fringes of Magpie Farm. There is nothing to hold people any longer; the evil has gone. There are police about and the manor house is burning. A man and a woman walk across the yard to their car. A BMW.

He holds her tight.

That man was you, Harry Morton and she of course is you, Maisie Price. I know one day I will make your acquaintance properly. Isabelle's curse walks the world on different paths now. You will be the solution. Then I will finally find out the reason why I can't die.

I had been lured to the farm so I could finally see you both, not to send Elizabeth into the Hopelessness. That had been my own action.

I turned to my companion, the woman in yellow, who I think you know. She smiled. Then we stepped into the Hopelessness.

"You think you can control me?" The Hopelessness un-said.

"I have done so before. I will do so again."

"You foolish man. I allowed you to do what you did. Did you think by purely channelling hope you defeated me? I am nothing, you cannot defeat me. I am the conduit for the one to come. Forget the Magpies, Robert. Beware the Crows instead. They are legion."

I laughed as we disappeared, and later, I wrote this letter to you both, because I heard that, like me, you both like strange cases.

THE EMBROIDERED HANDKERCHIEF

Twelve-year-old Maisie Price looked out of the passenger window of the Land Rover as the fields rushed by. It was warm outside and the air was stifling.

Maisie and her father were travelling down the A38, approaching Lichfield in the County of Staffordshire, where her paternal grandparents lived. Her twin, Daisy, was poorly in hospital with appendicitis back in Yorkshire; Maisie was making the journey to be looked after by her grandparents while her mother was shuttling back and forth to the hospital.

Perched up high in the Rover, Maisie took in the beauty of the countryside as it whipped by. Thousands of roadside trees broke up the late summer sunshine like giant vertical blinds, eventually giving way to undulating fields of rapeseed and wheat.

"Nearly there, sunshine. Thank God," her father muttered, more to himself than to Maisie. He had been driving all night down from Scotland, where he was currently working, to see Daisy, then to take Maisie to Lichfield.

"Are you tired, Daddy?" she asked sympathetically.

"A bit. Keeping an eye on me, Em?" he smiled.

Within minutes, they had hit the Birmingham Road and were heading into Lichfield, where they pulled up in the small car park at Lichfield City station. As people rushed about them to catch their morning trains, her dad retrieved her case from the back, gave her a quick peck on the cheek and a hug.

Thump.

The sound was concussive, reverberating like a faraway explosion. Maisie staggered, her vision a blur. The air became thick. Another loud resonant thump detonated in the distance; she looked for her dad, but he was gone. Why would he just vanish like that and leave her? She was only twelve. What was happening? Was it a bomb – had he been blown away from her? Was he looking for her? Yet she could see no damage. Just an absence of people.

Maisie was a practical girl, so she decided to go and meet Nanna and tell her she'd lost her dad.

As her eyes cleared, she became aware her surroundings had changed. Not physically, just the colours, like a faded, sun-bleached seaside billboard.

The people *had* all vanished, it seemed. No activity whatsoever. No one near the train station. No cars on the road. No milkmen, postmen, or women with pushchairs as you might expect.

Maisie had known she would have to wait for Nanna to finish her early cleaning shift at Victoria Hospital, so she had planned to go and have breakfast at the old tea shop on Bore Street. They would go there regularly when visiting Lichfield; Maisie and Daisy would eat massive slabs of cake and slurp thick milkshakes through straws.

Would Nanna arrive at the café though, or had she vanished like all the others?

Undeterred, Maisie made her way into the city centre; it too was as quiet as the grave. Could she call Nanna at work? She could see no phone box, but in any case, she wasn't sure she knew Nanna's number. She supposed she could call Grandpa.

Maisie looked up and down the deserted high street. No shopkeepers in their shops, as you would expect at nine-thirty in the morning, nor customers. There was literally no one about.

She headed off towards the tea shop that was situated next to the Civic Hall, all the while scanning the streets for signs of life. Still no one.

The flags adorning the local government hall hung limply in the still air. Now there was not a breath of wind; how different from the trees swaying on her drive to the city with her dad. The café was closed, no signs of life within.

Maisie shivered, feeling a distinct chill. It didn't feel like summer any more, which was strange; it *was* the end of August and it *had* been so warm, they had driven since dawn with the windows of the Land Rover down. Now it was positively icy. She put down her case and did the buttons up on her cardigan. Should she get her coat out of her bag? She rubbed her freezing hands together.

"Cold, Miss?"

Maisie nearly jumped out of her skin.

"Sorry, Miss. Did I make you jump?"

Maisie turned in the direction of the voice and as she did, she felt another surge of light headedness, a dizzying discombobulation. She steadied herself with one hand on her upturned case. The strange man caught her arm, *a gentleman hopefully, and not someone who is going to steal my bag. Or worse.*

Feeling giddy, she pulled away and tried to draw in a deep breath, whilst she focused on the man before her. He was in his late thirties, possibly early forties. She wasn't so good with judging adults' ages. He was not tall, "of middling height," as Nanna would have said. His hair was a mix of blond and brown and his face was bright red, like he had been drinking for years or recently crying for long periods. Bloodshot eyes looked at her from a kind face. *This man is possibly more of a danger to himself than to me.* Probably a vagrant, although his clothes looked well-made if not flamboyant, like she imagined an actor might wear. Why was he here when no one else was?

"Are you okay, Miss?"

Her heart had been thudding on her rib cage like a pneumatic drill on concrete. She pulled in another deep breath. She still felt strange, like the feeling of distance one got in those moments between sleeping and waking.

"Yes, I'm fine, Mr...?"

"Call me Ned. Edward really, but friends call me Ned."

He handed her a handkerchief. It had the initials EW carefully embroidered onto one corner. She politely accepted and dabbed her brow. Absent-mindedly, she put it in her pocket.

"Thank-you Ned. I was on my way for a coffee. I've been a passenger for the last four hours and I'm parched. But the café's shut." She needed caffeine. It was the start of a lifelong habit.

"Follow me."

Maisie followed Ned as he walked, muttering and mumbling names as he went. She could make out two names: Frances and John. He repeated them by rote, but he also kept interjecting his mantra with, "Sorry, so sorry".

Ned stopped at the far end of the church, by what should have been a bright red phone box, which presently looked dirty pink and did not contain a working phone. They were now situated opposite the Drum pub, where Grandpa used to take Daisy and her for a cola after the market had closed.

Ned pushed open the little side door. He disappeared inside, but did not call her in, so she felt it was better if she just waited for him outside. Her case seemed to be getting heavier and her day was getting stranger.

"I've found you some tea, no coffee," Ned shouted.

Maisie looked up to the sky. It had turned dark grey and looked like rain. Had it indeed promised thunder earlier? She caught sight of the clock on the corner of Dr Johnson's birthplace. It said five. Strange: it had been just after nine-thirty moments ago. There was the distant rumble of thunder again.

Suddenly, a feeling of unease rolled over Maisie again. She felt like she was going to faint. Maybe she was coming down with something? She quickly sought out a washed-out green bench, one of many around the city square and sat down. For a moment, she closed her eyes.

So sorry, sorry, so sorry." Maisie woke to the sound of Ned's voice. He was sitting next to her, repeating his mantra. She looked at the clock; it said a quarter to four. Was time going backwards? She breathed again very deeply, to forestall another wave of panic.

"Feeling better, Miss? Here is more tea. Better for you than that coffee, apparently."

"What is happening, where are we Ned?" He smiled- and it was such a lovely smile- but she just wanted to punch him when he answered, "Lichfield Square, Miss."

"What year is this?"

He laughed, this time raucously, as if she was the lunatic. "Nineteen ninety-nine miss."

"Are you sure?"

"Yes, it was on my chip paper last night." He was smiling. Then he got up and moved away slightly, muttering. "Hot, hot, hot," under his breath, before switching to "Frances" and "John" by rote again.

"Do you work for the church?"

He stopped, and the smile returned. "I have turned out for them on a couple of occasions," he said. "It was like mummery too, I tell you," he confided, with a hint of sarcasm in his voice.

"Sorry?"

"My clothes!" He did a funny little turn. "You think I am an actor. A guide?" He said this last word as if he was uncertain of it; as if he had snatched it from somewhere, but did not know what quite what it meant or implied.

"I have performed in this square many times. On the last two occasions, they could hear my voice for miles around, apparently."

"Where do you live?"

"Here at the church. I have a place not far away. I look after the square; I have done for years." His voice was tinged with sadness. "I look after the others who have gone before. You can't see their resting places anymore; they built on most of them. They are here, however, sleeping. Sometimes they pop in for tea or a cake."

There were beads of sweat on his brow which gathered and rolled down his face, spotting his off-white shirt. She looked at his hands; they were blistered. What had he been doing? She stood, partly to see if she had regained her sea legs and partly to stretch them.

"Where were you born, Ned?" She asked. "You sound like you are from around here."

He looked up and smiled. "Hinckley, Miss, Leicestershire, but I was brought up in Burton upon Trent."

"Are you married, do you have children?" His smile was wiped from his face and he scowled. "I didn't get the chance to say goodbye." It seemed she had hit a nerve. Perhaps his family had died, or left him. Poor man.

He suddenly got up and moved across to the side of the church directly opposite Dr Johnson's house, climbing a small set of steps that she hadn't seen before; they looked like they were there, yet not there. Once at the top his whole demeanour changed. His chest slowly rose, then fell more calmy as he exhaled.

"Preach you from scriptures of shining gold?" he shouted at the top of his voice. "Take your icons and lay them waste. For that is not a religion, it is superstition. Your soul shall not transcend, I say.

Luther spoke of such. Thy soul shall sleep for eternity, not raise itself to heaven. Dear Maisie." He looked over to her. "No one goes toward the heavenly light following forgiveness, confessing sins to a man wearing his vestments does not absolve, but damns you to eternity, an eternity of wanting."

Maisie could not believe the transformation. From the nervous, weak man who had brought her tea, to this preacher declaiming from his glowing, wobbly, pulpit made from light. His arms were held aloft, but she also thought she could see him bound, in a kind of double image. Then the feelings of discontinuity hit her again.

She was five and she was with Grandpa as he sold fruit and veg on the market. She remembered running in and out of the stalls, waiting for the time they would go to the pub and she would get her reward for helping to tidy up. Maisie recalled a long-forgotten memory - playing with her old imaginary friend; what was his name again? With a jolt, it struck her; Edward...

She came to again. Ned was there, trembling, looking even redder of face. She glanced again at his hands: the blisters looked worse. Pustulating, she thought.

"It's time for you to go, Miss. I've got things to do before *they* come." His voice was dismissive, confident once again, as if he were still atop his pulpit. Maisie wondered if he had to get ready for his day's work, acting, guiding, whatever it was. He certainly was a confident speaker.

"Yes, of course. I'll go and see if Nanna is ready."

She looked at the clock on Johnson's birthplace. It was just after half-past nine again. Across the street there were people, milling about. They had not been there before. What she saw was vibrant again, full of colour, not washed-out grey. She turned to say goodbye to Ned, but he was gone.

She no longer felt cold, at least. The sun was high in the sky and not a cloud in sight. Things still felt a little unreal, as if she were dreaming. Then she passed out.

That was the first time she had suffered one of her migraines. Nanna had found her shortly afterwards. Her father had turned his back and apparently, she had wandered off, with her case. The doctor had said that people with migraines could exhibit erratic behaviour, could have very vivid dreams.

Every time Maisie returned to the marketplace, she looked for Ned – but he was nowhere to be seen.

"Maisie wake up! Telephone. It's Harry." It was Teddy, her fiancé-she hadn't heard the phone go; she must have been so deeply asleep. She pulled on her dressing gown over her short nighty to cover her decency and raced downstairs."

"I'll make you a cup of coffee," Teddy said.

"Hello Harry, what's wrong?"

"Have you heard?"

"I've had a migraine, I needed to sleep it off."

"There's been a murder. Lichfield Market Square. I'm on my way there now."

Howard Maple had been killed outside what used to be St Mary's church, now a library and tea shop. He'd been doused with petrol and burned alive. Days later, they had the murderer in custody. It had been a big case for such a small city -and it had been horrible.

She had decided to call in and see the tea shop manager, Charles. She wanted to say goodbye, and finally ask him about Ned. It hadn't seemed appropriate to enquire earlier, while she was supporting the investigation at Maple's home in Whittington where she, as Detective Sergeant, had a secured base of operations.

She remembered her childhood visit. Being dropped off in Lichfield, on a trip down from Yorkshire, to see her Nanna. She had been about twelve at the time. She had suffered such a headache that day.

She opened the doors to the former church, now tea shop and entered. Charles was down by the old altar with Agatha, his wife, who was refreshing the flowers; they had been in situ during the time the murderer, Roddy Burt, had wreaked havoc inside. He maintained a voice had told him to kill Howard – the voice of a witch he referred to as 'Isabelle'. Roddy had been sectioned.

"Detective Sergeant Price," Charles said, in obvious delight. "The genius who saved our fair city from that murderer." He reached out and hugged her.

"I've come to say thanks."

"Oh, thank you. Such a shame about Howard. Such a terrible way to go."

"It was." She paused. "Can I ask you one last thing? Does Ned still work here?"

"Ned?" Charles asked.

"I know it's a long shot, but he made me a cup of tea when I was a girl. When I came to Lichfield as a kid once, back in the late nineties. He looked after me when I had a migraine. I think you were the church manager here then."

Charles looked perplexed.

"I was indeed in charge of the estates here during the nineties. Describe this Ned to me."

"Some sort of actor type. Quite an enigma, one of a kind I'd say. Initially he seemed quite nervous, mumbling a lot, but when he went up these stairs and started preaching, he was impressive."

Charles shook his head, frowning.

"We do not have a Ned here- never have." Agatha said, simply.

"You must remember him. He was so distinctive. Thirties or forties. Really odd-looking, old-fashioned clothes. Very red complexion - he had nasty burns on his hands and arms too. They were very blistered. Oh – and he gave me this, after I had a funny turn with my migraine." Maisie retrieved the handkerchief from her handbag and showed Charles the initials. "I've kept it ever since." Charles studied it carefully.

"I wonder." Charles said to himself. "Follow me."

Charles led Maisie around to the front of the church and pointed to a plaque.

"The only E.W. I know who has been officially linked to this church is that one. Edward Wightman. You mentioned his burned hands. Wightman was the last person to be burned alive for heresy in England. He was in fact burned twice, recanted the first time but then recanted his recantation."

Maisie studied the stone.

"Edward Wightman. Died 1612?"

"Being a former man of the cloth, I'm not a believer in ghosts, save one, Sergeant, but I'm not sure I can readily come up with another explanation."

"A ghost who gave out embroidered handkerchiefs?" Maisie replied incredulously.

PART TWO: ROBOTS AND THE FUTURE

IMPOSSIBLE FRUIT

Endure and Eternity wanted a child. They had wanted to be parents for thousands of years. Unfortunately, robots couldn't have children - unless they made them.

Yet neither Endure nor Eternity wanted to fabricate a child from lifeless components. Nor did they want to grow one in a vat, like some lab clone that would eventually be brought to gestation in a false plastic womb.

They wanted to have a child naturally, silly as it sounded. Eternity wanted to conceive a child and carry it within her body; she wanted to deliver it into the world herself, feed it from her own breasts. Unfortunately, short of magic, it was not looking like a possibility.

Endure had striven to make it a possibility for his wife, however; he had scoured the universe for clues to a miracle that might change their physiognomy. Unfortunately, all the records stated that no android had ever been able to give birth to a live child.

Only one human had ever said he knew differently – but he was long gone. Killed at the start of the robot uprising, the eventual mutual destruction of most real and artificial beings.

"Magic exists." His creator, Dr Arnoldo, had once said when Endure was minutes old. *"One day my child, one of you will find a way to have real offspring. It may take considerable time and sterling effort, but you will succeed, or at least one of your kind will. Your mechanical family tree will bear its impossible fruit. One day you will have apples from your tree; real, living apples, not constructed but conceived, grown and born."*

Had it just been a "welcome to the world" speech by Dr Arnoldo? Had he said it to all his biomechanical children to give them hope? Or to assuage the ultimate fear of the immortal – loneliness?

Dr Arnoldo *had* been a type of magician himself, of course. He had been the inventor of the first self-replicating, artificially intelligent being. All the laws of physics, biology, and chemistry throughout the universe had seemed to work against him - until he had his first breakthrough. It had been as phenomenal as the emergence of the science of instantaneous travel through punctured wormholes. Clemency, Endure's brother, had been that first breakthrough.

With Dr Arnoldo's words etched deep within his psyche, Endure had spent thousands of years looking for the magic. Many had called him insane. He'd spent several centuries himself in self-imposed stasis, fully powered down, as he thought he was mad. Yet he emerged enthused, intent on finding the magic once and for all.

More recently, Eternity had ordered him many times to stop looking, maintaining that it was a fruitless task, that Dr Arnoldo had misled him. Endure had ignored her; he knew that she wanted the same thing as he did. She was just trying to protect him from doubt.

"All persistent, ruminated what-ifs will come true, if you live long enough. They will *come to pass,"* Dr Arnoldo had once commented in a lecture on immortality, as humans and robots prepared to live forever, side by side.

Then the madness emerged. The suspicion. The rise of Robot Freedom and the Wars of Indenture. Stupid humans: they would rather wipe out their creations than free them. What a waste of that magic they imbued, to be so destructive against the artificial beings that had been the key to human expansion - in a universe where other life was rare.

Endure sighed and fiddled with his seat strap as the Mindship - *A Controversial Punchline!* – spat out his shuttle. He watched through the front screen as it plummeted through the atmosphere towards the surface of the planet Melan.

As ever, on an approach to another planet, Endure felt an all-encompassing sense of doubt. Even though his brother, Tolerance - who protected the world below - seemed positive that he had found something.

The shuttle banked, then levelled out, its buffers dampening the turbulence. No doubt the abundance of vertical air currents was the cause of the eddying. Endure watched the gravid sky broil on the viewing screen. The mixture of dark grey, pinks, and purples like the mottled flesh of a drowned corpse. Lightning traced powerful, streaky patterns through the rainy vapours, but the absence of thunder made the experience strangely silent.

Would this be the place he was finally given some clue to the existence of magic? Tolerance said he had some information that he would share - if Endure brought him a gift. Of course, Tolerance had been joking, but Endure had still brought a gift with him: an ancient music device. Tolerance coveted such things. It would be small reward if this led to Endure's own glittering prize.

As the shuttle descended through the lower bloated, festering clouds, Endure surveyed the archipelago that stuck out of the major landmass, like an arm grasping a large egg.

"Please prepare yourself for translation, we have reached our *wonderful* destination." Punch, the ships AI, said theatrically. "Not that much is going on down there - other than a rainstorm."

"Sarcasm, Punch?"

"I have learned a new skill. It will aid me in conversation."

"So, are you talking to me now?"

"No. You are a shit for telling me to mind my own business."

Punch was grumpy a lot of late; she thought *he* was being foolish. That his search was a pointless exercise, that they wouldn't find a magic way for him to become a natural father. Punch was just being pragmatic, like Eternity, when she was lost in her rare moments of doubt.

"Okay, have it your way. If it's strictly business, are there any threats down there, Punch? Any Creatures?"

"Nothing sentient nor harmful, other than Tolerance, from what I can detect. Although we know those Creatures are wily."

"Good enough, I suppose. Please translate me to the surface."

Endure's skin was as near enough an approximation to a human's, without being real, that he could feel the hair on his arms and neck stand on end as he translated down to the planet. Eternity had worked such marvels on his body, but even her advancements were slowing. There was no denying they were approaching the pinnacle of achievement – as close to human as artificial beings could ever be.

The Creatures were the remaining harbingers of Switch-Off. They continued to scour the stars in search of Endure's kind, in order to end them all. They were fundamentalist humans, still following the orders of men and women who had been dead for what seemed like forever. If they could not stop the Creatures, then it would be futile bringing life to the universe.

Their brother Explore and his partner Aspire had set out on an almost military quest to discover the means to end the Switch-Off. Armed with Eternity's technological expertise and an army of android children, they sought to finally defeat the Creatures. Yet they had not contacted Endure or Eternity for such a long time. They were probably all gone, already switched-off themselves. All those children too. So sad.

Endure's pre-arranged rendezvous point with Tolerance was a deserted beach. As his molecules fully coalesced, Endure could feel the fine sand particles between his toes. Immediately, Tolerance materialised; Endure was horrified by his appearance. Tolerance's skin was flayed and was hanging off him in strips. Endure could see metal between the gaps in his hypodermis. The embarrassment of true nakedness for an android. Tolerance must be heartbroken.

"What has happened to you?" Endure cried, taking his brother in his arms.

Tolerance looked at Endure, faux tears in the corner of his eyes. "There must be a Creature here, Endure. It has already attacked me, and it is cloaked. How can they cloak themselves from us? Endure, my Switch-Off approaches, I am sure of it."

Endure cast his eyes about in response.

"Fear not brother, I am here." Was there still a Creature nearby? Endure knew it was unlikely a single Creature would attempt to Switch-Off Tolerance without another of his kind in support. The Creature would wait, or summon a fellow. Unless it was able to corner either of them, then it might try to pick them off, one by one.

How can we not have seen it, Punch?

It seems they have evolved their camouflage, came the response from the ship. *I said they were hard to detect.*

As Endure embraced his brother, he noticed the sensation of Tol's flapping skin touch his own; damaged as he was, Tol seemed more robot and far less human. Endure knew it was a horrible thought, but could not help himself.

"We can help you re-grow your skin. We have the means. Eternity has developed many updates to our operating schematics, growth and development algorithms that will help you."

Tolerance looked like he had been tortured physically and emotionally. Needless shame was writ large upon his raggedy, peeling face.

"I would like that." Tolerance sighed.

"Then it will be so, brother. We must soon be away."

Tolerance brightened. "Come, where are my manners? I will find you refreshment before we go anywhere." He led the way from the beach into the lush forest Endure had viewed from the shuttle. Thunder growled in the distance as they walked and rain pattered in large, loaded drops upon the tree canopy above.

Tolerance's abode was a small log cabin, set centrally in a green dulled clearing; it did not look big enough for his needs, let alone his ancient collection of music recordings.

As he crossed the threshold, a space opened- Endure could feel the dimensional parameters shift. A huge lounge and dining area appeared, far larger than the outer dimensions. One open door led off to a kitchen and the other closed door, no doubt, to sleeping areas. Endure laughed. He had been fooled. "I thought you might be staying in an actual log cabin."

Tol's laughter echoed from the kitchen area. "I would have nowhere to keep my discs, tapes and crystals. That reminds me. Did you bring me that cassette tape?"

Endure patted his pocket. There was a micro-woven stasis pouch in his coat, containing the ancient music storage device. Beaming, Tol entered with two cups of aromatic tea in ceramic mugs on a wooden tray, Earl Grey- Endure's favourite. It had been so long since he had smelled, let alone tasted the fragrant drink. As Tol set the tray down, Endure handed him the tape. Tol took it and with a broad smile on his lacerated face, stored it with the others that lined the east wall of the room.

For a time, they relaxed and talked about the immense stretch of time between their meetings, sipping tea. Tolerance had been composing; he played Endure a wonderful melodic excerpt.

Suddenly, there was a loud, ear-shattering bang: the music cut out as the speakers blew. An EMP pulse had preceded it. Endure's audio receptors became muffled, the effect of a drop in pressure upon his advanced hearing and balance system, caused by the explosion. Fluid sprayed him, yet it was not tea from his spilt cup- it was tepid and viscous. Servo life-fluid. The blood of an android.

"Dear Universe. Tol." En looked up to see as Tolerance staggered backwards. He had been shot. There was a Creature here in the room with them; he could now smell its fetid musk.

"System report, Tol."

"Damage, but not irreparable." He had one flayed hand on his neck- the projectile had gone through it, hopefully missing vital systems.

Endure readied his weapons. He had not ordered their stand-by for such a long time that he'd had to access his memory cache to remember how to do so. He alerted his bio tracking programs and scanned the surroundings, then linked with Punch for additional coverage.

Be careful, Punch sent.

The Creature phased into view, slowly, almost sarcastically - it knew how fast Endure and Tol could move. Although rusty in combat, Endure sent out two pulses of energy, enough to have fried an un-augmented human; this one, however, was fast. It phased out again, appearing behind Tol who screamed. His belly opened like the reddest of smiles, belly-lips parting in a parody of silent laughter. Internal plastic, semi organic components and wetware mechanisms spilled forth with sopping flops and splashes. The horror on Tol's face was non-deletable.

In that millisecond as the Creature withdrew its blade from Tolerance's back, another memory of death flashed across Endure's perception filters.

Dr Arnoldo fell to the ground, his face a ruin. General Torvind Carbid lowered the gun. His creator was dead. This was the zero event.

"The robots will evolve exponentially if we allow them to," Carbid said to his audience. "I want you to ensure we have a switch-off option. That option cannot be an automaton. It must be human.

Humans will endure; robots will not. Robots must not outlive humans. I refuse to let them bear Dr Arnoldo's impossible fruit. Make it so, 123674-6."

The General of External Affairs would not call unit 123674-6 by his given name, Endure. He called Endure One-Two.

The galaxy plague and the connect-virus the General then released, on behalf of the dying Imperial Code, wiped out ninety per cent of humans and artificial intelligence in the universe. Those viruses mutated beyond their original intended impact. The Imperial Code envisioned a time where only the elite survived, in a less populated and easier to control existence, but they had badly misjudged the way their viruses would work.

Only -by chance- Endure's remote cut-off kicked in. He had shut down and purged his systems in time, forever cutting himself off from the World Minds and the universal faster-than-light-fi connections; this insured he survived the AI virus.

"The Creatures will be the victors! Their advanced weaponry will put paid to any long-lived defences the remaining robots might have. Look at the weapons, One-Two. Look at how they work."

The General had never thought his loyal robot would rip out his heart when he had ordered its death. Neither did The General ever think One-Two had it in him to reduce the Imperial Code to so much charnel, starting with Kieros and the General himself.

Endure wasn't proud of his initial killing spree, although in those early times, he had taken thousands of human lives. Eventually he became distraught every time he ended one; perhaps, ultimately, this led to his drive to try and make life anew.

As Tolerance quickly bled out his servo-fluid, Endure reached the Creature, which had been blown across the lounge into the east wall. Endure tore out its heart, just as he ripped out the General's, all those years ago.

The laws of robotics were no longer valid. Humans had broken them all. Murderers disobeyed their basic programming all the time. Human and artificial.

Putting down the wet mess of a Creature, Endure reached Tolerance. Tolerance had been switched-off, that was clear; and as the last of Tolerance's back-up energy failed, Endure's brother smiled. Synthetic fluid spilt down his lips, like fangs of death threatening to bite Endure.

"I found a clue to the location of a magic-user, Endure. On Fidorax." Tolerance offered weakly, coughing. Then, a moribund whine filed the air. It was the noise early artificial models made when they irreparably shut down. Tolerance was ancient and had no energy remaining to perform back-ups; and so, he just turned off.

Endure screamed with rage, with loss, with exasperation. Trembling, he contacted Tolerance's House.

"House. Tolerance has died. Cease operation. Command 43509-XDR-8. Punch, take the house AI with us."

The outer plasmic shell of Tolerance's house that was the log cabin winked out of existence, leaving the body of Tolerance in the clearing. En wrapped his brother in a protective cocoon and translated them both up to the ship.

"Magic isn't real, Endure." Eternity had said eons ago, as she corrected subroutines that enabled him to access slow time upgrading in stasis. "If we are to have children, we must build them in our current image."

"Any scientifically advanced technology is indistinguishable from magic. Someone once said. I struggle to find who that was."

"Your programming is definitely decaying. I need to carry out a full overhaul of your systems." She laughed; they both knew there was really nothing seriously wrong with him. Endure was just a dreamer.

When he came around, he was in her bed, naked. Eternity was next to him. Artificially intelligent beings did not need to have sex, but they had come to enjoy the act of lovemaking and the subroutines of pleasure it gave. It had been one of Eternity's first successes. A robot sex life. It had been marvellous and had led to more partnerships amongst their kind, although they knew full well their labour would bear no fruit, impossible or otherwise.

He kissed her when they had uncoupled and told her he was going to embark on his final journey. If there was no magic left, he would return to her arms and he would remain with her forever; they would build -or grow- children.

Eternity laughed. She'd believe that when it happened; she was resigned to the fact that he would probably be leaving her for many years once again.

Fidorax was seven thousand light-years from Veelum, the world he shared with Eternity. Punch opened a hole in higher space and tunnelled through towards it.

Fidor was a single star system with four circling planets. One New Earth class, one partial New Earth class and two distant gaseous giants. Endure translated down to the surface in silence. Punch had ascertained his mood and did not speak to him, for which he was grateful.

Fidorax, according to the welcome data he received as he hit orbit, was one of the few scholarly planets remaining with a population higher than one thousand. The Fidorians were a learned race and they sought knowledge like Endure sought magic. He hoped they may have some information.

Endure coalesced in the grounds of the huge Fidoran library that had been a centre of study for millennia, according to Punch's info dump. He made his way up the marble steps of the stone behemoth. The structure looked like it was reaching upwards towards the sky, a hundred storeys or more of information and enlightenment, trying to effortlessly block out the greyness of the dull sky.

"Grata, scholar," announced the floating face, Endure approached the reception desk. En switched over to automatic translation. "Welcome, scholar."

The face was that of an ugly humanoid. En supposed that he should not be so judgmental of another intelligent being, but on the other hand, he was past caring. Tol's death still enraged him.

"I have an appointment with the Arch Librarian," he replied and in answer, the floating head nodded.

"Ancient One."

Endure turned, to be faced with the Arch Librarian. It said so on his large badge. The man was humanoid - in as much as he was descended from Earth colonists - but evolved enough away from the human pattern that he appeared to have distinct racial characteristics. He was grey- skinned and angular, with a mouth crammed with teeth.

"Are you well, Ancient One?"

"I am. My name is Endure."

"Yes, Ancient One. Please follow me."

They walked for what seemed like an age, but was probably merely a few minutes; Endure had switched his real-time sensors back on, so the human world seemed terribly slow. They reached an enclosed, windowless room with subdued lighting: probably to protect the ancient tomes, crystals, and data wafers from the stringency of natural light, Endure decided.

The Librarian opened a wall cache and pulled out a large mechanism that puffed and wheezed on its servos. A lectern in the form of an ancient space eagle was revealed; upon its slanted surface of wings was spread a massive book - all leather and paper. So rare.

"This is the Book of Heaven. What the Kastians would call the fourth testament, if they still existed. Like all fundamental religions, theirs died out when the Kastians realised there was nothing after death- other than storage or rejuvenation in a vat-grown body."

"And the relevance to my question about magic?"

"The fourth testament was written by one of their kind who could transform any physical object into another. Betem could also fly. His tomb was watched over by the descendants of his own family. The only family that did not ascend, or sublime or go into stasis. They are said to have the purity of magic in their veins. The only creatures left on Kastia. Or were. He..."

There was a dull boom and the Arch Librarian's head exploded. Endure was splattered with gore for the second time in recent history. He reacted immediately and threw himself down, rolling as he did so. It was time for *his* Switch-Off, it seemed. He engaged his weapons, thankful that Eternity had enhanced his dermal storage to include low impact grenades and drone singularities.

Endure braved a glance about the room and saw there were two Creatures standing on its threshold. They both looked cybernetically enhanced. Were *they* upgrading? The Creatures were the fiercest of single-minded humans, their purpose focused on the hunt for the "robots" who allegedly doomed the universe. Why, therefore, were they adapting themselves with metal exoskeletons? Was that not an anathema to them? Life regressing back to machine- it should be the other way around, he thought. Eternity would be flabbergasted.

The table/lectern shattered beside him, sending splinters of wood and slithers of metal everywhere. Endure felt those small bits of shrapnel pierce his skin. He checked his surroundings, ran a heat sensor check, then locked on to the Creatures, sending out two tiny drone-bombs. They burst from hidden pores and raced off, like mosquitoes towards their blood-filled prey.

A concussion hit him squarely in the back. He was thrown forwards, but he was accompanied by the remains of one of the Creatures- a head bouncing dully off the black, anti-reflective wall with a wet thud.

Endure quickly scrambled to his feet and scanned the immediate area. His systems were a little fuzzy and his vision pixelated, but soon that steadied and he was able to run a further heat scan. Too late: the other Creature hit him with an armoured fist so forcefully, he flew and hit the wall where the bloody ruin of its colleague lay.

En stood up, covered in a mixture of filth from the other Creature and his own servo fluid that leaked thickly from his head wound. The second Creature was racing toward him with enhanced swiftness. En switched to a faster-operating speed, raised his arm, and ordered a more percussive response.

Forty small rounds spat out of his hand at five per millisecond. The advancing Creature fell writhing, riddled with bullets.

Endure walked up to the Creature and looked down upon it.

"Are there any more of you on this planet?"

"Eat shit, robot." The response was punctuated with the middle finger of its remaining hand.

Endure sent a single, larger round into the Creature's skull. Then he went to retrieve the Book of Heaven.

It was a mere thirty light-years to Kastia, so Endure decided to remain awake and study as much as he could about the Final Family in the religious book. The last testament was written by the youngest family member. It was a call for any remaining Kastians to help them to protect Betem's tomb – a place of miracles, which could bring the dead back to life, heal mortal wounds. Was this a source of magic he could exploit?

En searched for two hundred and fifty years, give, or take, but did not find any sign of Betem's tomb nor the Final Family on Kastia, despite following the instructions in the Book to the letter. He had combed every inch of the large planet.

Frustrated, but with purpose, he found and visited any planet whose name could possibly be translated as Kastia into universal common; Kest, Nastan, Oestia, Hassin and Tian. He found nothing.

For a further six hundred years Endure searched. Finally, and with more frustration than he could bear, he decided that he would never find magic, and therefore he would never father real live children. Time to return to Eternity. Then he slept to re-charge.

He woke with a heavy heart and mixed emotions and asked Punch to send a link to Eternity. There was a ping from his comms unit.

"I have a message."

"Who from?"

"Eternity."

"Please play."

"I am trying to clean up the recording."

Endure snapped upright.

"Clean it up? Why?"

"It's nearly four thousand years old."

"What? Why didn't you tell me I had been asleep for so long?"

"You were asleep."

Endure shook his head, irritated. "I asked for an alarm call if any messages came through."

"Did you?"

"Yes!"

"I must have forgotten."

Endure thumped the side of the bed with his fist. "Play the fucking message."

"I object to your vulgarity."

"If you do not play me the message, I will wipe your personality and replace it."

"You would end me? You who wishes to create life? What would you replace me with?"

"A tortenhog from Jetah 6."

"They only grunt."

"Yet they work hard. Play the message."

Again, a pause from Punch.

"Play it now."

"En it's Et. They have tried to switch me off, but I intercepted a Creature. It was cybernetically improved, so I decided to deconstruct it. I had to do it whilst it was alive as it was transmitting. I have sent its corpse back to the Creatures' Earth, along with a sound-beam that carried a virus that should finish them for good. Apparently, their kind tried to switch off Clemency."

There was a pause. Clemency was the famed original member of their small family. He was said to have watched over Earth One since his brothers and sister had fled in the wars.

"My love. Residual memories from the Creature's hive mind suggest Clemency is alive. Ze tried to destroy the Creatures with something other than science. Ze killed forty-seven of them with what they could only communicate as magic- Ze called forth powers from around him and ripped them apart. I am going into deep storage for a while. Your journey to Earth One will take even longer and I am heartbroken to have to wait for you. So, I will sleep. Wake me when you are home. Sending Earth-One coordinates you will have to compensate for f-t-l travel. Message end."

Eternity would be waking very soon and he still had a four-hundred-lightyear journey to and from Earth. Luckily, Punch could navigate that distance in a few hundred linear years- with the right calculation of jumps through higher space.

How could the Creatures have travelled to Earth One? That part of the universe was not only meant to be sterilised, but well-hidden, awaiting re-colonisation. The Creatures must have been searching for Clemency, since Keiros gave those orders.

Endure sent a message back to Eternity to tell her to go back into stasis and set the ship to Clemency's coordinates. He was unsurprised for the navigation systems to show it as the centre of an ancient star-map.

"Wakey-wakey, rise and shine. We are in orbit. Earth One. You would not believe the fun I've had finding it. It is clouded from most navigation systems. I've have had to use old fashioned telemetry and star positions, so much has the solar system moved over the eons. I am home, Endure. This is where I was born." Punch sounded fervent- full of awe and wonder. She was probably one of the oldest living intelligent beings left alive in the universe. Most of her kind, the Universe-Class Mindships, had been the battle-craft of choice in the twenty-fifth century. It was now tens of thousands of years later.

The sound of klaxons filled En's ears.

"Wow, they still work." Punch sounded impressed. "What are they?"

"The ""Oh-No" alarms."

"And why are they called such?"

"Well, as you can imagine, if they go off, we are in all kinds of sh..."

"Punch, what's going on?"

"Something has got hold of the ship. It is pulling us down. Really fast. Some sort of force I cannot define"

"Is there any way we can reverse our thrust?"

"Engines are off. It is all tug force, high gravity. At this rate, we will hit the surface in four minutes and counting."

"Please don't count."

"I like counting."

"I like stripping ancient AIs from sentient ships too."

"I'll stop counting." There was a pause. "You wouldn't do that by the way?"

"Are you going to count again?"

"That will be a no from me."

"Marvellous. Any ideas? We've got about three minutes."

"So, you are allowed to count, and I can't?"

"Punch. Come on. I'm moments from destruction and I am really-"

And then suddenly, Endure was elsewhere.

He could feel the sun on his skin, he could sense slight changes in his melanin levels: his upgrades had developed well during his long sleep. There was a distant sound of many birds. He had not heard birds for some time. He looked up. Great floating beasts flew high up, intermittently shutting off the glare of the sun. He had to shield his eyes with his shade-lids to study them.

He was on an island beach, it seemed he had been brought down to Earth One. It was the only place birds had ever existed. But they had all died out before the initial expansion of humanity, hadn't they?

"Greetings, brother," a familiar voice said.

He turned to see Clemency standing before him, Dr Arnoldo's PhD study. Clemency was a beautiful creature: black curly hair glistening in the sun, sparkling brown eyes and dark brown, smooth, hairless skin. Clemency was non-binary, equally male and female. Only strips of cloth and a toga covered their nakedness.

"I heard you were set upon by Creatures," Endure said.

"I was, but Earth healed me." Clemency replied.

A table appeared on the sand; upon it stood a bowl of fruit, a jug and two glasses filled with a red liquid. They sat and partook.

"How?"

"The Gaia pulse. It is made up of extraordinary energies. It seems humanity should have looked deep within their world, rather than heading for the stars. Neural controlled energies, under the oceans of all things, hidden in plain sight."

"I have never heard of such."

"Well, that rather proves my point Endure. You still go by that nomenclature?"

"You still like a decorous flourish in your conveyed etymology?"

"Touché."

They both laughed.

Endure moved to his sibling and hugged them. It had been such a long time. Clemency kissed his cheek. His sibling was even more evolved than even he and Eternity were. He could feel the pure softness of Clemency's skin. Dr Arnoldo made Clemency to represent the best of male and female humanity, not to mention that the new android kind could replicate themselves. Clemency, however, was further adept at advancements than Eternity was.

"Well met. It's good to see you." Clemency said.

Endure was waiting for his sibling to elucidate.

"My message from Eternity said you had made a discovery, but what about? Creating life?"

Clemency nodded. "It can take energy and create anything with it, given the right practice and commands."

"So, you have found magic?"

"Yes, brother, I think I have."

"And it's not science?"

"It appears to thoroughly disobey the laws of physics as *we* know them. There is no energy depletion when I use the Gaia pulse - not as far as I can tell."

"Therefore, no entropy. You have tested the hypothesis thoroughly?"

"Indeed, many times. Mars, Venus and Mercury have pulses too, even Titan."

"What is the best thing you have created?"

"A new island in the Mediterranean. I have called it Home."

"Take me there."

There was no flash or feeling of ambulation, he was just elsewhere. It was dull, muggy; there was precipitation and thunder rumbled in the distance, like angry gods dancing a dance of war. A young man passed them, tall, muscular, red-haired, wearing a toga. He waved.

"Morning."

Endure looked at his sibling.

"You *have* created life?"

Clemency held out their hands, as if warning Endure to go no further. "I can't talk about it here."

"Then let us go somewhere you can."

They were transported simultaneously to a stone-walled room. It was decorated with shelf upon shelf of books. A fire waved from behind a glass panel; lights in the stuccoed ceiling were dim, but focused upon a desk where tomes lay aplenty.

"You cannot use the magic to create life. Adam, the boy you just saw, is like us. A simulacrum. A homunculus. Magic cannot create life from artificial life. It seems it is not allowed. I have visited other abandoned worlds where I have accessed their own Gaia pulses. I have not been able to create life for my family. Only the shadow of it."

"Can you talk to the pulse? Ask it what is missing?"

"It sometimes talks to me and tells me that I do not have it in me to create life. I am therefore not allowed. No one is allowed on their own. Unless … they know the key."

"You have found magic and it still needs a key?" Endure was exasperated and furious.

"You are confusing magic with creation. I can do anything with the magic, I believe, except to create the spark of life. I know how much you want a real child with Eternity. I know what Eternity has sacrificed to make you both resemble life so closely. How her work on multi-dimensional engineering and the creation of cold-fusion star traps suffered because of your whimsy."

Endure stopped listening. Disappointment again and again and again. He would have to return to Eternity and tell her he had failed. He loved her so much; he wanted to gift her life. He implored Clemency to show him how to tap into the worlds pulse and they did so, although Earth would not let Endure and Clemency wield the power at the same time. There was, it seemed, a limit to god-like powers.

A few years- or mere seconds- later, they were back in the library.

"Brother, I am sorry for my comments. You know nothing is impossible. Except for that one thing. I can open a window back to Veelum and sister Eternity. You and Punch will be able to step through, if she warps into her standard avatar form."

Endure nodded at his sibling and called the ship. Punch appeared in the library room by translating her physical form into a random avatar state: a tiny, green fairy, with huge wings.

"What's up, Clemency?"

"Punch. How are you? It's been an age."

"I'm cool now. Cooler, once I worked out not to crash. Earth is pleasant now, isn't it? I am going to stay a while. If Endure can step through back to Veelum so easily, I would quite like to stay on the world I was born."

"Punch..." Endure began.

"If you two can open gates with your magic, why would you need a ship?"

Endure considered her logic and found he could not argue with it, although he could not understand why she would want to separate from him. He had set her consciousness into the AI. Punchline had once been Eva Geller, a victim of locked-in syndrome, rebirthed in a ship's memory banks thousands of years after the ship's original creation and its former AI's destruction. He had been her father of sorts, she was his daughter, and now she wanted to leave him.

"I can come and visit at any time, Endure. Clemency can open a wormhole for me whenever." And she winked at Clemency, her green-skinned fairy-like aspect looking mischievous. Clemency was chuckling.

"You have been away from Eternity for too long, my brother. She is probably pining for you. You were always so well bonded. Leave cheeky Punch here, it has been such a long time since I have had a regular companion my age."

A coruscating hole warped open and Endure could see the familiar buildings that made up his homestead on Veelum. It seemed Eternity had added to the construction footprint. He embraced his sibling and kissed Punch, once she had ceased darting about on her wings, trying to avoid him, laughing. He then stepped through the hole, which winked shut behind him.

Eternity was asleep when he found her. Softly snoring the sleep of updating. She was covered by a fine sheet and below he could see her wonderful curves. His machine coded emotions fired up and artificial neurotransmitters like synthesized dopamine flooded his body. Checking in with Veelum's Gaia pulse, he felt the power and called it to him.

Endure then undressed and crawled into bed. Eternity awoke, a smile on her face.

"You found the magic?"

"I did."

"Can it make us a life?"

"No."

She kissed him. "It does not matter. We have each other."

"I love you," he said.

"I love you more."

"En!" screamed Eternity, through their connection.

There were no more Creatures about surely- she had said she had killed them all. He had been working in the grounds of their abode, making sculptures with the power of the Gaia pulse. His experiments were going very well. While he could not create life itself, he had been able to evolve it; he had made a treehouse from a living tree, encouraging a sapling to grow and to develop its cognitive skills. It now had had its own consciousness and could talk. He had named it Arbor. It called him Moving Daddy.

He dashed up the pathway, past the few animals they kept on their farm, as they called it now. He found Eternity in a bathroom and in his haste to open the door, he caught his hand on the frame. He felt something strange but put it to the back of his mind - En was in difficulty. Why was she in one of the bathrooms? Why was she sitting over a toilet- their bathroom did not have a toilet? She was she retching-they did not retch. Had she been evolving? Or had she introduced something to her system it did not like? She had done it before and he had needed to help her purge herself. That was of data, however.

"What are you doing?"

"I am unwell."

Endure absently sucked the blood from his hand. "So why not carry out a diagnostic?"

"I have, continually these last few weeks. I wanted it to be a surprise- once I realised it was true."

"What are you talking about?"

"Endure. I am pregnant. How. The. Fuck. Can. I. Be. Pregnant? I am a machine."

She smiled at him, colour coming back into her cheeks.

"I used the pulse to change my body. Not into a human- it won't do that- but to the nearest approximation."

"Yes, I have done the same, we talked about it."

"And it seems we can now procreate."

"Clemency said it could not be so. You have tried it too. The pulse cannot be used to make life."

I can. It was the voice of the Gaia pulse. It talked to them occasionally. This time it was to both.

"Clemency said it could not happen. They had tried and tried. It never worked."

Clemency worked alone. It does not work on its own. It needs...

And in that moment, Endure realised. He looked at Endure and she did too.

"Love."

Hope – the Impossible Fruit of the Android family tree – was born eight months later.

THE TINMAN AND THE LUNG TREE

"Progenitor beta. Look. The Lung Tree. And there's the Tinman."

Uksfvar, beta parent of the child Vivitcth watched as his little alpha hurried up the lilac and magenta hill towards the giant tree, as fast as her six hooves could carry her. The suns were up high in the North, the air was clear; no sign of rain nor wind and no weather front likely to ruin their pilgrimage.

This visit would do Viv a great good, as well as being an exciting experience, Uks thought. The pure healing oxygen the Lung Tree exhaled would hopefully heal her ailments. Viv's malformed air sacs needed aerating- and where better than here? Uks had promised, as all parents had for thousands of years, that his little alpha could come here and ask the Tinman for a story. He wouldn't answer of course, he never did, but that was the tradition. Uks would then buy her a wish gift, to reward her disappointment, like all parents would.

"The funny Tinman. Look progenitor beta. Look at his funny face."

Uks wasn't as young as he used to be when he was an alpha, before his change, so it took him a while to catch up with the little one. He would need aeration at the summit too, if he kept her pace. He was gasping like a marshland flobberbeast during the high summer season.

As he reached the summit, he could see the tree dominating the skyline, its white lung-like presence swayed, like scripture set forth, with the heartbeat of the planet. It was like any other tree, with its chaotic fractal patterns, but where most were green and purple, the Lung Tree was bone white, standing stark against the violet sky.

Viv was talking animatedly to the metal Tinman now. For what seemed like eternity, the Tinman's silence had held the joy of the children from afar, the promise of a gift for an unrewarded request.

A legend built upon single visits by children -and their parents- for millennia.

The Tinman was all gleaming and reflective, difficult to look at due to the refracted light. His humanoid face was bland, worn away; his button nose almost smooth, his once bright blue eye lights dimmed by wear and tear and years of atmospheric assault. He would once have moved and would have been called a robot or an android, in ancient common. Any original decoration upon the Tinman's surface had long since been worn away by the millions of childhood pilgrims, who travelled here to ask the Tinman for a story. Child after child, rubbing their faith upon his face with excitement or holy fervour. He would probably have been six spans tall originally, but now his long legs were entangled in earth and the Lung Tree's roots.

Uks took in a breath. The air here was so pure at the base of the Lung Tree. His eyes danced with the bright lights of headiness. He steadied on his hooves, trying not to overbalance, a difficult feat for Satpada.

"Tell me a story. Tell me a story. I don't want a present. Tell me a story. Please," Viv wailed.

Uks said a quick prayer asking the Lung Tree and the Tinman forgiveness for her eagerness and noise levels. Viv, however, continued in her fervour until she sat down coughing.

"Deep breath. Your air sacs will be healed, but you must breathe deeply. It takes time." He sat down beside her, happy to take respite from his own giddiness. A trace of tears could be seen around her manifold eye ridge. He patted her with a manipulator hoof.

His thoughts were suddenly interrupted by a high-pitched burble. The ground tremored slightly and Viv wobbled. He caught her just in time. A fresh wave of oxygen hit them, seeming even fresher than the first.

"Progenitor. My air sacs. I think I have healed. I can breathe better." There was surprise in her voice.

He didn't acknowledge her, more interested as he was in the sound of the burbling and whistling.

"Ghivarsisk wuly ipoltutim castans," a voice said.

"Progenitor. The Tinman- he speaks!" Viv screeched in pure excitement, getting to her hooves, and scrambling toward the ancient metal being.

"Translating into speech offered. Greetings. My name is Silas. I am pleased to be able to tell you my story."

Uks got up on his hooves and clambered towards his little alpha and the Tinman. He was amazed and a little beholden, if the truth were told.

"Hello, Silas. Will you tell me a story?" Viv asked. The words she had rehearsed each day since she knew she was coming to this place, although they had never known the Tinman's name. There was a pause. The Tinman spoke again, for only the third time in perhaps ten thousand years.

"Yes, young one. I will tell you my story." Silas answered.

"Get out the way, your stupid useless chunk of scrap metal and tidy something up," Trooper Dree spat, with casual bitterness. "As you won't tell us the reason we are fighting on this godforsaken planet, you need to be useful or get out of my way."

Although Trooper Dree was thirty years old, he looked barely older than a child. Yet the responsibilities of a man at war seemed to lay heavy upon his shoulders; he was always concerned, always busy. He was a super soldier, elitist and evidently upset that *he* had to "babysit" what *he* felt was a "sack of metal shit," rather than go fight with the vanguard against the Chund.

"Our mission is code locked and marked secret. I have been assured by the General that my usefulness ratio is high, therefore, you are assigned to me as part of the clean-up operation once the Chund hoard is vanquished. Which should be soon, Trooper Dree."

"Frack-bucket."

"That is not a word. It's hyphenated nonsense, Trooper Dree. Part of it is offensive too, so desist." Dree didn't scold easily; he was a stubborn man.

"I'm advanced trained, a super soldier, a White Warrior. I have killed hundreds, ingested tech, and subdermal weapons, but, and here's the fucking crux of it, my arsenal is disconnected by high command because I've got to babysit you. Silas. What sort of name is Silas anyway?"

"Silas was a companion to an ancient prophet. As for the mission, I will be allowed to reveal this to you as soon as I have clearance, nearer the end of the mission. Until then, please have patience." I was repeating myself; but Dree wasn't listening anyway.

Dree sighed as the rain started to pour down. It was heavy with the ash of destruction, a symptom of an ailing planet and of the devastation caused by the war between the Satpada and the Chund.

The two species of Satpadachund Three had co-existed in harmony for thousands of years. They had lived on separate continents, had kept themselves to themselves. Then, one day, a rich vein of carbon-based fuel had been found on the most southern of the two land masses belonging to the Satpada. Natural resources had become depleted: any fuel found was valuable and highly sought after. Days after the first trade discussion regarding the carbon seam, the Chund invaded.

Hundreds of years later, humans had settled on moon sigma (a designation rather than a name) with the agreement of both races; mainly because they had brought important technologies to share with both sides of Satpadachund Three. Unfortunately, they had also brought the curse of weapons.

At the time Trooper Dree and I landed on Satpadachund, its two sentient species had been warring for eight hundred years. There was only a handful of Satpada left, no more than a few dozen- most of the survivors had fled to the human moon. The Chund were in a similar position, but their low numbers were more to do with their dual war against the humans.

The Chund had been ruthless in their treatment of the Satpada. Concentration camps, weapons experiments, starvation, and execution parties were common. For this evil, the human and Satpadan governments had agreed to jointly attack the Chund, following the signatory meeting known as the Treaty of the Moon.

The final assault on the Chund capital had been raging constantly for eighteen months. The only Chund remaining were a few tens of warriors housed in a bunker, alongside the Chund government, under assault from the human-Satpadan alliance.

The final human and Satpadan push had struck a week before. Dree and I were just behind the front lines.

"Might be home to Gloucester for Christmas." Dree said. He was shampooing his hair in the rain. "If the General has managed to break through the bunker."

"That would depend on what our actual mission is, Trooper," I said.

He mimicked me sarcastically, in a language I did not understand. No doubt it was nonsense: high pitched and containing a lot of "me" sounds.

Suddenly, there was a distant booming noise, a percussion of ordnance far away, followed by the tell-tale sound of artillery speeding overhead. Our camp was small, but that did not mean it was safe.

"Get down!" Screeched Corporal Vance. She was the highest-ranking soldier still alive and as tense as a bow string.

"It's a few clicks away, Corporal Vance." Dree said. He had no time for the corporal. I will not repeat his vulgar sexist opinions about her here.

"You should still have gotten down." This voice belonged to Che, a tall biotech, his Earth-Asian features blended clumsily with his mechanical exo-skeleton, as if a painter had bought too much silver paint and did not know what to do with it. Dree had said that. I would have been more expressive, less literal about the amazing symbiosis of metal and flesh. Dree was what you would call opinionated.

"You have enough sensors, New-Yank, to tell how far it was away. You are just a kiss-arse." Dree said to Che.

"And you are disrespectful. I might have to pound some respect into your pretty little supposedly enhanced head."

"Enough!" Vance screamed. "As if the last two days haven't been bad enough." Her stress levels were high, I could tell through our bio-linkage. This was her first mission as corporal; she had ended up the ranking officer after our command tent had been hit a few days before, wiping out all the officers and troops who'd been using it as a mess.

"I've heard nothing from the General. I think we will move towards the bunker soon," Vance stated.

"We should await orders." Dree was pushing it a little, I felt.

"No. We move. Or we will be sitting ducks." She fetched an e-cigar from her pocket and sparked it.

Dree put his shirt back on and clipped his jacket, then over-vest in place. He fetched his carbine from atop his pack and checked it could un-lock following exposure to the soot-filled precipitation.

"We go at 0700," Vance said. "Get a few hours' sleep." No one could be bothered to argue at that point. I charged my cells.

Out of a troop of nearly 400 that had landed on Satpadachund Three, a few weeks before - including air assistance troops - only seven of us reached the estuary where the bunker was situated. We approached the jetty, and could see the remains of an industrial ferry port that was spread out like concrete butter, full of massive crumbs of buildings and rusted vehicles. It was a right mess, according to Dree.

I had recorded the approach with as much sadness as my limited emotion chip could provide me. Thousands upon thousands of human corpses littered the terrain, lying like discarded dolls, or bobbing in the estuary like bloated, erratic swimmers. Most of the humans had been wiped out- Dree and co were probably the last men standing. There was little sign that any Chund had survived; they also littered the field of death.

Unprepared for leadership, Vance was showing extremely high levels of stress and panic, her blood pressure dangerously raised again. There had been no sign of the vanguard or any rear guard. No orders from on high had come- I supposed, as others did, that the General and her team were most likely dead. By that evening, Dree was criticising Vance constantly, questioning her orders, her mental state and blaming her leadership for their current predicament. I was just grateful that he'd stopped spitting his venom at me for a while.

Dree approached me after he had been dismissed by Vance yet again for insubordination. He was uncharacteristically calm. "You okay, Tinman?"

Well, in those days I did not look like a Tinman. I had skin like any human. It was the richest brown and quite often humans mistook me for one of their own, even flirted with me. I knew it was a nickname. I know now it was an affectionate one.

"I am functioning to nearly full capacity. One of my plasma filters has malfunctioned, but I can work just as well with the other one."

"Any idea why we're here yet?" He'd lit an e-cigar, puffing out vapour like an industrial chimney. He was filthy, covered in the purple-brown soil of the region, his eyes staring out of two cleaner areas of his face, where his goggles had afforded him some sort of protection.

"I am still unable to unveil what our role is here, Trooper Dree."

There was a percussive thud, followed by a scream, but not from the person who had been hit. Vance screamed louder as Trooper Haden fell silently, partially decapitated by a Chund flechette, his fingers still curled round his gently smoking e-cigarette.

I saw the trooper go down. Half his face there, half of it mist-or mud. Vance was covered in brain matter, blood, and bone fragments. She screamed again loudly, wobbled, and fell.

"Silas! Shut her up," Dree hissed. This was the first time he asserted his leadership.

"Down!" I shouted, as I heard another round of the flechettes speeding across the water like little arrows of death. We all dropped this time.

"Thanks, Tinman." Dree said. A strong leader always acknowledges good actions or deeds, he said later. He was soon by the side of the corporal. "I think a bit of Haden's skull has gone through her eye. Sadlow, come and look. Is this fatal?"

Sadlow was the medic, a quiet but usually cheerful man. He silently got to work on Vance; she didn't look good. My visual settings could detect the bone fragment in her brain at the back of her eye.

Another round of flechettes came at us. The ping of death, we called it.

"There can only be a couple of them firing, judging by the amount of ordnance. Silas, can you give us a distance position based on the velocity?" asked Dree.

It took a few seconds for me to locate the Chund and let Dree know their position, but as I did so, Sadlow cursed quietly. Corporal Vance was dead.

"Che, with me. Silas, back up. Sadlow and Corden, you stay here and wrap the dead." Dree ordered.

Corden was one of the female civilians, assigned to make sure the military did not commit any war crimes. I had witnessed her kill a lot of Chund over the last few weeks. Not sure she was civilian anymore. War was like that, it seemed.

We skirted the left bank of the estuary, looking West towards the waning sun, keeping close to the buildings. I continually monitored the far side for assault, although long-range, high-velocity weapons would have been needed to reach us. Unlikely that the Chund had anything more than flechette rifles or guns, by that point. There had been no energy weapons used for days on either side. There was probably nowhere to charge them; the power net was most likely down, hence the team's use of percussive assault armaments.

An explosion emanated from the lower floor of the building we were marking. A small group of humans, civilians and two armoured Satpada came careering out of it towards us. Some immediately fell - hit by weapons fire. Others ran on. Twilight was descending around us, making the locations of the Chund rifle fire easy to pick out, as they lit up the darkening sky

"Silas, with me. Che, get this group to safety."

Dree and I entered the Chund bunker. I could hear our colleagues greeting the refugees. My hearing was still good, despite the ash; I could make out a couple of Satpadan children amongst the voices, although I couldn't tell if they were alphas or betas from their shrill cries of emotion.

Dree led me up another floor. We had run up two already. I'd turned off my hydraulic joint boost at Dree's request because I sounded, in his words, "like an asthmatic elephant crawling up a mountain on its elbows." Looking back, I could have laughed - I had enough of an emotion circuit for that- but I was discovering anxiety and how it was affecting me. I did like Trooper Dree; yes, he was "bombastic", but he had focus and small flashes of kindness pushed through that day too, like later when he sat with the Satpadan children and distracted them from their fears with his funny stories- mainly about me, of course.

On the third floor of the Chund building, we were closing in on our quarry. We had managed to get the building layout downloaded from the orbital linked into Satpadan intelligence; miraculously, there had been some bandwidth left. Dree had managed to get his weapons online, too.

We could hear the dull thuds of weapons, sound-proofed by thick layers of concrete. There was only one gun, by my judgement. Trooper Dree agreed. He clicked his safety off. I looked at him in case this would be the last time I could do that. His bleached blond hair was streaked with sweat, his fringe wrapped around his head like a halo above his bright blue almond-shaped eyes. They twinkled with mischief. I wouldn't have known that at the time, but I've had ten thousand years or more to go over every second of my life and my short partnership with Trooper Dree. With my now expanded emotion chip I would judge, that at that moment, he was excited. Excited for the assault. Finally entering the war on *his* terms.

An uplink image of the next floor pinged through, there were three heat emitting signatures, like little fires in the dark. One was firing the flechette gun. Two others sat at each end of the room, probably covering the exits.

Dree morphed, linked to the orbital, and translated a small, airborne grenade with his subdermal transporter systems. Without warning, he sent it forward into the entrance at the top of the stairs. The air thumped as the door blew inwards. One of the heat signatures split apart. I won't describe further, other than saying the one operating the gun was flung across the room. The third held its ground.

Dree charged; I followed him in, my hydraulics back on-no point in hiding any more- and I jumped up the final three stairs and tailed Trooper Dree into the room.

We walked through the mess of a Chund. Sorry, young alpha, I wasn't going to elaborate, but it's important to know it was a very senior Chund we had killed. The World President no less. The other two looked at us with less-than-fear. One was no more than a calf, the other a wizened old cow.

Trooper Dree shot the child immediately. It had been firing a gun and it was mortally wounded too, not that that is an excuse for killing a child, no matter its race. Trooper Dree recognised the final, older Chund.

It was Lord General Ghurrt. Leader of the Chund Military. She was weapon-less, thankfully. Too old to fight.

"It's over, Ghurrt." Dree said. "I am going to kill you; I have orders to do so." He didn't - but who would argue?

The Chund snorted through its flat nose, like a cross between a Highland cow and an alligator. Unarmed, Chund could be ferocious. Spit dripped from her maw, her red eyes glaring malevolently.

"I will not surrender," she wheezed. It was difficult to tell her sex, there was little to distinguish it, but she was infamous. The wife of the World President. "We have wiped out your leadership in totality-it should be you surrendering."

"Three sexes to make a baby and still damn ugly," Trooper Dree had sneered, shortly afterwards, over her smoking corpse.

I felt at that moment something had changed. I knew why I was here. I knew my mission. The ding of purpose landing in my memory cells was a disappointing sound.

"We need to get a boat across the estuary and then, on the other side, sail outwards towards the archipelago. Island 134 is our destination."

Trooper Dree looked at me as if I were mad.

"Just tell me why?"

"I cannot. I know why, but my command sub-routine will not let me tell you. We need to be together, though. We will survive if we are together."

"Cryptic, Tinman."

We had camped and made a fire in one of the big buildings, open and defensible from all sides. We believed there was no one left for miles, apart from our little "band of irregulars", as Dree labelled us. One of the Satpadan adults, a beta, approached.

"The children are frightened, Trooper. We cannot cross water. It is not safe."

Dree looked at Vheolox and sighed; he wanted to save as many of them as possible. He did, however, seem to believe me when I said that all those who wished to survive must come with us.

"The children will die if they do not accompany us. Something is approaching, some event linked to us, here." I was being prescient; I knew more than just my future. I knew about the futures of others.

The Satpadan beta looked at me, its eye ridge creased into a "v" shape – a look of disbelief.

"Take the children. My alpha and I will not go."

"You'd leave your children?"

"They are not my children. They are not even siblings. They are orphans. The Chund were keeping them to eat."

"What?" Trooper Dree asked incredulously. "You eat each other?"

The "v" on the Satpadans brow furrowed further and he spat on the floor. "We are not the same species, although we are the same race. We are herbivores, they are carnivorous. They eat carrion. Had we known they took our people and ate them as a delicacy, we would have wiped them out before now."

Trooper Dree looked at me, and his face was, no doubt, inscrutable to the Satpadan. To me, however, he looked like he was going to vomit.

We left Vheolox and Uksmart together. They were convinced they would be safe and if not, then they would take their lives in their own hands together. I shook my head sadly. The emotion chip was being challenged by the second.

Che, Sara, Dee, Sadlow, Corden, Dree and I, accompanied by the two nervous Satpadan children made ready to board a boat that would just about hold us all. I checked the mechanics and biofuel. We had found a fuel depot not far from the building where Dree had killed the last three Chund. We had filled the tank: it would ruin the engine, but this was a one-way trip.

We decided not to leave until morning, as the tide would be further in, allowing us to sail down the estuary into the main ocean and skirt round the islands of the Archipelago that sat just off the coast of the Chund landmass.

In the night, however, they attacked.

The children woke first; the sound of their screaming was "blood-curdling", I think Dree had said. Sadlow must have fallen asleep on watch - the Chund eviscerated him with a traditional sharpened metal implement that was more rake than axe. Corden's corpse lay nearby. There was almost nothing left of her abdomen but pulp.

Dree yelled at me to get the children on the boat, handing me a weapon and ordering me to protect them. I wouldn't have used it. My programming does not allow me to kill, even in self-defence.

There were two Chund -large ones at that, warrior caste. One of them bit Sara's neck out, the other killed her friend Dee with a single punch. Che and Dree retaliated and managed to get one down.

That was when Che was finally defeated. He wrestled the last Chund to the ground, screaming to Dree to run, while strangling the creature with his hydraulic arms. But the Chund fought back with pure aggression "that would have made millions of credits on the vid-screens back home". From the boat, we heard the sickening sound of Che's neck giving way, like a dry branch being snapped and the victory roar of the Chund echoing across the estuary.

According to Trooper Dree, the Chund wasn't smiling when the back of its head was blown off; but Dree was not triumphant- more weary and subdued.

All under his command, save me and the two children, were dead. The human armies, the Chund Host, the Satpadan family -as their collective were called- were lost. But it seemed to be the loss of Che, "the bravest man I ever knew," that weighed heaviest of all upon him.

I sailed the boat and we were all silent, apart from the gentle but strange "whuffle" noises from the children as they snored. Dree looked over the prow, lost in his thoughts. We cut a slow, chugging channel through the dark purple water and as the suns rose high in the sky, Island 134 hove into view.

134 was a large island, hills of green and purple vegetation, lush despite the damage this planet had taken over the last few decades. I could see the temple at the top. It would take us days to walk there from the beach because of the undulous terrain. We had no choice though, not even the children.

"Can you tell me yet, Tinman?" Trooper Dree asked as the boat hit the green, fine, and soft sand of the beach.

"We need to go to that temple," I pointed it out, miles away through low mountains and hills. "All will be revealed."

Two days later, we arrived, hot, tired, and thirsty after Dree had let the children have the last of the water the previous night. The Satpadans were normally used to the heat, however the little ones had complained.

The temple stood out proudly, halfway up one of the small mountains. It appeared to be constructed from marble, a green hued stone streaked with purples and pinks. Tens of feet tall, it was carved with intricate motifs of Satpadachund creatures- mostly mythical, according to the children who burbled in excitement, despite their predicament, as I translated. It was beautiful; I had never felt reverence before, but this was undoubtedly a holy place. A place of creation, the little ones said.

Inside the temple, there was a deep pool of cool water. Before we knew it, the children were in the water paddling, each of them with their six hooves splashing, giggling as if they had not been through the terrors of nearly being killed. Strange how Satpadans were fine in water, yet would not cross it.

"We should leave the creatures here- they will be safe," I said.

Then with a thud, the flechette hit Dree in the back and went right through, just missing me. He turned and looked at the old Chund, who had obviously tracked us after we had landed. Dree raised his left arm, connected with the orbital, translated an explosive bolt, and shot it through its head.

The trooper fell to his knees, blood welling on his lips- his lifeblood; ironic, considering what I was about to do.

"Initiate."

I knew without looking that the forcefield would protect the children. The programme would obey, the raw, sentient power filling me was so potent.

The programme interface looked at Dree through my eyes. "I cannot save him but can integrate him." It was my voice, speaking in my head, but not my conscience.

"Then do so. But let me speak to him."

The blood had stopped flowing and all of Dree, except for his head, was covered in this strange orange and yellow glow.

"What's happening, Tinman? I should be dead."

I sighed, evidently the emotion chip was working well.

"You are dying, but there is a way you can live. My secret is that I am a terraforming seed. I will transform this world into an image of its former self, as it was before the wars. Only the Chund will not be here, they are sadly extinct, it seems."

"I have killed so many. I do not deserve to live." he said, in what I thought was a heroic manner, despite his meaning.

"You are a hero," I said.

"Tell that to those families, whose loved ones I have killed."

"You saved the children. And the seed has offered you eternity; if you, in turn, help the sick and injured. Forever."

Dree had tears in his eyes. He smiled. "Death or eternity? I thought they were the same."

"Metaphorically perhaps," I replied.

"What will happen to you?"

Noticing my surprise, he laughed – realising I didn't know.

I placed my hand on his head affectionately, although I didn't realise until a few thousand years later, it was the program imbuing me with life.

"I will stand with you for eternity. First, however, tell me your name."

"I haven't told anyone my first name. Ever."

"Tell me."

He sighed. "Laing. Laing Dree."

I laughed at the massive irony.

"From now on we will be known as the Tinman and the Lung Tree." I knew what he would become. The healing element of the seed core, the balance of the planet. Its heartbeat, its breath.

Viv screamed in delight at the Tinman. He had given her a story. The original story.

"Write it down Viv. The story of Laing Dree." Silas said. "He was not a good man, but he saved the children. However hard life is, however bad things get, there is hope - the hope of renewal. Laing Dree knew that. He knew how important children were, but he only realised it at the end. Forgiveness, however late, is still forgiveness."

"But you told him the children should come here. What happened to them?" she asked.

"Thousands of years ago, the two children grew up and together, bonded and raised their own alphas and betas; they travelled and met others who had luckily survived- and the world was finally re-seeded."

Uks sighed. As a student of religion, he knew the damage that could be done if truths were revealed. He made a mental note to destroy her story as soon as she had written it. This would likely cause a religious war if it got out. This robot and the tree may have been the original progenitors, but they could not oversee telling the world the truth.

"My time has come. I will now be silent with Trooper Dree." Silas said. "Forever."

Uks sighed again, this time with relief.

"How about I still get you a present?" he asked Viv, on the way back to their skimmer.

She squealed with delight.

"But you must never tell another soul about what has happened here today."

"Okay, Daddy."

BONG

Jarlo Tord was not happy. His holiday was over, he hadn't been paid and he hadn't got any weed.

Almost two hundred million credits were owed to him by clients, half by Sturrock Claus for translation work. He had returned to find he was broke, his bank portal was showing no history of any deposits in the last few weeks.

Sturrock, a *former* university friend, now his largest single debtor- was a total pain in the ass, according to Jarlo's message service administrator, who had charged for extra bandwidth. Jarlo's portal was over its buffer limit.

It had turned out Sturrock wanted the translation job re-done for the damned manual for the damned ancient kit robot he had bought. Why hadn't he asked for it as part of the sale agreement?

Jarlo had spent weeks on the translation and it had been tricky. He'd had to cut a few corners because of the time, otherwise he would have missed his flight to the leisure planet he had just returned from.

How ironic Sturrock was building a robot companion; he was never the best at keeping friends. He was building a pleasure-bot, no doubt. Hardly a life-or-death project, Jarlo thought.

Jarlo dipped his left hand in the massive bowl of root crisps left out by his carer. She knew his joints would be flaring up after his journey to Tarl and that food would relax him. The crushing mastication was helpfully loud in his ears, drowning the blood rush of his stress tinnitus. When Jarlo was angry or wound up, he ate- which was most of the time he wasn't smoking weed.

Jarlo's three-week trip to Tarl had turned into five and boy, had it been bittersweet. He'd found a Luchian woman, fell in love and had showered her with gifts. Luchians only lived for eight weeks in their adult cycles, so he had spent a fortune making sure Chenisse remained his concubine for the rest of her life. He had paid for her funeral too, which hadn't been cheap, but he had done so expecting there to be two hundred million bastard credits waiting for him in the bank on his return.

Intent on trying to find the reason for the delay in his down payment, Jarlo opened an audio link to Sturrock. He got an "out of office" message again. Another handful of crisps was grabbed to allay his fury. Given the amount of urgent messages Sturrock had sent, he didn't appear to be in a hurry to take Jarlo's call.

Then he heard a *ping.*

"You have messages. All the messages are from Sturrock Claus. Do you want to me to download them all?"

Thank the goddess. Finally, he would get his money and he could spend the evening off his tits. The download was a few crystals worth; a big file. It was both video, audio, and sensory, although his immersive helmet was up the creek, so just sound and vision it would have to be. Jarlo hobbled to his faithful recliner seat and plonked himself down.

"Play," he commanded.

"It went bong - then nothing. After that first bong, the android should have opened its eyes and said hello - according to the build instructions *you* translated. Yet look at it, sat there, just a torso and a head, watching me, but ignoring me. The instructions specifically say not to fit its arms or legs until you are fully ready to respond to its needs. I think that might be a mistranslation, Jarlo. Strange terminology.

"I'll need help with that. I've shouted at the thing a lot over the last week or so. I've built it, stripped it back down, built it again, stripped it back down again and then built it for a third time.

"I've christened him Bong. Bong is always silent, never responds, I could easily slap him, but that would be like hitting one of my children - or the toaster. Did I tell you I got the kit from Gordon's Antiques and it is a male? Did you know, Jarlo, that he was uncovered during an excavation dig on the ancient Colony Planet called Diarmuid's World? Diarmuid's World is one of the early post-Earth planets. It seems that most of the technology from those times was not built to last- an absolute bag of spanners, to coin an ancient engineering phrase my dad used to use. You remember him, Jarlo, you dined with us once back in the day. He'd never seen such a thin man eat so much. Obviously one of your syndromes manifesting itself.

"The instructions need another go at, Jarlo. That's why I have sent you this live feed. I'm not happy paying the second instalment if the wording is wrong. That's not an accusation, but due to inflation that's just over thirty million Coriozone pounds. A year's wages for an ancient history professor like me. I know you like the whacky stuff J, but promise me you'll stay off it whilst you have another look at the translation. Bong will just have to stay in bits for the foreseeable future, until your return.

"We couldn't afford a modern android. They cost so much money, J. Ailsa and I just do not have the resources. We were taxed so heavily when the twins arrived. I don't know whether you know, it's a one baby population rule here and because we used unauthorised fertility treatments, they refused all the multiple birth rebates.

We need Bong to help us. He will be our electronic manny, so we can both spend time together."

<SEND>

"I am so frustrated, Jarlo. Finally, I got the fucker to say hello, but then shortly afterwards it went "bong-bong" repeatedly and wouldn't stop. It was so annoying. I went back to the translation you did- apparently this was the internal positronic brain trying to link with what the instructions said was the neural net. We call it a different name these days; our blue cloud ether link is the new version of that ancient network. The blue cloud has not been so helpful though, despite a million gig per nanosecond.

"I called a few antique technicians as you haven't responded. You are probably balls-deep and don't give a shit. The techs I spoke with said that, in theory, there should be nothing wrong with the connection. They were not familiar with the make and model, but there were early-form androids with positronic brains still operating within the Coriozone Collective when the blue cloud was established. So, in their opinion, Bong should work.

"I'm going to send more messages until your inbox jams and your message sub-space link provider manually contacts you. So read your fucking messages. Ah, he'll never reply if I'm rude. Delete last line. <deletion failure> Tonight's message might be delayed by the atmospherics. Boy, it's one hell of a stormy evening here.

"Bong has been stressing me out. I had a couple of beers for the first time in ages - and chilled a little. Then I re-read the translated instructions and eventually got the first bong stage to work. I had used a 3.0 positronic chip rather than a 4.0. I am such dick. However, listen to this clip:

""Accessing planetary language systems. Adapting ocular sensors. Morning, Sir. I am <insert my name here> - how can I help you? Before you answer however, please make sure you do not assemble my arms and legs until you are ready for me to assume my duties."

"Jarlo, he speaks.

""I am unit designated Bong, how may I help you?"

"Well, Jarlo, I laughed my pants off because I was so pleased. I laughed out loud and Bong copied me. He was obviously in a learning phase. We had been storming and now we were norming.

"I am Sturrock Claus. Pleased to meet you, Bong," I said. "Are you able to relate the rest of your construction manual to me verbally?"

"Guess what he said, J?

"Sorry Sturrock. I cannot access those files. I hope you have the original document files, as they are not stored within my systems, for obvious reasons."

"What does he mean, Jarlo? What would those obvious reasons be for Bong not to have the manual in his files? I told him to go into standby mode while I looked at stage three of its construction, according to your translation. It said the protocol needed to be installed appropriately and all of the failsafe protocols must be opted into. That if any were switched off, Bong may be harmful to animals, small children and the infirm. And that without further updates, his response could be challenging.

"That was not what I was expecting. So, I asked him:

"Challenging in what way, Bong?"

"Guess what he said? Yep. You are right, you win the prize.

""I do not have that information stored in my systems.""

<SEND>

"Jarlo. Its Sturrock. I've installed, via download, the ancient language update which was thankfully still available on the blue cloud. Unfortunately, a broad search has not been fruitful where Bong's safety protocols are concerned, or where the fully translated version of the manual might be. So much is eluding me. There must be one. I really need your help.

Can you run the translation again, Jarlo? There are still bits I can't understand and his warnings not to fully activate him, are worrying me, but we are desperate for our Manny."

"Jarlo, I thought I'd send another message to you. I know you are on holiday. Some success: I've got Bong to stream music and recite poetry. He spent hours answering the kids' questions yesterday. The twins taught him to swear in universal common and told him dirty jokes too. Guess what- he laughed and laughed. Must have a basic emotion chip.

"Are you male or female? Will you have a tinkle or a front bottom?" Joddo asked him. I didn't know whether to laugh or flush with embarrassment. Mira admonished Joddo for asking such questions. She's the eldest by twenty minutes and a better parent to Joddo than I will ever be. I can build things from their atomic weight upwards -if I have the manual I might add- but raising children is a whole other kettle of poisson, to coin another ancient phrase of my father's.

"When Bong went bong four times today, I tried to look it up in the manual- with no luck. To be honest, I had got extremely comfortable with how he was. I almost convinced myself that he was finished."

<SEND>

"It's been over five weeks, Jarlo. I know you are probably lying comatose in a pool of your own puke on Tarl - if indeed that's where you are.

"I understand now that five bongs means put on arms, six put on legs and seven switch the android over to full intuitive learning mode, free from the net. So, what the hell does four bongs mean? I tried you again Jarlo, but there was no response – as ever."

<SEND>

"So, four bongs is just his internal activation switch-over. "Yahhght" is a word meaning empathy, his empathy switch. Fabulous. Thanks to Vos, who came back to me. A longer chat with your clever friend Vos would be useful at some point.

"I know you've had another friend look at it for me too, but he's not got back to me either. I have run a further three tests off the back of your translation, but I'm having no luck with the final set up protocols. The translation seems to suggest Bong is a protector, hence the empathy switch, I suppose. It seems apt we're using him for our childcare.

"We might get a night out without having to pay a babysitter soon. Or am I being utterly naive, with lack of sleep tinting my rose-coloured spectacles?

"Honestly, Jarlo, I need the manual looking at soon. I'm going to sort the switch phase then add the arms and legs. You'd be welcome to come and visit to see Bong in action, any time you like."

"Jarlo, hi. I am seriously motoring now. Yes, another one of Dad's phrases. I am in the basement again with Bong. He is lying across the table. I attached his arms and legs and I've just attached the force grown epidermis. I have even grown the optional bits of skin that have made Joddo roar with laughter. Bong needs his male identity, he even asked for the full gender designation. The nipples and belly button miraculously fell into place as the skin settled onto his frame. Such clever tech, I bet his original skin wasn't this good. It's been guesswork though, without the full translation."

"I've heard back from your friend Vos again. He was so helpful- he said he couldn't get in touch with you, either.

"Bong is complete, Jarlo. I suppose I no longer need help, although I'll commit to having the full re-translation at ten million credits in total - no more. Just in case he has a fault and I need to fix him. I have sent the first one hundred mil.

"I watched Bong fully activate earlier. He's a tall, fit specimen of a robotic man- you'd like him. I know you like to travel on either shuttle. He sat up and looked at me; I was a bit embarrassed because he was naked. I looked into his eyes- they look alien, distant -a bit spooky. But as Bong said, he is growing into himself."

<SEND>

"Jarlo. Oh Goddess, Can you fucking answer your unit? There is something wrong with Bong. Do you have any friends who can help me? I need to switch him off. There is nothing I can understand that relates to switching him off. Neither you nor Vos are answering.

"Please get back to me. I don't know what to do... Dear Goddess... Listen to this:

""Sturrock, Creator. I am now complete. I can now download the final schematics, fail-safes and weapons of mass destruction."

"I asked him what he meant. He's just repeating it over and over.

"My name is now no longer Bong. I am a weapon master, designate Marus. I have been created to destroy."

"Jarlo, I think he is going to kill me and my family - my children, for fuck's sake -and he's said once this planet is dead, he's going to visit you to collect his manual translation."

<Messages send >

Jarlo couldn't believe the newscasts. The terror attacks on Tilan were horrendous. No wonder neither the messages, nor the money had come through.

He was sitting in his bedroom, planning his next trip to the Leisure Planets, when his vid-screen kicked into life.

"Jarl, its Petch. Your friend hasn't activated that android, has he?"

"Noooo?" He hesitated. Where was this going to go?

"It wasn't an empathy switch."

"Is that just a random sentence Petch? I'm busy."

"The translation Vos did for that annoying Sturrock guy was wrong. The literal translation is "turn off the empathy switch.""

"So?"

"So, I asked a couple of historian friends who work for the Vellums of Gha."

"You are well connected!"

"It's probably unfortunate for you we didn't get in touch with them earlier. Jarl, it's a fucking planet-buster. A colonisation tool used to destroy the Zeapon Hoard planets. Your friend just built an Armageddon machine. It won't stop until Tilan is a cinder."

"Thank fuck I live off world, then," Jarlo said. He thought, quite often wrongly, that humour could improve any situation.

"You are a sick man. We are the closest world to Tilan. The Android will come here next."

"Shit. Thanks. See you." He cut the call, not wanting any further confrontation.

Jarlo wondered if he could get a trip off-world as soon as possible. He opened a link and booked his flights on credit. He had enough faith his travel agent would get him out of the system that very day. He cancelled his carer for the foreseeable future. He would have to pay travel insurance because of his medical conditions- but it would be worth it to survive.

Whilst he waited for his travel agent to respond, he listened to the messages from Sturrock again with a mixture of curiosity, horror, and offence. Why hadn't Sturrock paid more attention to the thing he had been making? Why had he, Jarlo, rushed the translation? Worst of all, the message containing his credit dump still hadn't come through.

There was a knock at his door.

He got up from his bed, something that did not happen very often when he was at home. His knee joints cracked. He didn't dress, caring nothing for his near nakedness. Clothes were tight and restrictive. Anything he had to be embarrassed about had shrunk to nothing because of his disease. Thankfully, his urine bag tube was long enough for him to go from the bed to the door.

Jarlo opened the door. Standing in the doorway was the most beautiful man he had ever set eyes upon. Must be the new postman. Shame he had no money left.

"My name is Marus. Are you Jarlo, friend of Sturrock?" the beautiful man said.

Then Jarlo recalled the name. It was the planet-buster. He would have pissed himself, if he didn't have a catheter fitted.

Just before Marus crushed his windpipe, he heard his house AI confirm,

"I have retrieved a failed message from Sturrock Claus; he has deposited one hundred and ten million credits into your bank account. Would you like to order your narcotics now Jarlo?"

AS SIDNEY SLEPT

I am alive. Sidney thought, as he opened his eyes.

There was light coming through the opaque hood of his coffin-like cubicle. He had gone into cryogenic storage suffering from late stage metastasised cancer. It was a miracle he had revived.

Sidney shifted his body in the cubicle and was further amazed about what he didn't feel. He no longer felt constant pain, he could breathe better too; he'd only had limited lung capacity towards the end, his SATs dangerously low as his life leached away.

Sidney was one of the first people to be cryogenically stored as a living patient. Those who had gone into storage before him had been stored dead, either as decapitated heads or cadavers, awaiting a miracle cure -or science's ability to re-grow their bodies.

Reaching up with both hands, Sidney pushed at the cubicle lid, as he had rehearsed before he'd gone under; the mechanism hissed quietly, then opened with the whir of hidden hydraulics.

Two arms? How could I not notice I pushed with two arms?

His left arm had been amputated in 2094 as a result of sepsis. He'd lost toes and the tip of his nose, too. The doctors had said the sepsis took hold after he cut the bottom of his left foot, whilst his immunity was lowered following his first round of chemotherapy. That was after the skin cancer had spread to his lungs and slowly taken his breath away.

My arm. My toes are all there. I'm cured. Sidney touched the tip of his nose-it was whole. *Better than cured, rejuvenated.*

Sidney sat up with the flexibility of his youth; his left leg had been most strongly affected by cancer and his tibia had regularly fractured. There was no pain at all.

Looking down, he saw the tubes that had catheterised him had already been withdrawn. There was a slight breeze, he had goose pimples and his nipples were erect- but he wasn't cold. He ran a hand over his head.

I've got hair. So, they have also found a cure for baldness.

How long had he been asleep? Ten years, twenty years, a hundred years? The side panels to his booth opened outwards, lengthening into gleaming steps studded with little LEDs, like the gangways of old aeroplanes. Did aeroplanes even exist anymore? He had to admit he was handling this well. He'd always been pragmatic.

The Cryogenica Inc laboratories were near Lichfield, underneath the old Whittington Barracks, where ironically he had been trained for National Service during the latter stages of the Japan-China wars, which in turn had led to a distinguished career in the Army Engineering Corps.

When the illness had first taken hold, he had been posted in Hong Kong, so he had returned to Whittington, along with other troops who had suffered near fatal trauma. They had treated him as best they could, but to no avail. He was then asked by his commanding officer if he wanted to take part in the cryogenic experiment. With death approaching, it didn't take much for him to make the decision.

Sidney was surprised no one had met him after he had woken. Why were there no sensors telling the scientists that he was awake? There were other booths neatly stacked in towers of ten all around, set out in the catacombs that were constructed from steel strut racking. Just like a warehouse of bodies.

Sidney had been placed on the bottom level because of his illness-related disability. He climbed out: the floor was cold on the soles of his feet. At the front end of his booth was the box where his over-gown was stored; it was an oak chest that had belonged to him since childhood and where he had kept his toy soldiers. Like an ancient Egyptian, he had been encouraged to take keepsakes with him, so he had familiar things to hand once he woke up. Smiling, he reached for the lid. It immediately crumbled at his touch, disintegrating into a pile of dust. There was no sign of the clothing inside- apart from his flip-flops. He picked one out of the ash and examined it. Only the plastic soles remained – where once a leather thong had been attached, there was now only a void. How long had the material taken to rot completely away? Hundreds of years, he guessed.

His gaze fell on an unlit booth at the base of the opposite tower of cryogenic chambers. He moved across and wiped away some of the dust that had gathered on the viewing window, uncovering some writing. The word *deceased.* There was similar writing on other, unlit booths- but as he moved the lid back, not on his, he noted.

Well obviously, Sid, you prat.

Returning to his opposite and closest neighbour, he pressed what he believed was the booth release catch, lighting up the window section.

Thank God. I hope they know more than I do.

The now-familiar hum of hydraulics filled the air, but as the opening grew wider, he was hit with the most foetid breath of air he had ever smelled. A bouquet of decay.

As the lid swung upwards, the corpse was revealed. Despite being in an airtight environment, it was no more than dust itself and, unrecognisable as male or female, it briefly shivered, crumbled to nothing.

Sidney moved through the booths, checking them one by one; it seemed all the occupants were dead. How could it be that he was the only survivor? All those people, row upon row of them. The sobs that overcame him made him thirsty and his throat was becoming drier. He needed to drink, otherwise no amount of rejuvenation treatment would prevent him from dying of thirst.

He noticed a lift, moved over to it, and pressed the call button.

Originally, Sidney had been staying in the hospice on the first floor, so when the lift opened with a ping, he stepped inside and pressed the number one button. Hopefully, the lift was still functioning, despite the time that had elapsed, which had been long enough for wood and corpses to completely disintegrate.

The lift rose for quite some time. He'd estimated that he was a mile or so underground on his journey down all those years ago; the calculations of distance, speed, and time, familiar to him as an engineer, had kept him from thinking of his stasis treatment for a few moments. The owners had wanted the catacombs to be safe from harm, predators, or nuclear strikes, the publicity had stated- hence their depth.

Had he been a believer, Sidney might have felt like he'd awakened from the dead and was rising to meet his God, but he had seen too much of war and death to have any kind of faith.

The lift pinged again and came to a halt. Doors opening, he walked out into a well-lit corridor, which he remembered like it was yesterday. Other than the hum of the still operational air-conditioning vents above him, all was silent as he made his way down the long corridor, until he reached the reception area of the hospice. Two great big double glass doors swished open, revealing a rich carpet that felt warm under his feet. So, they were keeping the buildings fresh even if they had not maintained the catacomb area.

It was then he noticed the skeleton; he jumped, then found himself laughing nervously- it was no threat to him. The skeleton sat behind the reception desk, grinning as skeletons do, dressed in a uniform of sorts that was as pristine as when it came out of its wrapper. The lower jaw of the deceased was detached and lying on the desk; it was tidily arranged directly under the upper jaw, as if someone had placed it there very carefully. It looked almost as if the receptionist had been told a joke that had really made their draw drop laughing - but had also killed them.

Examining the jawbone, he shivered involuntarily – it was real.

Military and engineering training kicking in now, he began to assess on the situation. No scraps of clothing. No excessive dust or decaying rags, no trauma. It was likely someone had continued to clean around the dead body that had been left there with almost funereal care.

What could he use as a weapon, he wondered, as the animal part of his brain wrestled between fight and flight? Unless he took a leg bone, there was nothing to wield - and he wasn't going to desecrate a resting place.

Suddenly, he heard whistling, a tuneless dirge that was both at once appealing and frightening. It stopped as abruptly as it had started. He needed to find the source.

Two long corridors joined all the hospice rooms together, they stretched for quite a way beyond the reception. He remembered they were broken up by kitchens and lounges to accommodate family and friends as they made painful decisions for, or advocated on behalf of their loved ones.

Sidney set off down the left-hand corridor, towards where his hospice room had been. As he walked upon the deep pile carpet, he felt a growing angst. Out of the gloom, he saw the door to his old room eventually hove into view, the lights coming on to guide his way.

He tapped on the door pad for room 33 and it whooshed open. The air smelled of ozone, as if electricity itself was trying to escape from the plug sockets.

The room was just as he had remembered.: The picture of his fathers was still in its large frame. He noticed with sadness that it was faded. Very faded. He opened his wardrobe. Clothes. His City 2075 football top and his boot-cut Levi's hung neatly on a hanger. His prized Adidas Samba trainers were there too. *Why were they in such good condition, when my soldier box didn't survive?* He quickly dressed.

"Ah Sidney Saunders, you are awake."

He didn't jump because it was so nice to hear another human voice. He did his trousers up quickly, feeling it might be impolite to face someone with your flies undone, then he turned.

Now he jumped. The voice had sounded human, but it was clearly an alien who was standing before him. He staggered back in shock, falling on to his old bed.

It's a lizard.

"Apologies Sidney, I did not mean to frighten you." The lizard was of a variety he could not classify, despite all the old Attenborough cubes he had consumed as a boy. It held out a human like hand, with four fingers and an opposable thumb, like his own. Sidney took the outstretched hand and was pulled up by a strength he wasn't expecting.

"I am designation Gruss, I am a Kallienthi."

"A Kalli-what?"

"My race discovered your world shortly after the extinction event." It shook his hand.

"What?" It was becoming his favourite retort. Sidney had spent most of his military career knowing what he was doing; currently however, he was well out of his depth by about one lizard.

"Are all my people gone? Was it a war?"

The Kallienthi shook its head. "No, Sidney. Meteor strikes, multiple detonations. The first hit the satellite of this planet, tearing a great swathe from it, resulting in a bombardment of the surface and unmanageable tides."

Sidney sighed." And my people?"

"There are some left, although our reference point was limited."

"Sorry, say that again? In-fact a little more detail all-round would be helpful."

The Kallienthi blinked, it's under lids moving sideways and the outer eyelids down. Very disconcerting. Its forked tongue spat out of its lipless mouth once every few seconds. It was beautiful, in a reptilian way, all blues, and purples with a great pink fleshy crest. It was bipedal in overalls too, no sign of a tail. To Sidney it was a holder of secrets.

Sidney waited.

"It's probably about a thousand years ago since we found this world. The meteors had subsided, but there was still a lot of debris in orbit, preventing a physical descent. If you look during a clear night, you can see a fine ring. Our Exploration Bird hung in the weak gravity field and we translated down to the surface. We estimated it was approximately seventy years since the extinction event. The dust was thick, but we managed to speed its clearance from the atmosphere by cloud seeding. The oceans had risen and the atmosphere had warmed. Mammalian life was all but extinct. We managed to save and catalogue some of the species, but few survived; those that did were mostly waterborne, or underground habiting creatures Humanity was all but extinct- then we found the life signs underground in the catacomb below.

Unfortunately, the dust had silted up the cryogenics, meaning most booths malfunctioned. We found you here and maintained your booth; you have slept peacefully ever since. We healed your genetic discrepancies, in order to assure a perfect sample of DNA."

Sidney thought of his arm and his hair. Then his mind flicked back to the creature.

"Am I alone, then?"

"No, Sidney, you are not alone. There are other humans, but they are all genetic copies of you. This world is populated by copies - both male and female - of Sidney Saunders. It was the only way. We are conscious this was done without your consent and we apologise. We will extinguish the experiment, if you so wish."

Extinguish? The hair on the back of his neck rose. "How many copies?"

"Sixty-six."

"All descended from me?"

"Cloned, not descended. They do not reproduce; we do not allow them."

"How many of you Kallienthi are there?"

"Only designation Gruss now. Just myself. I have recently laid a clutch of eggs, so I will not always be alone."

"Why do you not let them reproduce?"

"Our ethics and governance committees always forbade the development of mammalian life. We seldom interfere with other types of life forms whether they be silicon, carbon or gaseous based in origin."

"Why did your people not settle here?"

It laughed, a drawn-out clicking noise, neck fins flashing open in a display of blue fan-like membranes.

"We do not interfere. I am a Remainder. I have chosen to watch over this world. My people come from a remote galaxy; it took the Exploration Bird over seven hundred years to reach here."

"So, you and I represent the only original life on this planet. We will be companions... until we die?"

"You will not die, Sidney. You are immortal. Should you end your own life, you will be backed up and re-cloned. A perfect copy, no different."

Many would exalt at the promise of immortal life; Sidney was all too level in his pragmatism.

"What if I do not want to live forever?"

"I am afraid you have no choice. It is done."

"From nearly dead to immortal. How ironic." His humour masked growing concern.

"Feel free to explore. This is your world. I need to continue to clean the bones of the dead. A Kallienthi is bound to do this, during their respite breaks. Ancestors are the most important, even if they are of another race."

It was very disconcerting to see the group of *Descendants,* as they called themselves. They welcomed him as if he should be venerated. There were three children, including two little girl Sidneys, both blonde. Thirty-one male Sidneys of various ages and thirty females, who resembled him precisely, but with their female genetic markers switched on; they all wore tight-fitting, Lycra-like underwear. It was a temperate land now, no need for woollens or leather coats. Could he let them procreate? The little he knew of genetics led him to believe inbreeding would lead to abnormalities. He guessed there must have been gender manipulation, otherwise all of the Descendants would be male; if they were not to procreate, why bother? He would have to ask Gruss.

One of the little blonde girls ran up and took his hand. None of the adults stopped her. She asked if he would like to go on a learning walk. She led him up a big hill and then further on, for what felt like a couple of miles. She told him of all the place names and monuments, most of them ruins. He did not like to tell her he knew most of them from when they were brand new. They eventually came to the pagoda on the hill he remembered as a child; they must have been near Borrowcop Lane, by his old school.

Lichfield Cathedral had been a wonderful example of the gothic medieval; he remembered the intricately carved stone figures at its entrance façade. Now, it was a ruin. It wallowed like a beached whale that had rotted in the sun, leaving only bones behind. Two of the spires had long-since fallen; only one remained, pointing in disappointment to a silent unresponsive heaven.

Sadness welled up in him, sadness drawn from his predicament and from the memories of all his friends, his lost loves, and his wonderful fathers. The little girl tightened her grip. He took her through the forest that had grown about the city. The Churches of St Mary's, St Michaels, and St Chad's had long gone. The two pools now lapped against the outer walls of the cathedral square.

The little girl told him about their society. They lived in the forest, close to the underground base. She was pleased their God was awake and that they would prosper under his reign. The melancholy Sidney was feeling an overwhelming sense of unease. These people

– these *Descendants* - were not Sidney's friends, not his family. He was still very much alone.

Gruss was his usual charming self when he gave permission to let the small group of humans procreate. Sidney had asked about abnormalities and was assured the Kallienthi would ensure they would receive the help and support they needed to develop their genetic resilience. It had taken him three weeks of living with the Sidneys to make the decision. He could not stay with them, it was too difficult, and the expectations thrust on him were more than stressful.

"I will leave this place. I cannot be a god to these people. I might return but it is highly unlikely. I cared nothing for religion when I was alive, I'm not going to subject the last humans on earth to it."

"You are alive!" Gruss said his crest rippling. He was nursing a chick, a baby Kallienthian, who was eating from a handful of insects. "I have told you, you are truly immortal."

Sidney hated being reminded of the fact.

"I may be immortal, but this world is not mine. All I love and lived for is gone. The remaining humans are disconcerting to say the very least. I have looked at every aspect of my being over the last few weeks; I can see what I would have looked like as a female, young and old. The best thing about not seeing yourself from all angles is that you do not see your whole soul. Just the bits you can come to terms with."

He'd had many philosophical discussions with Gruss over those few weeks, but Sidney felt no meeting of minds, no connection to the Kallienthi. He needed to leave.

He asked the Lizard if there were any forms of transport he could utilise. Gruss appeared excited to be asked and offered one of the Kallienthi hover vehicles. Sidney took the next few weeks to familiarise himself with the controls. Fuelled by advanced solar batteries, the "anti-gravity" machine could take him anywhere he wanted to go. Gruss had uploaded all the remaining information left from before the extinction event, so Sidney could look over it at his leisure.

Then came the day to say goodbye to Gruss and the Sidneys.

The small group of humans wept to see him depart. Although he had kept himself apart from them, they continually angled to spend time and converse with him, boasting to one another about the amount of time they had stolen, like the stupid bragging rights one might have had on meeting their favourite celebrity.

Eight weeks had passed since Sidney had awoken. He had become immortal, a god, a father – but still he felt like an experiment. He had secretly put his stasis booth in the hover. It was far better to be in control than be controlled, he thought.

Sidney took the hover ship into the air and directed it towards the Cathedral. He wasn't going far.

Part of the Cathedral crypt had collapsed, revealing a large oblong gap. He was able to park the hover within it, managing to secrete it from view. The next week or so was spent walling himself in. Exhausted, nine days later he entered the booth, reconnected a stasis cubicle to the hover to monitor his life signs and commanded the machine to let him sleep again.

For seven hundred and sixty-three-years, Sidney slept.

He woke thirsty as before; but this time the hover, which had been self-repairing over that time, just as Gruss had said it would, provided him with sustenance.

The crypt was silent. The wall had been built from double-thick cathedral stone, cemented with quicklime the hover had reproduced and sand he had sourced himself. He'd had to dig down more than six feet to reach the sand he'd recalled below the slides and swings at one of the city parks.

Although Sidney had been reluctant, Gruss had insisted on providing him with a weapon, which the Kallienthian had explained worked by manipulating sound. Sidney pointed it at the wall and fired. He blew himself across the room with the blast reflection, bouncing off the hover, before scrambling to his feet, sore but still apparently alive. Discovering a lower setting in the data banks, Sidney tried again, this time managing to use the gun to clear a big enough gap for the hover.

The hover ship started up the first time. Despite some inexpert manoeuvring and a few broken branches, Stanley eventually coaxed the ship out of the vault and through the now lush, dense forest that covered it, rising into the sky; the lone spire of the Cathedral visible below him, covered in sigils of a language he could not decipher.

He skirted around the immediate area for a while, then headed out towards what would have once been Tamworth and the underground base. It wasn't long before he found the outer reaches of a huge city.

Suddenly, the communication screen in the hover ship sprang to life.

"Lord Sidney. We have been expecting you. The Lord Gruss' scriptures said you would return. We are blessed."

This almost prompted him to turn the ship around immediately, but curiosity got the better of him. He supposed he could stay a while, assess the situation, and move on, if he so wished.

Regular exchanges with what he could only guess was flight control saw him land his hover on the top of a great ziggurat. All the buildings as far as the eye could see were pyramid in shape – some pointed, some with a flat top – all with the same lettering upon them as the Cathedral spire.

He exited the hover, to be met by a small group of Kallienthi, dressed in red and gold armour and carrying weapons with deadly looking spearheads. Granted, any civilisation would have its rules and would wish to protect themselves.

"We are to take you to Lord Gruss, Venerable Sidney." The tallest of the guards motioned with a spear towards a double glass-fronted opening that cast out much light.

Sidney moved through the opening with the guards, immediately recognising his surroundings - an extension of the underground base where he had first been cryogenically frozen. The walls, the floors the carpets- all the same.

As he was led down corridors, Sidney could hear singing all around, the most beautiful keening – remarkable, but very alien. The place was unrecognisable as *his* Earth.

They entered the original base elevator and descended. When the door opened, he saw humans for the first time. To his joy, none of them remotely resembled him. They were beautiful too, men and women, some slim and muscular who looked like they were servants, others of all shapes and sizes who were lying about; Gruss had obviously re-introduced racial diversity. There were people from all the cultures and creeds of Earth, as there had been before he had slept for the first time, engaged in various pursuits: playing music, relaxing playing cards and in one corner there was cushion filled pit, next to a screen. The video upon the screen was very sexually explicit and some of the people were coupling. Sidney blushed.

"This way," one of the guards said. Sidney followed.

Not once, however did any of the humans take notice of him. They were less curious than sheep and quiet with it; he couldn't hear any of them speaking. The guards led him to the area he recognised as the Hospice, where he had first met Gruss, and brought him to Room 33 - possibly not a coincidence- and took him inside.

The room was bare, save for a computer screen- or rather a flat surface that resembled one.

"Gruss," announced a guard; immediately they all left, closing the door behind them.

The screen turned on, the image of the Kallienthi filling its view.

"Sidney, it has been over seven hundred years since we last met."

"I see your children hatched and your society has grown up alongside my clones' descendants. Where are you?"

"This is me, Sidney. I have ascended past the constraints of a physical body; I live as perpetual energy now."

"Nice." Sidney wasn't quite sure how to respond to that. "How did you manage to diversify the clones' children into separate races again? Surely not from my DNA? I am of mostly African descent."

"We didn't. Your clones all died, Sidney."

Sidney went cold. Was its relief or sadness? His eyes welled. He wasn't the crying sort, yet the tears flowed.

"We knew there were others, Sidney, I just needed your assent to breed them."

"What, the clones?"

"As the last remaining person left linked to the military command of this planet, we needed you to agree. Governance and ethics. Even a warrior race still has red tape."

"Warrior? I thought you were scientists."

"A little misconception."

"Or lie. And what do you mean, breed them?"

"What else would we eat but mammals? We are reptilian for Zorth's sake."

Sidney had gone even colder. He was beginning to realise he had been duped. Humans had survived, and they had been bred for meat. To feed the Kallienthi.

"You mean to say you came here to find food?"

The image that was Gruss click-laughed. It didn't sound so quirky now. It sounded threatening.

"You took this world after a disaster, you subjugated its remaining people and you have bred them, to eat?"

"I saw you walk through the human level. How happy were they, how passive? We bred out the larynx and forbade the use of texts and information centres, so they could not evolve a meaningful language of their own. With no communication other than the grunts they make and the screams of their pleasure when rutting, they have been easy to farm. They go to their deaths with some awareness, but the bolts we use are quick and painless."

Sidney stared at him in disbelief. Although he had no connection to this creature in its original form, he believed it had been a compassionate, ethical being.

"You had the choice, Sidney. Had you said no, had you ruled over your clones, we would never have found these other humans; we would not have gone looking for them at all. We could have eaten cloned meat once you had got used to the idea. It made us sick, but ethics would have demanded we do so, until we moved onto another world to conquer."

He did not think he could get any colder.

"Conquer?"

"Who do you think fired the missiles at the Moon? I needed somewhere that was warm enough for forty million Kallienthi." Gruss raised his voice. "Guards, kill this man."

The doors to Room 33 opened, two Kallienthi with blasters walked in, and Sidney died, for the first time in his life.

Gruss had told a pack of lies from the start, although Sidney *did* wake up -in a new body- in a booth underground beneath the old Whittington Barracks site.

As before it was quiet. No other booths had been used.

Had Gruss forgotten he would be rejuvenated?

Sidney tried the lift, but it was in disrepair this time. He managed to find the stairwell and climbed thirty flights of stairs, clambering over debris, and picking his way over gaps in the damaged structure. It was a good job he had his new body. It felt similar to the last one, although Sidney could tell somehow that this was obviously a copy, despite no obvious physical disadvantage that could be discerned. He just felt more powerful, his sensory perceptions enhanced.

He navigated the rubble into the hospice area, which was littered with corpses – or rather skeletons. A battle had taken place here, but evidently a long time ago. Discarded weapons were strewn about the floor; clearly no-one had come to survey the battle scene or to bury the dead.

The upper lift was functioning and Sidney's path to the surface was easy. He shrank from the sunlight as he emerged from the surface building. Now he was no longer in a forest- all around were fields, lush with wonderfully green-purple grass. The sun was high in the sky, but it was cool, like early winter, with a North wind bite. Sidney could see no vehicles about that were road or sky worthy.

He heard a clicking noise and turned to see what could only be described as a half-human, half Kallienthi. She was beautiful: human face and torso, Kallienthi head, complete with a wonderful green crest. She wore a diaphanous bodysuit that shimmered in the light.

"How can it be?" she said, in English. "You are a survivor from before the catechism? You are like Sidney-our god."

She prostrated herself on the ground.

Goodness me, Sidney thought. *What happened this time whilst I slept?*

PART THREE: THE SKYFLIERS

THE DREAMS OF AEFLYNN VALKSLANDER

PART 1

Flynn the Sorcerer opened his eyes. He was in his private accommodation in the Magedw Capitol. The sun was streaming through the partially open glass windows and the curtains fluttered in a light breeze. Vanvear was next to him, lying on her side, looking at him, smiling.

"Good morning Flynn." she murmured, sleepily.

Vanvear was the most powerful sorcerer in all the world bar him- and the most beautiful of women. He was a lucky man to call her his wife. Her red hair fell about a perfect angular face framed by high cheek bones under lightly browned skin. Her chin rested on one hand, propped up on an elbow.

"Morning, Vanvear," he said, still a little disoriented.

"Dreaming again?"

"The Nightmares afflict me once more. It seems we are at a crossroads. I'm dreaming of the past, but not how it really happened. My name wasn't Flynn. I was so scared. The dream cut out before the ceremony. Clem wasn't the wild. It was me."

"They are warping the past. The Gold Lord, whoever he or she may be, grows in power." It was a well-rehearsed warning. "You must tell me if the Gold Lord appears."

Flynn nodded. He had never seen the Gold Lord. He probably never would.

She read his mind as she stroked his hair soothingly.

"Go back to sleep my love. It is only just after dawn."

He felt the comfort of her nakedness as she spooned him and he was soon asleep and dreaming again, this time of another version of the past that had so shocked him.

Aeflynn Valkslander looked to the early morning sky. The orange and blue block of dawn appeared to be pushing up the deep red half-globe that would be a fiery ball of heat and light come eleven of the clock. There was still a faint chill in the air, but this handsome, biting dawn gave promise of another warm day.

Flynn had been born in the snowy wastes of the far North, but he had been a Chendran citizen since his mother Gretan brought him here as an infant eighteen years before. He thanked Torin he did not have to toil in the snows of his homeland day after day, looking after his grandfather's sheep. He would take the odd early chill morning over eternal snow any day.

Flynn was clerk to the Privy Council of Chendra and his attendance at the Calling Ceremony was essential. He was there to make an official note of the proceedings for the royal records. He momentarily glanced at his mother Gretan; She smiled encouragingly as always, her warm face helping to comfort his nerves, if not his cold hands. It was his first official Calling Ceremony narration; his nerves bubbled in his belly, like a bag of burping toads.

Gretan was the king's mistress, still as beautiful and youthful looking as she had been in her late teens, when she first came to this land. Many saw his mother as the queen in all but office, but most at the Calling Ceremony—and the Lawmasters—would rise in civil war before bending their knee to her.

As he drew out the seating plan with his pen, for prosperity, Flynn's eyes naturally flicked to the skinny, elderly, demented King Aledro, who sat on his makeshift chair-cum-throne. He did not understand what his mother saw in Aledro. The king's first wife Shennine—Gretan's sister—had died in childbirth at the age of sixteen, just after she had bravely presented a royal heir to the Crown. Aledro had invited Gretan to come and nurse Vanstos, as she had a young baby of her own, and he had then fallen in love with her. They could not wed as she was legally his sister by marriage; something that was not acceptable, even for a king, in the eyes of the Chendran Lawmasters. Instead, he had been permitted to remarry from within noble circles and had done so- with Gretan's blessing.

The King's cousin, the Crown Prince Vanstos, was the legal ruler, following the King's stroke and subsequent lack of capacity. Vanstos sat, serenely as ever, on his throne. He was a kind young man, if a little too serious, but a wicked swordsman, always willing to spar in the yard with the students. Princess Serah—Vanstos wife—sat to the Crown Prince's right: a staunchly religious member of the Iyan imperial family, who looked down her nose at most people.

Priest Kitis—the King's second son—was seated on his left. A jolly member of the Pantheon Church, he was nineteen summers old and already developing into the rotund, hairless man his father was. Kitis's mother, the second queen, who the king had taken when he could not marry Gretan, had died of the wasting a few summers before.

The other members of the royal party sat behind the king: Duke Dedron—the King's nephew and Royal Chamberlain crammed his tall thin frame into a small chair. He was a nervous type, eyes darting left and right, then to Flynn, as if he were seeking reassurance that the ceremony would go to plan. Duke Sedris—the Castellan—sat next to him. Sedris was a muscular warrior, more at home in a smithy than at royal occasions.

The final member of the Royal Privy Council was Vanine—niece to the king—although the exact family ties were known to a few, other than the monarch and his eldest son. Vanine was the reason Flynn wanted most of all to be a mage. He wanted to be her equal and dreamed one day of taking her hand in marriage - such was her beauty. To be fair, it was the dream of most men—and many women—in Chendra City. Vanine charmed all who came before her: bearing no falsities, she was the most generous of souls. Despite Flynn and others had seen Vanine vaporise a murderous spy from thirty yards with a bolt of white light, their admiration knew no bounds.

Flynn caught Vanine's eye as she readied the applicants with a few words of support. She winked at him; it was all he could do to keep writing. He felt blessed to work with her most days and was amazed he wasn't a simpering wreck by the end of each of them.

A royal herald trumpeted the dawn, jolting Flynn from his reverie. It was just after six of the morning. Vanine would soon begin the ceremony, as planned.

"Your Majesty, Royal Highnesses, Graces, Lords, Ladies, and Commoners alike; welcome to the Chendran Calling Ceremony, in the year of Torin, Three Hundred and Thirty-Three of the Seventh Age. One of the young men here will be chosen as our candidate to join the Tavander at the Academy of Magedw."

Vanine paused, nodding encouragingly to all the young men before her. They were all in their eighteenth year and Flynn often wondered how Magedw knew their ages, before scolding himself and thinking of the powers that Vanine had at her disposal.

"To please his Majesty and Royal Highnesses, would the candidates announce themselves fully to the Calling and the audience?"

"Prince Earnstos, Duke of the Fell Lands, Third son of King Aledro, brother to the Regent and Priest Kisit."

His friend was finding it hard to stand for this length of time. Earnstos had been a cripple since he had fallen from the back of his horse when he was four summers old, leaving his left leg bandy and turning inwards. He was of plain features, resembling his father as opposed to his eldest half-brother.

"Lord Keffen, Of the House of Dedro, Baron of the Dedron Manse, second son of the Chamberlain Alrec Dedro."

Flynn winced; Keff was a nasty, slimy, big bastard. Keff's group of bullies were known across the kingdom as the Lords of Misrule. He stood a head taller than Vanine- and she was taller than most men. His dark skin had helped him to reach a full beard by his eighteenth year, Keff had it styled in the fashion of Magedw, all pointy and waxed. *Torin help us all if he gets the white robes.*

"Lord Malac Of the House of Kirn."

Flynn did not know Malac well. The young lord spent his days in the royal army with his father, Lord General Malac, on the borders of the Desert of Souls fighting the nomadic Desert Roaches. Stoic and to the point, Malac seemed amiable nonetheless.

"Baron Charn Alec of the House of Alec of the Borderlands." Malac's friend and supposed close companion, if rumours were to be believed. Charn was an effeminate man in his ways if not his build, which was nearly as broad and tall as Keffen's.

"You all know why you are here." Lady Vanine continued. "You represent the major families of this kingdom, in blood and in stature. One of you will travel to Magedw before this year is out. Please present yourselves for the Rod and Helm of Calling.

Little Clem slowly walked upon the steps of the stage, dressed in his best jacket and hose. The ginger-haired, deaf, and mute royal valet smiled as he presented a velvet cushion, upon which rested the Helm and Rod of Magedw. Each nation under the alliance had a set. He carried them proudly.

Poor Clem was always smiling, despite his difficulties. He had been mutilated by his father, who had served the king. Clem's father had been dismissed for embezzlement and he had battered his son, severing his little tongue between snapping teeth with an uppercut. The beating was so brutal that both his eardrums had burst as well. The boy's mother and sisters had not been so lucky.

"As is the tradition, the more junior applicants will go first. Therefore, Baron Charn, will you please step forward? Place the Helm upon your head and hold the Rod in your left hand, then kneel and ask the honoured question. *Tavandar, am I called*? Then, as when Torin was first Tavandar, either you will feel the Calling- or you will have your residual power drained and you will be neutered."

Charn took the rod and helm and knelt. The Helm was nothing more than a silver circuit, Vanine had explained to Earnstos and Flynn the previous evening. It was the receiver, for the Download of the Permission. The rod was the antenna which would allow a conduit to be formed, bringing the Permission, the life-force link that enabled an individual to access the Net of Power. Whatever most of those words meant however, was long lost in history.

"Tavander, am I called?" Charn asked.

It seemed nothing happened, then Charn went a little red faced. He put his right hand to the floor to steady himself. Then he lowered his head. Those with exceptional eyesight would have seen the tear fall and splash on the stage.

"Baron Charn has not been Called," Vanine announced, her sweet, deep voice laden with disappointment as it carried over the massed crowd. At first, there had been a lot of noise, not befitting the ceremony; now you could have heard a clipped bronze sovereign drop in a turd.

Vanine went to help Charn up, but he pulled away from her touch. She said a few words that were lost- or magically warded- before her voice could be heard once more.

"Baron Charn, as befitting a failed applicant, Magedw gives you your reward. You are now Heir to the lost Dukedom of Melsea and granted a stipend of ten thousand gold sovereigns a year."

As Flynn watched with bated breath, Malac also failed and was rewarded with the role of a Lord-Lieutenant in the Chendran Royal Army.

It was Keffen's turn. There were groans from the crowd when he knelt, and Flynn was sure he heard someone in the distance ask if people could explode during the Calling. Vanine's smile was lost as she called out Lord Keffen's details. He took the Helm and the Rod, knelt, and confidently asked the question.

One of Keffen's biggest faults was his self-aggrandisement. He was a natural boaster- and liar too if, mistruth built up the part for him. He was smiling as he knelt, awaiting the power to come through him. Keffen asked the question again, with the flourished intonation of a showman, or a mummer, *or a wanker*. Expletives were not allowed in the record, unfortunately.

Keff's smile became fixed now; for a short while, it looked like the power might be flowing through him. Then, to Flynn's joy Keff pissed himself and fell over sideways as the Helm of Chendra hit the wooden planks of the stage with a pleasing ring- although not quite as pleasing as the thud Keffen's head made as it hit the floor. Flynn made sure he noted everything down for posterity.

Duke Dedro called out, and his other son—the Captain of the Royal Guard Banatras—rushed to the aid of his younger brother, accompanied by some gasps from the crowd – and undeniably, some laughter.

Vanine stepped back and did not help. *Was there a faint smile on her lips?* They said the reward from a failed Calling was always deserved.

"Get out of the way, witch." Banatras said under his breath, his comments clearly indicating that he supported the One God. Ironic, considering his brother was part of the ceremony. Had he too failed a Calling? As approached his prone brother, his anger was plainly visible. "Is there a healer in the crowd?" he cried.

Ignoring the commotion, Vanine said with her magically enhanced voice,

"The Calling's reward is sometimes painful-we have all seen such reactions in the past. However, Lord Keffen will be rewarded with the Vice Captaincy of the Royal Guard, serving under his gracious and helpful brother the Lord Banatras." Sarcasm: Flynn could feel it, if not entirely hear it in her voice.

The ceremony paused for a time to allow the mess to be swilled away from the stage. Flynn felt bad for Earnstos, who had been standing all this time; the pain in his legs must have been unbearable.

It was now Earnstos's turn. Taking the Rod and Helm from Clem, the Royal Prince struggled to kneel.

"Poor bastard cripple," a voice in the crowd said; a little louder than planned, perhaps.

"Tavander, am I called?" the prince asked. There was a pause. Flynn held his breath.

"Come on," Kitis muttered, which prompted Vanstos to raise his hand. Moments before, the Regent had indicated to the guards to seize the woman in the crowd who had made the derogatory remark about his brother. Vanstos was thorough and fair in calling any in the audience—commoner or lord—to order.

Earnstos wobbled and Vanine moved towards him with an outstretched hand. He steadied himself and held up his right hand to stay her. "Cramp in my leg."

Then the Rod lit up and the Helm glowed as the circuit was made and the power flooded into Flynn's friend. Earnstos was the first mage to be born to a Chendran king for many years. The crowd recognised the situation for what it was and cheered loudly.

"Prince Earnstos of the Royal House of Collandine, you are the first-born royal mage in two centuries. Pull forth your power. You will be travelling to Magedw in the next twelve months to receive your reward."

Vanine's voice carried across the noisy crowd. Vanstos and Kitis had joined their brother and were hugging him and shaking his hand, shortly followed by most of the royal party; except for Aledro- who was sound asleep and snoring despite the noise, his head, and much dribble on Gretan's shoulders.

Flynn, wake up. She's here. Clem signed at him, using the language Flynn and Earnstos had devised for him. Flynn stirred.

"Aeflynn," Vanine called again, impatiently. "Are you well?"

Flynn came to, his head pounding. He was starting to get one of his legendary headaches and had got lost in himself for a few seconds Vanine looked amused.

"I know you hoped one day this might be you, Aeflynn, but you know commoners don't get called."

He hoped no one would remind him. He was pleased for Earnstos, yet disappointed it would never be him. "If only my dad had been from a royal house."

Vanine laughed. They had had this conversation before. Nowhere in the Books of Torin and the Pantheon did it explain why only the elite families answered the Calling.

"Torin's will, Aeflynn. Can you store away the Rod and Helm, then come and meet me in the Privy Chamber ready for the Celebration? I need an escort and so do you. A lady such as I should not be unescorted to the beginning of such an occasion. You are an important secretary too, you should not attend alone."

There was a pause again as his head blossomed with pain. He felt he was going to heave-he needed some powders.

"I am sorry my Lady, but I may have to decline." And much to his embarrassment, he left to be sick.

Later, Flynn awoke in the room he shared with Clem. He sat up quickly; a feeling that he was very much in trouble settling over him. *Shit, I didn't put them back!*

The Second book of Torin and the Pantheon lay upon Clem's immaculate bed. He wrinkled his nose at the chamber pot of vomit, which he nearly kicked getting to his feet. His clothes smelt too, but changing them would have to wait, because on his bed along with his shoes were the Helm and Rod of Calling. He carefully put the circlet on his head and held the Rod in his left hand.

Tavander, am I called? he said in his mind.

As expected, nothing happened. He would need to put them away before they were missed, then get ready for the party. First, he needed to take more powders to relieve him of the pain.

Then, he felt the circlet go warm as power filled him. It was divine.

Then it cut out, he panicked, swore, felt like he might vomit again- and decided he needed his mother.

Vanine had not always been her name. She had adopted it for the role she was playing in this age. Once, she had been known as Vanvear, and before that the ancient name she had been born with. Thankfully, her chosen role was that of a Sorcerer. It meant she would not have to relocate or change identity for at least a few hundred years. She liked her current life. It was simple, straight forward; she didn't have to follow the machinations of her peers in the eternal war of the One God and the Pantheon. She sipped her wine, popped a piece of bush fruit on her tongue, let it dissolve and relaxed back into her bath. What a nonsense the ceremony had been. When she had first walked this world, they had all used the powers as was their birth right. You did not have to be of noble birth. Torin would be turning in his grave, if he had one.

She had spent the morning reflecting. The boy—no, young man—Aeflynn was such an unfortunate lad. She recognised his potential, and he had the temperament to be a great mage. The power was in him, she could feel it. But the net did not allow a commoner to pull. She would get to the bottom of that issue one day, if it were the last thing she did. Closing her eyes, she cleared her thoughts, and drifted.

Suddenly just after she had drifted off, she felt a power like nothing had felt before. Only Adeus or Torin could have matched it. It was coming from the Castle-Palace. *Was it the young prince?* No, he was in his room asleep - she could feel him. She counted those with power. Her sister Fay, just out of town with Rollo the Magedw Ambassador. The low-level weather mages and the wood keepers were there. Yet there was one other and the size of his or her power was immense. She keyed into the lines of magic. Wait – dear God, was that Flynn?

Oh No. He said he was having headaches. Vanvear, you fool. Headaches. A key indicator of a wildling on the Calling day. Today of all days, you had to go and trust Flynn with the circlet and the Rod.

A portal opened before her. Fay—her twin—and Rollo stepped out. He immediately turned his back.

"What the fuckety is going on sister?" Faenvar—or Fay as the mortals knew her—was to the point as ever. "There's a mage who has made a power chime so loud half the civilised world would have heard it."

Vanvear stepped out of the bath, pulled the power about her to dismiss the water, and with a flick of her wrist brought her clothes about her. "You may turn, Rollo."

"Magic users are all accounted for. It's a commoner pulling on the power" Rollo said as he turned. "We need to arrest him. He needs to be neutered."

"In good time, Rollo," Vanvear said. Fay looked at the portly mage in disgust. The Tavander would not want that. This boy could be their Saviour. The end to the immortal curse of the Pires.

"We need to inform the Regent. Hang on, and I'll try and see who it is from his life force," Rollo said.

Quick as a flash, Vanvear diverted the searching spell and negated it. Unaware of Vanvear's intervention, Rollo huffed in frustration and tried again. Vanvear had kept him from finding out it was Flynn, but only for the present. She glanced at her sister, who rolled her eyes.

I could kill him. Fay's voice filled her mind.

No.

Fay's morals were less defined than her own, but she couldn't let Flynn be killed.

"I shall try to find where the perpetrator is," Rollo announced, with as much puff as he could muster. Vanvear and her sister Faenvar were in control – for now.

A little while later, there was a knock at her door. Vanvear had managed to compose herself by this time; she had applied her make-up and was sipping tea. Fay huffed about being a door valet, but still attended. It was Lady Gretan. The normally balanced mistress of the king was clearly upset.

"Lady Vanine. Many apologies for my unannounced arrival."

"Nonsense, my Lady, we were expecting you."

"It's Aeflynn," she said, as Vanvear bade her to sit and poured her some tea; adding some beet sugar to help with the obvious shock. Gretan picked her cup and saucer up with shaking hands and took an anxious sip.

"My son. My stupid son decided to put on the Circlet and hold the Rod of Power. He came to my rooms in a stupor, having just put them back in the vault. He didn't want me to tell you. He thinks he has been called. I need you to persuade him otherwise. He is not thinking straight. Rollo will interrogate him for this- he will want him strung up."

She said the last words wryly. She and Vanine had discussed this before and Vanvear had felt sympathy for her at the time.

"He's just a boy."

Don't tell her, Fay sent.

She needs to know, Vanvear replied.

"Listen, Gretan. And please do not take this the wrong way. Could you be mistaken about who his father was?"

Gretan was aghast.

"Dear Gods. He *has* been called."

"Was his father a commoner?"

"Yes. Harlan and I married for love, much to the chagrin of my father. When it didn't work out, I had to flee. Think of it. One daughter married to the King of Chendra, the other to a sculptor."

"And Harlan: Was he perchance of royal birth, by accident?"

Gretan shook her head.

"No, he's from peasant stock. I was forced to divorce him; on grounds of caste."

"Flynn has the power, Gretan. He's wild."

The king's mistress began to sob.

Now look what you have done. Tears and snot. I hate tears and snot, Fay sent.

"You have to pretend you do not know. Until I have a plan, I must take him away from here. I will look after him." Vanvear's thoughts turned over in her head rapidly. They would need to get away-soon.

The Tavandar will help him. What if he is the Saviour? Fay asked.

We will cross that bridge when we get to it. He will either burn out and dissipate, like all uncontrolled wild ones, or he will inevitably become the Saviour. We will then break the curse.

It would be good to end the Pires once and for all.

How many lives have we lived? I would be happy to live out the rest of my life as a mortal if we could do so? Vanvear's thoughts carried feelings of relief.

Then you are a fool.

Gretan raised her head and dabbed at her eyes with a kerchief.

"Tell me what I must do."

Goodness, Vanvear thought, *this woman is immense.* All the aversity she has faced. Despite her kindness, she was strong, stoic, and hard as diamond.

"You must be quiet. He is cousin to the king; this will be highly embarrassing. Think of the political fall-out. Vanstos loves Flynn like a full brother- this would decimate him. Same with Kitis. However, duty will mean they will have to denounce him. Our problem is not with anyone in Chendra, however. Every witchfinder who was casting last night will know about Flynn, or that someone is casting without licence."

Gretan sighed.

"I will do as you ask. When will you leave?"

Vanvear looked at Gretan.

"I'll not say, just in case. Go and see him. Say a silent goodbye. If he learns you will be apart for some time, he will likely break down the shield walls he will have subconsciously built around his power. He mustn't do so, or the power I felt will level the city and all who live here, including Flynn."

The pain in Flynn's head had receded a little. He had studied too much history not to know what he was. Moreover, the power that danced between his fingertips at times like the Northern Aura was confirmation. He pulled the power back into himself and winced.

He was sitting in his bed, sweating. His mother had gone to see the Lady Vanine, who would most likely neuter him or have him killed. The lovely Vanine. She wouldn't, would she?

Clem was sitting in the opposite bed, watching him. Many mistook Clem for an idiot because he couldn't hear or speak. Nothing could be further from the truth.

Are you okay? His little friend signed.

Yes. I think I've got winter fever.

Already? It's a bit soon.

Perhaps it's earlier this year. It does not always wait for the snow.

It's rare. Clem paused. *You slept with the Rod and Helm, didn't you?*

Not with them on. Flynn's body language would be giving him away to Clem.

You put them on, then.

Yes.

Idiot! Clem's hands jerked the sign rapidly.

They are only for show; the power would still have come to me.

It's been floating around you while you sleep. You need to run. They will kill you, or cut off your balls, or whatever they do.

They will neuter me, possibly execute me. Flynn signed, accompanied by an audible sigh.

Then you need to go now.

Without the help of a sorcerer, I will be dead in days.

Fay is an assassin. And Rollo will kill you. Vanine too.

No, Vanine would help me. She wouldn't kill me, would she?

Soon after, as Clem went about his duties, Flynn dozed despite his concerns. He was jerked from his slumber by a loud knock on the door. His mind cartwheeled. *Was this Rollo or Vanine come to take him to the gallows?*

Flynn wished his power silent. Unbeknownst to him, it became so. He opened the door, resigned to his fate: it was his friend, Prince Earnstos.

"Having a day off, scribe?" Despite the sarcasm, Earnstos loved him like a brother- and vice versa.

"Lazing around in your bed. What about your state duties? Have you written up the occasion when the world-famous Sorcerer Earnstos first got his calling and Keff pissed himself?"

"I've got winter fever."

"Urg. No tongues then."

Earnstos hobbled over to the bed as best as his gait could manage and climbed aboard. "I could do with winter fever, a few days off state duty. Now that I've been called, every in-bred girl from across the kingdom will want a piece of this royal arse. The meetings will be endless. I'll be promised to some poor wretch of ten who can't marry me until I have passed the Magedw test and come out the other side alive."

"There will be plenty of noble boys you can fool around with at Magedw." Flynn replied. His friend and liege was a lover of men, not women. Once Flynn had knocked back a few youthful advances from the prince, a line had been set in the sand for them both; it had not affected their friendship one jot. They'd accepted each other from that point.

Earnstos put his arm about Flynn's shoulder.

"Just one kiss – to give me the fever."

Flynn shrugged him off playfully.

"Never. Vanine and Vanine only for me." He knew she would likely neuter him, or worse.

The room he shared with Clem was quite large. Opposite the bed were ceiling to floor bookcases, a copper bath and a large scrivener's table. There was an area of soft cushions for relaxing; it was here that Flynn noticed the coruscation.

"What's happening?" Earnstos, newly enriched with the power of sorcery, could obviously feel it. To Flynn, that area of the room was fizzing like a shaken bottle of ginger pop.

A man appeared - obviously, a sorcerer- dressed all in black, like a desert nomad from the Desert of I. He held a wicked sword of light in one hand which thrummed with power, like a giant tuning fork.

The man pointed his sword at Earnstos. A blast of white light flew from it and struck him squarely in the chest, wrapping around him like a lasso. At first, Flynn thought his friend would be torn in half; instead, he was thrown across the room, crashing into the copper bath with a groan and a clang.

Flynn fought to resist unleashing his power on the man. He had never studied sorcery, other than reading the old scriptures of the time of the Skyfliers. The assassin – a tall person, whether male or female Flynn could not be sure - advanced.

"Wild boy, I have come for you. Surrender and you will be relieved of your suffering." The voice was male, guttural, speaking in the common tongue, which placed it from the Last Islands, maybe – certainly from further south than the Desert of I. The power was known to be strong in the sorcerers further South.

Flynn's response was instinctive and immediate. He thought about a small opening in his power shield and pictured a thin thread of power reaching out from his core, which could slip through the assassin's shield undetected. He visualised it approaching the advancing sorcerer and presciently saw it take down the man's shields and render him unconscious. With the fervour of relief that his plan would work, he let the power loose. It worked, but not only that, the detonation lifted the man into the air, destroying a bookcase, blasted the sorcerer clean through the wall.

Earnstos sat up, rubbing his head, inches from a sheer drop of thirty feet into the main bailey, surrounded by kindle and ash, which were all that remained of the bookcase.

"You are wild!" Earnstos laughed. Flynn had not expected his friend's reaction to be so accepting, but Earnstos was punching the air.

"I knew it. You can come with me to Magedw."

The young prince noticed the fear on Flynn's face.

"Oh. They will hang you in Chendra. Shittery. I barely felt any surge from you when he was blasted. How did you do it?"

Flynn's response was curtailed by the appearance of Vanine. She floated toward the young men and stepped onto the bedroom floor. She narrowed her eyes at Flynn.

"Who else knows?"

"The Prince now- and Clem guessed." One did not lie or delay an answer to Vanine.

"Shittery, indeed." She pointed at Flynn. "Did you do this?"

Flynn nodded his head vigorously before Earnstos could lie for him. The prince cast him a look of despair, his eyebrows almost rising off his forehead.

Flynn felt an imperceptible shift and a hole appeared, just like the one through which the desert sorcerer had arrived. It was Rollo, the court magician, with Vanine's sister Fay. The two women exchanged glances; Flynn was sure there was an uncomfortable look in Vanine's eyes, but before anyone could speak, Clem burst into the room, followed by a couple of guards.

"What in Torin's teeth is going on here?" Rollo looked between the Prince and Flynn, who both did their best to look as surprised as he.

"There is a wild at play here. The Prince is called, so it must be Flynn."

Rollo pulled on his power; Flynn could feel it, a sudden flash of heat around him, as if the air were burning.

"He has a massive shield up. I can't find the source. Vanine, assist."

Flynn could feel a pulling in of power- but not just from Vanine – from two other sources. One was clearly Earnstos, but his was just a small stream. The other was like a river, churning and broiling: Fay, Vanine's sister. Yet she was a master assassin, not a sorcerer. Was she also wild?

Flynn reached over to Rollo and turned off his power. He thought as he did before: small hole in his own shield, find the source, cut it off. Simple

Rollo's eyes bulged.

"I've been cut off. Neutered! How can that be?" Squealing like a stuck pig, Flynn thought, as he noticed a smile briefly cross he lovely Vanine's lips. It didn't end there. The large man was picked up and dumped out of the window into the moat; the two guards fell unconscious to the ground.

"I've wiped Rollo's mind and those of the guards, but the Privy Council will still be able to put two and two together." Vanine let out a breath- of relief, or anger? Flynn could not be sure.

"Because of the massive hole in the wall?" Fay as ever was sarcastic.

Flynn glanced at Clem, who signed, *she has powers too. And a nice bottom.*

Vanine signed back to him. *And she understands your sign language too, little boy.* Clem blushed red as Fay winked at him.

Suddenly Flynn felt Vanine draw her power to her. Then they were all somewhere else- somewhere completely different.

Flynn found himself in a small holding, in a clearing surrounded by trees. Koralia, Vanine declared, a principality almost four hundred leagues North from Chendra. She had transported them all with a thought. *What power she had. What a beautiful, powerful woman.* He should have been more scared, but the strength that now rushed through his very being gave him confidence he had never thought possible.

The house within the holding had at least six bedrooms; more like a small mansion. The grounds were expansive, tidy rather than opulent: lawns flanked by olive bushes, the yellow, orange and greens of the citrus trees giving an air of other-worldly exoticism. Apart from his infancy in Valksland, now long forgotten, Flynn had never been anywhere other than Chendra. Encouraged by Vanine, he explored the house, almost in a daze; the rooms were mainly functional, rather modest for a building of its size. There was a small staff and he had already made friends with the jolly young cook, Maere, who was probably no more than nineteen summers. Her bread and spread was excellent and she had winked at him earlier when he came down for something to eat. He wouldn't mind a kiss and a cuddle with the voluptuous cook, even despite his devotion to Vanine.

He knocked on the door of the room Earnstos was using. The prince opened it and greeted him with a smile.

"We've just had a magical conference with my brother. We've told him that you were killed by the assassin, that Rollo burned himself out defeating the man with Vanine and Fay and that Vanine has relocated me because my powers are *wobbly,* to protect others from me."

Flynn let out a tremendous sigh of relief. He immediately thought of his mother, Gretan; how distraught she would be, feeling that she might not see him again and how relieved she would be later when she found out that he was still alive. He hugged his friend.

"Whoa. Don't kill me, big fellow. Are you feeling the love suddenly?

"You have saved my mother from a lot of embarrassment and shame. I thank you."

"Vanine thinks it could all unravel. Fay has travelled back to see Rollo, to make sure his memory is short and to let your mother know the pretence. Who'd have thought Fay also had the power?"

"Do you think she is wild?"

"No more than you, Flynn. I'm not sure how you blasted the assassin out of the building like that, or neutered Rollo, but you did it so easily. All the wilds I have heard about have limited powers. I could feel Rollo, Vanine, even Fay pull on their power; but I could not feel you."

Flynn shrugged. He wasn't sure how he did it either – he just seemed to know what to do.

"I feel better. No more headaches. I feel powerful." *But it is as if there is someone else in my head, helping me. I know that sounds mad. Probably is.*

I am helping you to not go mad. Do not react or panic. Don't let on I'm here. Even to Van, and most definitely not to Fay. A strange voice, filling Flynn's head.

Earnstos cocked his head to the side.

"You okay? You're thinking of that cook's breasts, aren't you? You've gone cross eyed."

Flynn shook himself.

"You know what? I think I'll go and see if she has any milk. I mean, water."

Earnstos laughed.

"I'll see you at dinner. Six of the clocks. Don't get smothered."

Flynn returned to his room, stepped inside, and shut the door with a sigh. He suddenly felt ridiculously hot. He looked at the ground; his shadow was acting strangely. It detached itself and formed into the shape of a man standing opposite him in the room; a tall, dark, handsome man with deep brown skin and a beard, dressed in green and blue. He looked like a mummer.

"Bargo the Cat," the man said, holding out a hand which Flynn shook. "Sorry that I hid in your shadow. You can have it back now."

"How did you do that?"

"How did you blast an assassin and neuter a powerful sorcerer without any training?"

"Well, that's just it, I don't know."

"Fancy a drink?" Bargo said pouring two glasses of wine.

Flynn couldn't believe what was happening. *Who was this man?* Politeness never hurt and wine would help. *Does the power help me take it in my stride, or have I simply lost my mind?*

Bargo the Cat moved gracefully, like a court dance tutor. He surveyed his surroundings as if he were watching for the merest hint of danger, sniffing the air.

"I'm not really here." Bargo said sipping his wine. "I'm what we used to call a hologram, albeit semi-corporeal, but what you lot would call a magic lantern show."

"How are you able to drink?"

"Because I am amazing."

Bargo necked his wine and poured himself another. Flynn opened the drapes, flooding the room with sunlight, but Bargo the Cat still did not fade; if anything, he seemed brighter. He was smiling, his grin infectious.

"Who are you?"

"I was one of the Skyfliers." He said

Flynn laughed. Bargo the Cat laughed with him. "What's so funny?"

"How can you be a Skyflier? You would be as old as the first settlers on this world."

"I have worn well."

"You would be thousands of years old."

"I use a lot of unguents and make-up."

"You are quite funny too. Are you a mummer? An actor?"

"I thank-you. Yes, guilty as charged. Just an actor who can hide in the shadows and appear at will," Bargo said with a bow.

"A sorcerer?"

"Nothing so coarse. Vanvear is a sorceress, Faenvar is a sorceress—or witch depending upon how many members of your family she has killed. I am a magician."

"That's just semantics."

"You - young powerful man - are a smart-arse."

"I am a court clerk."

"Same thing."

Bargo walked over to Flynn's bed, threw himself upon it, plumped the pillows and settled cross legged with his hands behind his head. Flynn was trying to ascertain what he had just heard.

Vanvear and Faenvar were the Skyflier Twins, the daughters of Adeus—or Torin, as the One God Scriptures called him. Vanine and Fay? The names were close, but it was a far leap from there to immortal goddesses. He looked at Bargo, who was nodding.

"You catch on quickly, my boy."

"You aren't much older than me."

"I'm over fifty-seven thousand years old; older if you count the periods of stasis. The twins are my nieces. I am Bartholomew Gordon, or Bargo."

"The brother of Adeus. You're telling me that the second most important man in all of history decided to attach himself to my shadow?"

"Adeus, as you call him, wasn't my brother. He was my best friend." Bargo seemed sad even though he knew the One God and called Torin friend. "I felt your power. You are the Saviour."

Flynn spat out his wine.

Bargo laughed again. "Well, you might not be the most couth saviour. Torin's not about to be able to confirm, but I think you are he. I might be wrong. Yet I rarely am."

"Why are you here?" Flynn cut the man off; he was getting a headache again.

"I have a theory that Vanvear or Faenvar will not be able to prevent all the attempts on your life. If the Pires know about you, we are all in trouble"

"Pires, as in Whampyri? The Children of Gustav? Just tales told at Witch's Sunset, surely?"

"They will all want to kill you. You are possibly the Saviour. Do you know what you are meant to do? Think about the stories."

"The Saviour will turn off the Whampyri magic and lead us into the Building Age. He will fly us back home to Earth." Flynn knew his scripture. "The Pantheon of Skyfliers will do the Saviour's bidding."

"Turn off the Whampyri magic, yes. Quite an important bit. They will all want to be the ones to find you, influence you and control you. Not all the Skyfliers are like Vanvear, Faenvar even. Many have used their power for ill intent."

There was a knock at his door. Before Flynn's eyes, Bargo vanished and a little black cat appeared in his place. It snuggled into the pillows, purring.

He opened the door and Vanine, or Vanvear, or whatever she was called, stood before him in a rich mustard dress. Her hair was braided in a long tail that hung over her left shoulder, a ribbon interwoven. Her emerald eyes sparkled. She was so beautiful.

She strode over to him and gave him a hug. He reciprocated, and when she pulled back to look at him, there were tears in her eyes. Flynn had never imagined he would see Vanine cry. *Vanvear?*

"I am so sorry I did not see it before." She retrieved a handkerchief from inside her cuff. "All the time we have worked together over the last two years, I should have seen your power. Even with the wonderful shields you spin about yourself. There are probably only a half-a-dozen people alive who might see past them and I struggle to be one of them. And you can see and feel when we draw power from the Net?"

Flynn nodded.

"That is a skill a mere few have. Only I really know what Fay is. She hides her powers for her own reasons, but you saw past that. You are an incredible young man, Aeflynn. You *could* well be the Saviour."

He shivered, thinking about what Bargo had said. Vanine looked surprised

"Flynn," she said, calmly. "The scriptures of the One-God are just one interpretation of the codex. Your powers *are* strong enough to carry out the tasks of the Saviour based on the prophecy I have read, but there might be other interpretations."

Vanine placed a hand on each side of his head.

"I believe you are possibly the Saviour. So, until I am proven otherwise, I will protect you with my life." She kissed his forehead. She smelled wonderful, of lavender and a spice he could not put his finger on.

Part Two

Clem was dead.

It hadn't taken long, but the young boy who had suffered so much would now live forever with the blood of the Whampyri in his veins. He had been taken in the grounds of the Chendran castle, a day after the Calling Ceremony.

He had masked his true nature from the witches over the last few weeks, even disguising the fact his tongue had grown back and that he could hear perfectly again. His master had bidden him watch the boy Flynn and feed doubts into his mind. If this were the Saviour, he couldn't be allowed to fulfil his destiny. The Pires pulled power from the Net too; their ambition- now they had awakened for the first time in this age - was total enslavement of the humans. Controlling the world and their major food source.

You have left Chendra. Where are you? Gustav's voice sounded in his thoughts shortly after they arrived at Vanine's secret, magically cloaked house. The place reeked of humans. Sweaty, horrible creatures.

I am somewhere in Koralia. I know not where, sire.

You are to watch and listen. You are to drink from the Ladies Faenvar and Vanvear. Turn them to our side. They will help us defeat those who would raise the Saviour and put obstacles in our way. This is our greatest opportunity in the seven ages.

Then the voice of Gustav left Clem as quickly as it came.

The thirst had been dreadful at first. The three weeks since he arrived at this house had been torture, until he befriended one of the stable boys, then a maid and then the cook. Simple suggestion enabled him to drink from them. They submitted to him and never once suspected. He had urges though, the greatest of which was to drain one of his victims. That would be foolish; however, he would reveal himself too soon.

Two days later, he heard that the post boy had arrived from Westbank, the nearest town. Delivering post to the rural villages, he had wandered onto the Lady Vanvear's estate. He did not see the big house or the great gardens because of the magical cloak about them. Clem—or the thing that had been Clem—had watched the post boy, tracked him across the gardens, then out of the estate heading east. Oh, how Clem could now run for hours on end without wilting. He caught up with the boy, not much older than himself and took him off the back of the horse with the help of his preternatural strength. He drained his victim of life force, feeling the euphoria and lust as the horse bolted, screeching as it recognised something that was alive but also that had been dead for some time. Clem though about trapping the horse and draining it too, but animal life force did not satiate him at all.

We are older than them. The Skyfliers brought us to this world. Then we fed.

Clem was sometimes happy the voice of Gustav came, but at other moments it could be an irritant. He would have to learn to control it. When it was time, he would take one of the women sorcerers as his bride and they would be powerful. He would find a way to resist the power of Gustav. Clem would be his own man.

Faenvar would have cut the boy's throat if she could and be done with it. There was no way she was going to live with another wildling. She had nearly detonated many times when the power initially came to her in the First age. Van was fawning around the boy like a love-struck maid. She was thousands of years old and should know better. The lure of his power was clearly a magnet to her; Fay could feel it too, and it *was* attractive. She couldn't spend more than a few minutes with Flynn without beginning to want him herself. She had to resist. He was no more than a child.

They were preparing for the trip to Magedw; things would be easier once they were there. Hopefully the Tavandar would see through him and execute him on the spot, otherwise he would corrupt them all. She doubted the legend of the Saviour. So many had come before. Van was sitting opposite her in her private apartment, communicating with the Tavandar via a whirling pool of water.

"I can use his powers to enhance my own. We should be able to open a portal link directly to the Magedw lobes and translate across to you."

"And will he be able to mask his powers?"

"We cannot detect him now, even when he uses them. He is quite extraordinary. He has no knowledge of Magedw, so cannot visualise a materialisation point; otherwise, I would think he would be able to translate himself and the rest of our merry band quite safely."

Fay heard the Tavandar laugh. He was enjoying this. How could he not? He was the most sensible of them and even he was looking forward to seeing if Flynn was the Saviour.

Fay had spent thousands of years with Gustav before Van took away the Whampyri virus; she had killed millions as the Bride of the Whampyri King. It wouldn't be that easy to end the creatures of darkness. She was itching to fight; she had spent days training the boys when they were not receiving magical instruction from Van. They were both surprisingly strong, especially the crippled one. When Flynn had healed his friend's leg, Earnstos had taken to his room, seemingly distraught that he was no longer lame. Then a few days later he had emerged- within a week of instruction from Fay, his swordsmanship was shining through. He would be a skilled fighter.

"When do you think you will arrive?" The voice of the Tavandar cut through Fay's thoughts.

"A few days, maybe Moonday. I have a few things to finish here first," Van replied.

They said their goodbyes and Van broke the link. That was when the Witchfinders attacked.

Bargo had remained as a black cat for weeks without morphing into his human shape. Vanine seemingly accepted the fact Flynn had adopted a stray. He was curled up on Flynn's bed and Flynn was in the bath chamber washing when the shouting started.

Warlock bounty hunters. It seems your shields have not kept out all magicians, he sent his thoughts to Flynn.

How can they see through? Flynn asked, pulling on his trousers, the material sticking to his wet skin. He put on a fresh shirt and his boots.

Witchfinding skills. They smell magic. They detect it differently to how we do.

It was pretty much the same tactics as the attack at the palace, but this time it was a group of three Witchfinders that appeared in his rooms.

I cannot reveal myself. Bargo sent. *It's up to you, I'm afraid.*

A tall woman and man—brother and sister by the look of them—appeared on either side of a shorter man. They all seemed ageless, with white hair with pale, almost pink skin. Their eyes were grey, as if the colour had drained from them. Had their clothing not been totally black, one might have though them mummers' ghosts.

The shortest threw a spell at him. It wasn't like the magic the attacker at the castle palace used, or even his own power; this was more feral. Flynn staggered in pain as the attack battered against his shields. He felt the threads of magic weaken as they were peeled away. He watched the lines of the magic and learned. He pulled his power about him despite the pain and caught the threads that tried to bind him, yanking them. The little man screamed as he was shredded by the magic. Skin, blood, and shards of bone flew in all directions.

His two companions looked at each other in terror as the short man was ripped from the world. They yelled a battle cry and came at him, swords in hand. Flynn dissipated their weapons with a whim - their swords fell apart. Bindings fell away and metal rusted in moments.

Then they both hit him with that strange, threadlike, debilitating power as they neared him, kicking furniture away. Flynn gasped and fell to his knees, in agony. He tried to grasp the threads like he had with the little man, but he couldn't overcome the two assailants at once. He screamed as the threads of magic started to pull him apart.

Clem burst into the room, hitting the woman from behind with his short sword. She shrieked- the line of power between her and Flynn dissolved. Wheeling around, she slashed Clem across the face with her nails. He was spun about by the blow, falling to the ground with hands covering the bloody gashes she had left. Flynn gathered as much power as he could and thought of a bar of white-hot magic, of intense power and threw it at the woman. She shrieked in agony as she stood over Clem, glancing back at her twin as her body began to glow with the same heat as the metal, burning from the inside. Then Flynn watched as she vapourised, leaving behind nothing but an after-image burning on his retina.

There was an agonising cry from her brother. While he was distracted, Flynn created a blade of fire and slashed out, decapitating the white-haired man. Before the head could hit the ground, before the corpse fell, both body parts transformed into energy and dispersed.

Fay ran into the room, her sword drawn and dripping blood, covered in blood herself too. There must have been other attackers then. Hedging their bets, a multiple attack on the inhabitants of the house. There were probably more of them. This was not over.

Another hole opened; a massive, feral looking giant crashed through it, raising a large sword high above Fay. He made to crash the blade down upon her when Flynn threw another bolt of white-hot energy, blowing a hole through the giant's chest. The giant looked down at the smoking hole and fell over backwards. The smell of cooked giant meat was almost unbearable.

Flynn, help. It was Vanine.

Find, was all he could think. A coruscating hole opened before him; on the other side he could see Vanine and Earnstos. The Prince was fighting one of the Witchfinders as Vanine engaged with three others; she was being pulled apart.

Flynn stepped through the portal, followed not far behind by Fay. He looked at Earnstos's assailant and sent a thread of power through a gap in his shielding, piercing the man's heart. The Witchfinder fell, with little more than an instant to fathom what had happened to him.

Fay quickly dispatched one of her sister's opponents, but a second had set those debilitating threads on her. Flynn grabbed at the threads and pulled- the Witchfinder unravelled like the first had. The final one was the most powerful. Flynn scanned the female witchfinder's shielding but could not find a gap. He deployed a tiny thread, but to no avail. There was seemingly no chink in her defences.

From below. Vanine communicated. He knew immediately what she meant. Who needed shields on the soles of their feet? He sent power through the ground in two thin threads and then pushed them upwards into the legs of the woman. She screamed and fell as the flesh was flayed from her legs. Fay strode over and finished her off with her blade. The attack was over – for now.

The black cat sauntered up to Flynn, rubbing against his legs. *You are truly terrifying.*

Flynn had to agree as he looked about at the carnage.

Magedw was the shortened form of Mage Dwelling, said to be the original landing place of the Skyfliers' Boat.

Their group arrived at midday; the sun was high in the sky. Flynn had shared his power with Vanine, who almost wilted as she opened the hole in the night sky in Koralia for them all to step through.

The last few weeks had been difficult. Clem took some time to heal after the attack and had taken to his room. Fay was distraught for not picking up the signs of Witchfinders earlier. Vanine was elated that Flynn could control his powers so well. Flynn, meanwhile, was dealing with the most unimaginable headaches. They were debilitating, giving him lights behind his eyes and a sickness that was comparable to the night he and Earnstos drank five Head Smuggler ales on his sixteenth anniversary day. And then there were the physical changes taking place in him.

Flynn had never been small; tall since his twelfth year, he was thin and rangy. He had worked hard at his fighting lessons with the Captain of the Home Guard, but he had remained wiry. In recent weeks though, he had developed a full beard. His body—particularly his shoulders—had broadened and his muscles had tightened over his increasing frame. He was probably three or four inches taller now, making him tower over Clem.

"It's the magic of the Net. Once you link to it, it removes all the imperfections in your body and you become optimal. It requires you to be fit, strong, and clear of mind." Vanine regarded him differently now, particularly after the fight with the Witchfinders. She seemed to want to spend more time with him, questioning him intently; he felt like one of the rats the physicians used to try out their latest herbal concoction. He wondered if there was more there, a certain attraction from her too, but he decided he would not push it; even though his confidence had rocketed like a firework during Skytide.

His head was killing him again. He looked across their little group to Vanine- she came over to him.

"It's hurting you, isn't it?" She placed a gentle hand on his forehead. His body started to react to her closeness. He nodded, strangely finding himself close to tears. *How could his body and mind improve, but the pain gets worse?*

"We need to find your reservoir valve. There is a side effect when we use our power-an element we cannot keep within our bodies, lest it taints us. If you continue like this, you could go mad or vent power that would flatten Magedw in a moment. I am hoping the Tavandar can help you." She put her arm in his. He felt her power and then some respite. He breathed and the waste power shone silver as it left his lips. He immediately felt better.

"Thank you."

She wants to jump your bones. Bargo—in his cat form—was weaving around his legs. *To be honest, now so do I. It's the power. You have an aura of attraction.*

He flung the cat away in annoyance. Not because of his overtures—that was just like Earnstos—but more the intrusion while he was spending time with Vanine. *Vanvear.*

Now do you believe she is ancient, like me?

Yes.

She's had more men, killed more men, toppled more kings, and seduced more queens than you've had hot dinners.

Flynn tried to kick the cat again.

We can't help what or who we are. It's how we carry ourselves and treat our friends and family that is important.

You are wise beyond your years. This time, sincerity. *Torin would be proud of you. You truly are the Saviour. I believe so anyway.*

Magedw was a sprawling city of white fresco and copper-stained rooves. A light rain fell as they approached, but the temperature was high between showers. There were towers everywhere. *Magicians liked towers*, Fay had said. *It helps them to forget the world they live in.* Despite Fay's power being strong, she seemed to have a distrust of any other being with power- save her sister.

The city was circled by the biggest, most complete wall he had ever seen in either life or in scripture paintings. It encompassed the entire circumference of the city with no breaches. The palace at Chendra had not had a complete border wall for centuries.

As well as the towers there were turrets and temples, all similarly white and copper, but reflecting the different architectural styles of the cosmopolitan sorcerers who had lived there over the ages. It was said that there had been a settlement here for over one hundred thousand years, although it had at times it had been razed, during the magic wars of the first and second ages. Then it had been under the thrall of the Emperor of the One God in the fourth age. More recently, however, it had been a centre of learning and sharing, where all sorcerers came to receive their instruction.

At the East Gate they paused, not to speak to guards, but so Vanine could spell open the magically guarded gates for them to walk through. Nothing could get through without the cipher.

Vanine's Magedw residence was large, but even more basic than the Koralian one. They were greeted by an old couple: Rey and Rian, twins, and her seneschals. They had managed her accommodation for years, both part of the non-magical population of Magedw who serviced their powerful masters.

Flynn and Earnstos were shown to a room they were to share with Clem.

Just over a week later, they were all chatting together. The adults were attending official engagements, and so the youngsters had been left to their own devices again. Clem was snoring softly on his bed. He now seemed to sleep a lot during the day, Flynn had noticed.

"I'll probably change it back when I can," Earnstos said, gloomily.

"What's that?" Flynn was lying back with a cold rag on his head.

"My leg. It doesn't feel right that it has healed."

"I'm sorry." He had apologised a lot for healing his friend without permission.

"I'm not looking for an apology. It's the curse of the power. It would have healed anyway. Look at you; so big and handsome and so hairy now. It just doesn't feel right. I'm growing again too. It's weird."

"My head constantly hurts. I think my brain is trying to leave my skull via my ears."

"Can the Tavandar help?"

"He thinks he can. He is looking at some of the old texts regarding wilds, from back when we didn't neuter or execute them.

Apparently, there is a temple where the spiritual atmosphere can help the mind settle and open up."

Earnstos sighed.

"I am not so sure I'm going to like being a sorcerer. I just saw my daily timetable as a novitiate. Up at dawn, followed by instruction in magic, instruction in arms, scripture, scrivening, followed by bed. Repeat for two to three years. And that's just the first bit. You can already do most of what a fully trained sorcerer can do and with far more power. I've got a candle flame compared to your sun."

"You can vent though. Apparently, if they can't sort me out at this temple, they'll have to take me somewhere far away from people and let me detonate."

Earnstos winced. "Ouch."

"Ouch indeed."

Somewhere on the streets of Magedw, a figure appeared from a magical doorway, followed by two others. Silent and dressed entirely in dark colours, they blended into the shadows of the night.

Anyone watching would have observed them set a course for a large temple: The Temple of the One God, the main house of worship to those who did not believe in the powers of the Pantheon, the children of Adeus. These were the religious fundamentalists who believed only in Torin, the chief Skyflier. Their temple was famed for its temperate grace, an almost living calmness that aided prayer and meditation. In Magedw, the temple was renowned for its serenity and helpfulness, despite its fundamental doctrine. No other temple of the One God worldwide would have let sorcerers in.

One of the dark figures tapped out a code on a sturdy oak door; seconds later it swung inwards. The black figures were illuminated momentarily by candles, lit for the evening séance. The person who opened the door was an acolyte in the service of the high bishop. He was naked save for his evening loincloth, skinny and shaven headed.

"We will see the High Bishop," one of the figures said.

"His Grace is sleeping."

"Then wake him!" the figure bellowed, followed by a slap that knocked the acolyte to the floor. The thin man gazed up in fear at the visitors, then lifted himself up with one hand, stemming the flow from a bloody nose with the other.

"You could have just asked." You didn't become an acolyte of the One God without a certain steeliness.

Bishop Henrik of Magedw was the third most important person in the city, after the Tavandar and the Arch-Sorcerer. They ruled the city as a triumvirate. Henrik was not used to others disturbing his sleep. Barefoot, he padded down the corridor of the Temple to find his guests waiting for him.

"Do you know the hour, Sir?" he said to their leader. All three of them were in Witchfinder garb, rags tied about their pale-skinned heads.

"Why hasn't General Skidar warned me of your visit? This is most irregular, not to mention foolhardy. No finder has stepped foot in Magedw for quite some time. Your lord commanding officer should have notified me. I cannot broker any sort of peace."

"Gustav is our Lord."

Henrik went cold. Such a statement could only mean two things. Gustav had reawakened and he, Henrik the Pire, was being called back into the Whampyri fold. He had been for some time a sleeper agent. Magically shielded, his true appearance and nature were suppressed. Few knew the majority of Witchfinders were also blood drinkers.

"You are reactivated. The Saviour is here."

Henrik had heard the rumours. The blood of the young he sucked was full of their secrets and he carefully chose his victims from the capitol staff.

"The ancient rite is written. Gustav shall bite the Saviour and *he* will be destroyed."

Henrik knew that the scripture could be interpreted many ways. He generally forgot his nature; such was the power of his magic. Only when he needed to feed did the ancient blood lust and pure hatred of mankind surface. It was his part to play, however and he would have to play it- or be subject himself to Gustav's cruel punishments.

Henrik nodded.

"Tell our Lord Gustav welcome back. I am due to meet the Saviour in a few days. It will be done."

PART 3

The cat rubbed himself against the Tavandar, who went to push him out the door before recognition was writ large across his face. It was a concerned face. The Tavandar was a concerned man. He looked young -a side effect of his ancient magic- but his grey eyes were as old as Bargo's.

"You've got a cheek coming here after all this time, Bartholomew."

The form of the black cat wavered and in its place soon stood Bargo, in his human form. They had known each other for millennia, but hadn't encountered one other for centuries.

"We haven't seen each other since the fifth age. That's what? Three thousand years or so? You should have forgiven me by now." Bargo held up his hands in defence. It had been a long time since they had tested their powers against each other. If they did, it would surely rip the University apart.

"You smug bastard, I should slap you. You stole my son. I haven't fathered since because of it."

"We were in love."

"It was perverted."

"You cannot apply old Earth morals to this, Dafydd, he was a legal adult and had been for two hundred years."

The Tavandar frowned. Bargo smiled conceitedly. Two could play at the *I will say your ancient original name game.*

"If he really is the Saviour, we will have to work together to ensure he is victorious," the Tavandar said, drawing an agitated hand through his long, ash-blonde hair.

"If Gustav does return, we will need more than just one young man. We Skyfliers will need to unite. And you know the characters of some of our brothers and sisters are questionable."

"It will all be for good, my dear." The Tavandar sighed. He had always been a good man- the best of them and the most powerful, after Adeus/Torin. It was only right he monitored the centre of power on this world. Bargo was more erratic, always where the danger was. The *fixer*.

"We cannot go public with him yet. We cannot wake the others," Bargo asserted.

"There are rumours, Bart- and they are rife. Van and Fay would not be here for no reason. Their colleagues and friends all know it. They have both been on deep cover missions for decades, monitoring the Chendran alliance, not to mention the issues a demented king and a regent pose us. All those dukes who were deposed by the Chendran royals will want their revenge. Without agents there, Magedw will struggle to control tensions."

"It's too soon. We need to solve his venting issue."

"I cannot break through his defences and he will not let them down. The amount he can download from the Net is frightening, Bart. Can you not feel it?"

Bargo nodded.

There was a banging on the door. "I said no disturbances!" Dafydd the Tavandar shouted through the door. Bargo shimmered and became a cat again.

"Come near me and I'll kick you."

The door opened and the Tavandar's secretary entered.

"My Lord, it's His Grace, Henrik. He demands to see you now." Dafydd shook his head wearily, Bargo had never seen him this disconsolate; not since Torin left them, anyway.

"Tell him I am indisposed."

"He is most insistent. He said if you do not let him enter, he will shout about the Saviour Aeflynn from the ramparts."

Damn. thought Bargo.

Flynn stood in the Temple of the One God, shivering. He didn't like it here, with its high, vaulted ceilings like the Pantheon Cathedral in Chendra. The place was too calm; funereal. He could feel apprehension pouring out of the magic users.

Henrik was looking him up and down like a piece of meat. Earnstos had commented about what a salacious old queen he was. Flynn had to agree that he didn't feel quite right-there were too many dark threads about the man. Vanvear was next to him, her arm through his. Fay, Clem, the Tavandar and somewhere the cat Bargo was in attendance, skulking in the shadows. Bargo had told him he was most concerned- something was awry.

"You can stow your sword, Fay. You are in a House of God. Your Pantheon deities might allow the drawing of weapons, but Torin does not."

I can hold it. Clem signed. Fay ignored him, but neither did she sheath the weapon. The Tavandar had requested her attendance out of necessity, as one of the few who knew about Flynn. She would have to lend her secret powers to the shielding they would need.

Van had been unhappy to have Henrik in their midst the evening before. The Tavandar thought the calmness of the environment might enable them to get to the bottom of Flynn's venting issues, so the bishop had insisted they go there. The threat that the bishop would tell the world who Flynn potentially was, if they did not, had infuriated her. But, because Flynn's head hurt so badly, she had acquiesced. "Let's just get it done," she had barked at them all.

Flynn had guessed that the Tavandar was one of the ancient Skyfliers, although Bargo had not confirmed it directly. He wasn't sure about Henrik, however.

He's a worm.

Shhh. Bargo was not helping. Although Flynn knew who the cat really was, the others did not, as far as he was aware.

Earlier they had all admitted their unease. Fay felt they were walking into a trap. Van was worried the venting ceremony was too soon. Bargo agreed, but felt like they might flush out a rat- the Bishop. How had Henrik known about Flynn? They had kept it close. The Tavandar insisted they had to comply, or face more interference; life would be extremely difficult for him if Bishop Henrik started to accuse them of harbouring a wild.

The Tavandar quickly took control of the ceremony. Normally, this was a big thing for a mage; but they needed to cut through the religious nonsense.

"Vanine, would you open yourself to the Net?"

Bargo and Fay did the same. Flynn could feel all of them open. The Bishop did too, but his magic was a weak flow. It was dark. so dark. Flynn's magic flow usually had the girth of tree trunks, all erratic and free flowing, while the others' flows looked like ordered ropes, steady and uniform.

"Flynn, would you open up to the flow?"

He did so. It felt good, but the pain increased.

"Flynn, can you feel the source? Can you feel around the flow and see those black threads?"

He had noticed them before, but thought they were part of his power. In his tree trunks, he could see the black threads, like the grain in a milled plank.

"Try to open the gaps between the threads. Your flow is made up of those life threads. The black bits are the death threads – anti magic. It is those you need to vent."

Why did Henrik have so many death threads?

Flynn felt between the threads; he could sense foulness, like waste, the smell of a festering wound.

It took hours. Every time he thought he had grasped the damn anti-magic threads, they slipped through his fingers, like a bar of soap. His head throbbed, his nose began to bleed and he was forced to pause. He could see Vanvear and Fay shoot sidelong glances at the Tavandar; did they think it was taking too long, did they think it was better to remove and detonate him?

Van gave him words of support. Fay wished they would all hurry the fuck up. The bishop, Henrik, looked at Flynn as if he were a possession about to be returned to him, all washed and cleaned. The man was rubbing his hands. Earnstos' mocking words about the bishop were ringing in Flynn's ears.

The Tavandar brought them back together and encouraged Flynn to get hold of the death threads again. This time he grabbed them confidently and pulled, as instructed.

Then, he vented. He felt shields come up from Bargo, Fay, Van and the Tavandar. The flow was tremendous. Yet the Bishop did not raise any defences. The vented power filled the room and the Bishop screamed.

"Whoops," Fay said.

They all breathed a sigh of relief, except for the Bishop, who was gasping rapidly. All the candles had been doused, the black-silver light of vented death magic filling the air.

The cat appeared; surprisingly, he morphed into Bargo in front of everyone.

"You are in trouble," he shot to Flynn.

"Bargo! What the fuck are you doing here?" Fay screamed. She made for him, sword raised.

"Stop!" commanded the Tavandar. Fay froze. Flynn felt the room shake and sensed he had grabbed the power. The Tavandar winked at Flynn, seemingly calmer than the others. The Bishop, his back to them, shook with fright.

"The Bishop is a Pire," Bargo announced.

The creature that was formerly the Bishop turned, his form altered, the once-human face now replaced with something more akin to a snake: smooth features, no nose, slit pupils. Henrik flung out two death threads at the Tavandar and Van. Both crumpled. The Bishop might have been weak in magic, but he was extraordinarily strong in the power Flynn had seen the Witchfinders use during their attacks.

Fay flew at the Bishop and would have taken his head if the acolytes had not arrived. The death magic in the air stripped them of their humanity as they entered the chamber. They hissed and charged Fay as their own death magic threads struck her.

Flynn could see threads reaching from Henrik to the acolytes, the snake within him connecting through the magic to the snakes they were. Pires, all of them; Whampyri. He whipped threads of power at them and the chamber filled with their screams as they burst into flames. Moments later, all that remained of them were two pillars of white ash.

Henrik unleashed an inhuman scream and launched himself at Flynn. The younger man was taken aback at the power radiating from the Pire. He could feel the Bishop exerting his very life energy with his attack. He needed to use his death force to kill Flynn, who could read the creature's mind now that Henrik was so close.

Kill! Kill for Gustav! Kill for the Gold Lord!

Clem's own thoughts rang out with the same words. Dear gods, Clem was unravelling like the Bishop. He was a Pire, too.

The Gold Lord? Had Flynn heard the name before? Gustav was in the scriptures: The snake who came with the Skyfliers, best friends with Torin, a parasite that nearly ended the world before it began.

Henrik landed on Flynn and knocked him back, hitting the marble floor- and despite his shields, the wind was knocked out of him. He heard someone shout.

"That's too much power for Henrik- something is coming through him."

Flynn felt the dark threads and pulled. The Bishop Henrik screamed and twisted in place, flesh, and muscle flaying apart. Louder and louder the man's voice grew, filling the halls of the temple and echoing back upon them, until finally Henrik's body exploded in a shower of gristle, bone, and gore. But before he did, Flynn saw golden threads reach towards Clem.

Clem flew at him, swerving away from magic both the recovering Vanine and the Tavandar threw at the boy. The heat was so intense as Clem landed on him; he could barely hold him back. The boy's gaping maw and razor teeth sought the blood in Flynn's neck. Flynn could not gather his power. It was being nulled by the Witchfinder magic. Why was it so close to the Pires magic? Were they one and the same?

He glanced down at the Pire who had once been his friend. It hurt his eyes. There wasn't much of Clem left; he was screaming, burning beneath his own shields as he fought for life essence.

Flynn felt his power surge. *Here's a little help.* Bargo's voice filled his head. Flynn felt for the dark death threads and pulled. Nothing. There wasn't much left of Clem to pull apart. Flynn felt again and found threads imbued with such power that he recoiled. He grabbed hold of them and pulled with all his might, sending what was left of Clem skidding across the room to crash against an opposing wall. The boy slid into a statue, shattering the base, and toppling the figure over on to his now-prone figure.

Heal. He thought for his little deaf and dumb friend.

The scene before Flynn became one of devastation: his friends were fighting acolytes, all of them Whampyri. They were getting the upper hand; however, at last the Tavandar finished off the final one, pulling its death threads apart.

Within the rubble of the statue, something was gathering; Clem had regenerated, pushing the marble remains aside as he dragged himself to his feet. Flynn threw his power at the boy and looked deep inside at his threads. There, he found the snakes: one black, one gold. The gold snake hissed and left Clem. Flynn ripped at the black one, tearing it from his friend.

The snake is the virus.

Destroy it and the soul returns. Clem will live. You have healed him. It was the Tavandar who had spoken. Not Bargo.

Then time seemed to stop. There was a collective sigh. The air reeked of burned flesh and bonfires. Ash floated in the air like snow; Flynn did his best not to get any in his mouth, as if the Whampyri taint might reach him. He vented his death magic. He could do it with ease. He would not detonate. Relief. It was over.

Then he heard Vanine scream.

"Faenvar, No!" Flynn had lost track of the golden snake.

It seemed the fight had taken its toll on the assassin. She seemed almost torn apart. Yet, as they watched, the golden snake writhed within her. She healed; the death magic within her.

"No, Fay." Vanine screamed, her sister was a Pire again.

Yet there was more to come. Fay's eyes were golden, her skin turning gold. He knew who she was, without knowing why. The Gold Lord. An enigma, from where no-one knew. He would have to destroy her now. He pulled in as much magic as he could.

"Flynn, no. Aeflynn. Too soon." Vanine's voice again- but he had released his power and already it coursed towards her. It would obliterate her. He watched the entirety of the power in his being flood towards this creature that was Fay, a Pire- the Gold Lord.

And Fay laughed. He felt her stop the power and reverse it. It was heading back towards him. He felt it strike, with a pain beyond all that he had felt before. He could see, after the initial shock, that he was being unravelled by his own power. Some of the energy had been diverted towards Bargo, the Tavandar and Vanine. They, too, were unravelling.

He had failed.

The last thing he heard before he exploded was the manic laughter of the Gold Lord and her final words as he died:

"You might be dreaming, Saviour, but I have found you. And soon I *will* destroy you."

He awoke screaming. Van was holding him. He couldn't have slept long, but the details of the nightmare were so real. And her words...

"Van, I've seen the Gold Lord in my dreams. He's coming. And Fay. Fay was a Pire."

"Dear gods," Van gasped. "Here we go again."

IMMORTAL

Elizabeth was tired, even though she had only climbed half the steps to the great tower.

How preposterous that she should be perspiring. It was not right for someone of her station to perspire. Perspiration was the sole providence of servants, or athletic gentlemen.

Her father had ordered her to Magnus Heights to see the old Lord of the Tower. Much to her chagrin, they had blindfolded her. She'd asked the two soldiers their names- she would remember them. Young and Smith. She would have their heads, if ever she became queen. She would also get her revenge on her father, whenever he could be bothered to visit her again. At least one new dress, or a new roan mare, although she would more likely get another stepmother nearer her own age.

She had felt the transference to the Parallel, as her father called it; it made her stomach feel strange, like when she was in the presence of Lord Cecil the younger, only Cecil made her stomach flutter for days, as opposed to the journey to the parallel, which was fleeting. She sighed; she liked that feeling. It had unsettled her horse, Athena however. She was a flighty one at the best of times.

Nearing the summit, Elizabeth studied the pits and flaws in the stone and mortar. The tower was ancient: the steps deep, wide, and furrowed, where thousands of feet had often trodden.

Once the steps ran out, she reached two large oak doors that seemed to appear as if from nowhere. Elizabeth marvelled at the intricate carvings around those doors, if only for a few moments. They looked Viking in origin, all swirls, runes, and dragons. It must have taken days for the artisan to complete; but then, the working class had hours and hours to lose. She would never have the time to take up carving, not with her social programme.

She knocked.

"Enter," came the muffled reply.

Elizabeth felt put out; she did not normally open doors. A lesson in humility, no doubt, from her father, who had visited the tower many times as a boy, apparently. So how old was Lord Magnus?

Elizabeth turned the handle, releasing the latch on the other side and pushed with all her might. And it took some might- her strength was limited to needlepoint, lute-playing, and the odd dance. Ladies of the court never opened doors.

She was greeted with a noxious smell of strangely scented smoke. It seemed at first that the room was on fire. Gagging slightly, she stepped inside.

The room was semi-circular, as large as half the circumference of the tower. There was the main sitting area, with annexes or enclosures made by bookcases and piles of colourful books. A chimney rose through the middle of the room, a suspended fire beneath it hanging in the air, as if by magic- or probably rather some clever feat of ocular engineering.

The fire, although casting out light, was not the source of the smoke. It emanated from something in his Lordship's mouth. It looked like a brown carrot, or a turd.

That wasn't the strangest thing. His Lordship was not very much older than herself.

"Welcome, your Highness." His accent was English, but his vowels longer. Like someone from the middle of her father's kingdom.

The man looked tall, although he did not rise to greet her. His shoulder-length yellow gold hair shimmered, even in the half-light of the room. He obviously had no need for windows, this Viking-like lord. Yet why was he shut in here and not at court, for he was the epitome of beauty? Elizabeth felt the frisson, like the Transference; he was better looking than Lord Cecil, much better.

"My father has said that you may call me Bess. I would prefer your Highness, although many would doubt my claim now. It seems I am a seasonal bastard, depending on who my father is now rutting with. Why don't you call me Fitz or Fitz-Betty?"

The handsome Lord of the tower laughed, but his face did not smile. Another reason not to smoke turds in your mouth. He crossed his legs, eyeing her like she was a prize heifer at a market.

"You are funny, Elizabeth. He said you would be."

"What? Pater said I was funny?"

"No, the historian David Starkey, I met him a few hundred years ago. He said it was alleged that you were of strong wit, a prankster at times. I thought you would be more like Queenie from Blackadder. It seems you are indeed highly intelligent."

"You talk nonsense, my Lord." He still had not offered her a seat, even though there was about half a dozen scattered about, rather than placed at the table. All had books piled upon them. It seemed he could have an intricately carved doors created, but had not commissioned enough bookcases for his plethora of tomes.

"Would you like a seat, Elizabeth?"

"What- and deprive an anthology or two of their resting places?"

His smile grew even wider and he rose, mercifully tossing his smoking turd on the floating fire. He was very tall and, Elizabeth noticed, muscular under his coat; the veins stood out on his neck like the acrobats she had once seen at Hampton Court. He moved deftly across to one of the other dining seats, unceremoniously knocking the pile of books from it, then dragged it over with a dreadful noise of wood scraping on stone floor that set her teeth on edge. He placed the chair before her.

"Sit."

Unused to taking orders, she paused longer than necessary, which elicited a veiled smile from him once again.

"What did Harry say about *why* you were required to come here?"

He was very to the point. Like her father. She hesitated, not used to being addressed in such a manner. She wanted to swear at him, but that would just get back to "Harry". The impudence of the man.

"Go to Magnus. Listen. Be polite, but not fawning- and ask questions. I did the same when I was your age. He will test you. I failed."

He nodded to show approval of her curt answer. She sat, despite her clothing hampering her. She wished she were in breeches.

"My name is Magne Magnusson. Here I am known as Lord Magnus; I think Alfred started it. It is not my real name. You will learn that if you are to be Queen."

"Alfred? King Alfred? Moreover, how can you have spoken with father when he was a boy? You are no more than twenty-three." The words vomited out of her, like the worst of the flux.

"I was going to ask you if you had any questions. Obviously, you like being ahead of the game."

Her eyes widened: *answer the bally question, then!*

"I am cursed. Quite possibly immortal. It took a long time for me to figure it out, but I know why now. It was all a lesson in humility. The world you live in isn't the only version."

"Pater said I would be surprised."

He smiled, kindly this time. "I want to tell you a story. Then I will ask you two questions. I have asked it of all the potential heirs to the monarchy, back to Alfred the Great, prior to their succession. Some of them worked it out. Will you?"

"You have already seen Mary?" This was said bitterly. He sat back, as if she had bitten him. He looked at her a while, his eyes vacant, as if they had been hollowed out like boiled quale eggs, scooped with a spoon.

"Yes, I have seen Mary."

"And?"

"Elizabeth," he said calmly. "I ask the questions."

She smiled. Warmth replaced the threat of his impudence. Was he some sort of demon? He looked like an angel. Oh, here we go, that feeling again. Was she losing control of herself?

"No, you are not losing control. Listen to this story of a young man. It will take an indeterminable time to tell. It could take a day, or all day and night or four nights. However, you must agree to listen to it all, Bess. Then I will ask you a question."

She did not know why she would accept, but she did. He was halfway through pouring them a drink for the journey when she realised- he could hear her thoughts. He ignored her glare.

"Someone made me immortal when I was young, created this man you see before you from a broken wretch. Many have even tried to kill me. Why?"

"I could give you a few reasons and I've only been in your presence ten minutes."

"Remember, this is about teaching you humility."

"I'll drink my tea and listen."

I was born Magne Thorn Magnusson in the ninth century. A bastard son of the Lord of North Jutland, in the Danish territories. My mother disappeared when I was about three and I was taken in by the family of Magnus an old Yarl under Jutland's rule. I had been found naked in the snow, alive and thriving for some reason. Magnus thought I had been sent from Valhalla. He died shortly after, but his son Ander, who also believed me as gods-touched, raised me as his own, instilling the nature of the warrior and the honour of the old Norse gods in me. I came of age as they sacrificed volunteers to improve the yield of spring. Human sacrifice was common in those days. It was a strange atmosphere; sadness and joy mixed in a heady celebration of death, then birth. The families of those volunteers were revered and never went hungry or unsupported until the parents of those chosen died, despite Loki.

We lived close together in our village. There was a witch - or a seer you might call them today - who gave me lessons in arcane magic, linked to the power of Odin and his host. It was dark magic though; many thought they were most likely the tricks of Loki's art.

Agnete was the name of the seer and she was most beautiful. Most think the women touched by the supernatural or the power of the gods as crone; but they become as such only through age or isolation. Any madness they cloak themselves with is just to hide their true natures. Whilst Ander educated me in the ways of a Viking warrior, Agnete taught me the ways of the flesh, then had me teach others, both male and female. We were not so ruined by gods and churches in those days, we loved who we wanted to love and chose a life partner thereafter.

Sif was one such woman I loved. We both married other people and had children with them when we were older, but when we were teenagers, she used to take me into the mountains and show me a rare flower that allegedly had the potency to heal wounds far quicker than any other remedy. She brewed me such a tea following a practice battle, where I received a sword wound to my chest. It cleared in a few hours. We regularly made love upon that mountain top away from prying eyes, next to the small fires we would build to cook the fish that we'd caught in the lake before the mountain climb. We would then say our prayers to Freya.

By the time I was eighteen summers, I was partaking in raids upon the English coast. Nothing like the conquests of the 10th century, but significant nonetheless. We captured a woman, one day, from a raid upon the coastal towns of what we would now call

Norfolk. She was a Saxon woman, a nun, a woman of God. Her name was Aedith. She scratched me so badly I endured infection which left me with a scar in the shape of a "v".

In time Aedith, despite her original calling, became my wife; we lived alongside my adopted brother Fliri, who was now Lord, after Ander's death in a raid. We had children and we raised them as Christians. I was one of the first of the old Danish people to be baptised. Aedith had a cross made for me and blessed it. It was crafted from a trinket we had taken from her church, which was reportedly linked back to a Christian saint whose name I have now forgotten. Agnete did not like Aedith; she made that plain.

Trusting that my new wife and twin babies would be safe with my adoptive sister-in-law, I raided with Fliri; unfortunately, upon my return I found that Aedith had been murdered and the babies drowned. I had other children, but this made me despair and I fell into a period of depression, which led me to leave my home and travel to England with the bones of Aedith and the babies, to bury them on consecrated soil. This was to atone for my leaving them unprotected; I had not been a good husband, nor father.

Time went by and I ended up working for Aethelred, King of Mercia, as a mercenary in his royal guard. He was a weak man and soon bent his knee to Alfred, the godliest of Kings. Aedith would have loved Alfred. I met him many times and he once blessed me for helping his son practise in the yard. We had a short conversation about our lives and he was impressed to hear I was baptised. He suggested I go to Winchester as my first pilgrimage, to pay homage to Swithin, who had died in recent times; I did as he said, ending my time with Aethelred. I did not miss him; his kingdom was a mess.

Edgar was a monk at the cathedral who I met on my first visit and we became friends. I settled in the town and took up employment as a weapon smith. This had been my trade back in Jutland, when I was not on raiding trips. I had a purpose once again. I felt good. I missed Aedith and mourned my babies, but now I was a godly man. I vowed I would not take a woman again, for fear of loss once more. I worked in Winchester for more than twenty years. For most of those years, I led a healthy life, although I had regular headaches. One winter, I had an ague from which I could not seem to recover; I felt weaker and weaker. One thing that was certain, despite my illness, I did not age. People would pass comments about my good skin and strong physique. Edgar still visited me, but he was old by now, over fifty summers and riddled with arthritis. He had such trouble with his back and would do forever; only in death would he be free.

November that year, as I lay ill in my bed, Edgar died and I felt like I would follow. It was a cold winter, bitterly so. Then one day I had a visitor. It was the day I thought I would die. A young woman came to see me, sent by the Cathedral Bishop. She could be no more than twenty and she had the look of the seer Agnete. Agnete had apparently perished in a raid on my old village. My eyes had failed me by now and I felt that death and God were calling. The young woman nursed me through the night, but I when I woke, she was gone again. Her name had been Ethel and she was accented with a western brogue, even though I did not know exactly where she was from.

By the equinox in December, I was well again and healthy, although I could not get warm during that winter, no matter what. This passed as spring came; the warmth of what seemed to be the brightest sun I had ever known made me feel young again. I had decided to move on from Winchester; the local rumour was that I was a magician, as my hair had not greyed nor my body become infirm, despite twenty-five years as the weapon smith. The Bishop had tried to get me to stay- he had even baptised me once more, saying my healthiness was because I was so godly. He put me under the protection of a nun and she made me better; her skill in healing minds was tremendous. Her name was Dora.

Years passed and I realised I could live without drink or food. I occasionally had cravings for beef, grains and certain green vegetables and I had to make sure at those times I did eat, but other than that I needed little sustenance. I had invested wisely and moved from place to place every fifteen years or, that I might evade suspicion as an ageless warlock. I watched England grow into one Kingdom; I saw the Normans invade. I got into a pattern of moving between two landholdings and posing as my son and grandson. I became a landowner and swore my fealty to King Richard shortly before he went on his campaign to the Holy Land. I became a templar knight, but I remained in England, keeping Richard's kingship supported, although, as you know, it was short-lived plan.

As I travelled through Nottingham one day some years later, I was attacked by a group of bandits who were impressed by my accoutrements and believed I would have gold upon my person. You don't live for hundreds of years without gathering a few skills, so I defeated them. I did, however, receive a sword thrust to my abdomen. Believe it or not, in all the time I had been alive, I had never had more than two serious injuries. The first healed by my friend in the mountains of my homeland- this second one, however, felt like it would kill me.

Great fear fell about me as I lay dying; the fever was strong. I stripped the bandits of their clothes and made a roughshod set of blankets to keep me warm as I died, convinced I would go to hell.

Night after night I lay there, sweating, but not, after all, dying. Did I need something from the old gods, perhaps some manna?

Eventually, I was rescued by a farmer and his lad. Edward and Henry Collier put me upon their cart and carried me to their holding: it was a large farm, their fields of barley for ale and pasturelands, home to a hundred head of cattle.

After a week of my labours, the fever broke and I felt better than ever. Then, the strangest of things happened. I shed my skin. Yes, the whole of it sloughed off, as if I had been purged and the sickness had taken my skin from me. My hair fell out, just like it had with Norri in my village, who had the shock of seeing his wife impaled before his very eyes. But that wasn't the most bizarre element of the process. The skin and hair came together, wrapped around a skeleton of air, and created my former self; it stood before me, a person, albeit supernatural in its birth.

"I am your servant," *it said*, "I am your familiar, what would you like me to do? Would you like me to change my appearance to something else, or would you like me to dissipate in coda?"

Any revulsion I should have had at that moment was gone. It was as if the process that had led to this creature was natural and I should not be worried at all.

Furthermore, the familiar told me this process would repeat itself during each full moon. I would have the chance to create a familiar, if I had an illness to expel.

Happily, I wished the familiar gone, knowing that I had the option to create another, although I could not comprehend for what purpose I would use it. I later discovered they could age like a normal human being, if you asked them to. They were sterile and could not bear or sire children, but they could live life- under instruction from their master or mistress- or me.

Ordinarily, this should have rocked me to the core.

I was stronger then, more than ever, but how?

Summoning all my strength, I regathered my thoughts. I could no longer be a Templar Knight in the employ of someone else. I was immortal: the world was my oyster, as they would say today. I stayed with the farmer and his family for another few days, before making my way back to Winchester, where I found there was a need for a smith. Without further ado, I took up my old post at the same forge, as a master smith, with documents I had created myself.

I needed to understand what I was. What sort of supernatural creature was I? I studied scrolls and texts at the learned houses and establishments up and down the country for years, but I could find no answer, other than the label "demon". Was everything that was not explainable named as such, I wondered?

Valiant as my learning journey was so far, I needed to re-establish myself, to forget what I was and to make me who I am now. I set up my business and decided to reach out as a master weapons-smith. I travelled to London, arriving just as it was announced that King John had died and that his young son, Henry VI, had taken the throne. I made my way into court as a weapons master and over the next hundred years, I became a member of the royal court; I was there when Edward V was deposed by the nobility, and Richard III came to power. I sloughed a familiar for the first time to replace me as the Duke of Norwich and I set myself up as my own younger son, befriending the king again.

After a period when I could not have been happier, Edward died and I set up another familiar to continue to be me. I fought in the Wars of the Roses as my own son, but for some reason unknown to me I let slip my guard and a pike man managed to stick it through my belly, effectively ruining the arrangements I had.

My body took a while to heal. I crawled from the battlefield, sloughed again, and ordered my remains to look dead, until they was buried or burned, when they would dissipate without supernatural fuss.

I was fighting a war in my mind. I lived forever, I had loved or made love with hundreds of women, but I was hollow emotionally and physically. By the turn of the century, I had been alive over five hundred and forty years. All I wanted to do was sleep. So, I did. I found a smallholding and built a tower. I sloughed a familiar which set itself up like me, managing my weapons-smith business and trade. Then I slept. I slept for fifty years at a time, only rising from my slumber to create another familiar, to then go back to sleep in my catacomb.

I awoke one-day, smelling fire. It was the early part of the century, 1505 or thereabouts. My familiars had always transferred their memories to me, so I knew of the passing of time, but the latest it seemed had dissipated. I went to look for the source of the fire to find a group of people attempting to burn my household. It seemed, upon confrontation that my father (they saw me as a younger version of the familiar) had dissipated in front of the Parish Council, leading to cries of witchcraft. They set upon me and although I was strong, they overpowered me. Watching their reaction as my cuts and scrapes healed before their eyes, I knew that I was in trouble. They set a stake: they cut the faggots and they set me aflame.

Rightfully I should have died on that pyre; I burnt and it was painful, but I dissipated instead of dying, coalescing in another place, becoming whole again. I realised I had the power to transport myself massive distances in this way-naturally, I wished to explore this. So, I went to the colonies.

I returned a rich man, after establishing land in far off parts of the world, which I now sell off to settlers and prospectors. On the day I returned to England, I was sitting in my garden when the young woman who I thought had been Agnete appeared. It was obviously her familiar. She sat and drank with me. I discovered, however she was not Agnete; she was something else. Something that I couldn't comprehend, or attempt to guess.

Magne Magnusson had finished the tale.

"What am I, Bess? Who created me?"

"Agnete? Or the monk? You are supernatural, of that there can be no doubt. Unless you are an Angel?"

"I ask the questions, Bess."

Elizabeth sighed. She may well be queen one day; therefore, she would have to understand the question. Mary had failed. She might be queen, if Edward did not last long. He was such a sickly child.

"If you have asked these questions of all the monarchs going back to Alfred, then some of your story must be a lie. Lots of it."

"I only said it was a story. I didn't say it was my story, or a true story, nor the same story told to different heirs."

"Is it written down?"

He smiled and she took from that she was close.

"Yes."

"Then I will study the story."

"Excellent, I will prepare your copy. Your Majesty."

Well, she wasn't bally Queen yet, so that was a bit presumptuous.

Time moved on; her father, then Edward died, then Mary took the throne and the religious upheaval was considerable, as was the threat against her life. Then Elizabeth succeeded as Queen.

Every day at first, she studied the story of Lord Magnus, determined to answer it. She had her code breakers look, but they could not decipher it. Then Walsingham, the horrendous self-centred bore, introduced her to William Credence, a young man of many talents. He had the story for a day and then came to her with the answer.

The next day Elizabeth I climbed the steps to the tower to confront Magnus.

"Your Majesty." He bowed eloquently; he didn't look a day older than her last visit here. She meanwhile had aged twenty years. Her hair was sparse and she was losing her teeth. Too many sweetmeats and sugars.

"Do you have an answer?"

Elizabeth nodded.

"Are you going to tell me who discovered it? Was its Walsingham's young star?"

She was flabbergasted- how could he know?

"It doesn't matter how you did it. You employed your common sense," he said, kindly.

"It's too far-fetched sir. William agreed."

Magnusson laughed again but the smiles did not reach his eyes he looked disappointed. "No."

"Do not interrupt a queen, Sir, I have not finished. The tower, your surroundings - floating fire. Vampires do not exist. Vlad the Impaler overdid his mummery. Agnete did not bite you."

He looked at her and flashed a beaming smile.

"You traverse many parallel worlds," she said, firmly. "It was hidden in the text - William found the cipher. I worked it out with him, I questioned William to find out what it meant."

"Did he reveal anything?"

"No. Because you will. You are not of this world; whether of Heaven or Hell, I do not care. You are a wonder. Now, reveal yourself."

Lord Magnus stood. A coruscation of blinding light surrounded him and then fell away. In his place was a strange, blue-furred beast, even taller than his human aspect and just as beautiful. The room was filled with strange odours and a voice emanated from a box hung about the creature.

"Your Majesty. My name is Perfume Factory Large Pockets, and I came to this world to protect it. Your kingdom is a nexus. I watch over it. It is a gateway to many other worlds that could endanger it. I hold the nightmares at bay. It is my reward for the healing nature of your waters. My boon is that I enlist the best of people. Walsingham is one of them. William is the other. Now, do you want your prize?"

"Immortality could be a curse. Everyone you love grows old and dies."

"Let me demonstrate how it can be done."

Large Pockets (a miss-translation of his actual name into English. Earthlings apparently did not have the physiognomy to pronounce it properly) came to her and kissed her, not passionately, but functionally. Not that she was complaining.

When he stepped away from her, it seemed she could see him from many angles. She jumped. This was more surprising than him revealing himself as a blue, furry, bear-like creature. She stood there looking back at herself: another Bess.

He had moved across to a jewelled box on his writing-table. He brought back a mirror. She looked in it. It was her reflection, but that of her as a much younger woman.

"Your prize is to join me protecting all the England's, in all of the known parallel dimensions. All you must do is accept and your avatar will remain and rule as you would have done. Refuse and you will go back- and you will remember nothing of this."

"How long do I have to decide this, blue furry man-thing?"

His smile was a sad one.

"Seconds."

"Then I must agree to it."

There was a clearing of the throat and red-haired William entered, looking very well, considering he had been on the rack that morning.

"Bess. Let me introduce you to William. Also known as Rufus. Once King of England."

Bess and her avatar curtsied.

"Sire," they said, in unison. She hid her surprise better this time.

"Now you must choose how your avatar dies. I know the date."

Bess laughed.

"I knew you would say that. You must live outside of time, Mr Large Pockets."

"Clever girl." He replied.

Impertinent oaf.

Three hundred and fifty years later, Bess stepped through the wormhole and into the royal apartments in Buckingham Palace. Her namesake stood in front of LP. Her smile was regretful, but firm.

"No, Sir. I choose not to go. I love my husband, despite his flaws. I choose to forget." She turned to look at Bess. "You already have a Lilibeth. You need no other. Just protect my kingdom, Sir. Are you known to Parliament?"

Bess saw LP nod. Elizabeth the Second looked at her ancestor and smiled wanly. "Such erosion of power. He's had Parliament in his paws for hundreds of years, no doubt."

Bess nodded in affirmation. Then the audience was at an end and LP was stepping through the wormhole with Bess. Back to one of the worlds they both now protected.

PARALLELAPOCALYPSE

ADAM

The sky was pregnant with snow, its yellow-orange hue promising another inch or two before the day was out. Adam cast his eyes upwards- it looked like the world was ending.

The wind was bitingly cold; he was freezing, despite the thick itchy woolly scarf that was wound tight about his neck like a boa constrictor, his hands thrust deep into pockets clutching at warmth. He wondered if he should keep them there or have them out, ready, in case he needed to arrest a fall on the slippy, compacted ice of last night's snowfall.

He walked a mile each day from home to his job as a postal worker at the Garrison Lane Post Office, then ten or twelve miles or so on his delivery round before trudging home again. Other than driving rain, this was the worst kind of weather to be out and about in.

His ears were warm from the foam Walkman headphones, his Ultravox cassette providing the tunes. Adam had been a postie for six years. He'd taken the job whilst at university but, much to the horror of his now-deceased parents, he had enjoyed it so much, he had stayed. Ironically, now that his parents *were* gone, he had his own home and a bit of financial security- albeit under sad circumstances.

His parents had died in a freak motorway accident. Dad had let the dog out for a wee, but it had run into the carriageway; a car had swerved to miss it and then careered into his dad, then into the car where his mum was sitting. The dog, Maurice, had never been found.

So, his life was sorrowful for a while but now stress-free. Unless you counted Moira.

Moira was his new boss. Six feet of Scottish woman, bearing down on him daily, like a wrestler in a carbs queue.

They just did not see eye to eye. It all started when Moira – who's surname was Lech, pronounced 'Less'- was weighing herself on the shop floor scales – usually reserved for parcels. Davey Giles had shouted out 'more or less a tonne'. Moira had thought it was Adam. So, he was on a warning- and her watch list.

Today, he was late again. Moira would no doubt bust his balls. It was taking too long to get to work. His tape had finished, so he clicked across to Radio One. The news had just begun.

Breaking news: Margaret Thatcher, the Prime Minister, has been killed live on TV. Mrs Thatcher had been visiting a Staffordshire coal-mining community, when a masked assailant decapitated her with a sword. Programmes will be suspended for us to concentrate on this terrible occurrence. Michael Heseltine has been sworn in as temporary PM. More detail as soon as we have it...

Blimey. Probably a disgruntled miner. The old bitch was breaking the country apart, but he wouldn't have wished that on his worst enemy. Decapitation? With a sword?

When Adam entered the Post Office Yard, he could see that most of the vans had already gone out. He had chosen to stay on foot, rather than lug massive parcels in and out of his van all day. His colleagues in vans were locked into a set timetable, having to return to base two or three times a day to reload, whereas he could take the time to talk with his customers.

As he approached the depot building, there was an explosion in the distance that made him jump. Was it a car back-firing? He almost slipped over on the road, but he reached the gritted kerb just in time.

Adam stamped his feet to get rid of the excess snow, took off his headphones and stowed them in his ruck-sac. He could see green lights flashing to his left, contrasting with the orange sky. It had started to snow again - lightly - and the flashes were lighting up the flakes, making them look like little falling green leaves.

"Hurst, you are late."

That was the Haggis' voice. Shit.

"Sorry. It took longer to get here than normal."

Moira hove into view, stuffed into her Royal Mail regulation suit, which always seemed a size too small for her and made her look bigger than she actually was. Her frizzy red hair was tied up in a splat on her head and her green eyes - framed with wonderful pink-winged NHS glasses - bored into him like, two diamond headed drills.

"Then ye should have started out earlier, Hurst. Ya wee gobshite."

It was going to be one of those days.

"Sorry, Moira. I'll make the time up." *I wish the man who had decapitated Margaret Thatcher was here,* he thought.

"So, you will. Get on."

Adam made his way into the depot, stowed his bag away before picking up his delivery sacks and going to visit his colleagues in sorting.

Jaz Gill saw him coming and smiled. Jaz was funny, he had to be. A Sikh man in a predominantly white workforce needed to have his wits about him – especially when most of his colleagues were closet racists and the remainder were outright ones. Adam had got stick from the racists for socialising with Jaz down the pub. Nothing like the grief Jaz got, though.

"Alright, mate." Jaz cried. "Nice to see another friendly face." Sarcasm was heavy in his voice.

Adam saw Josie and Ray, the two other sorters, look at each other with hate in their eyes. Josie was forty, but looked in her seventies, smoke cured by Benson and Hedges cigarettes. Ray was a bald man, who looked like the little fellow from Taxi, the American comedy show.

"Morning Jaz, Ray, Josie. Good weekends?"

"No, wife left me. For a Polish acrobat." Ray said crestfallen. It wasn't the first time. It seemed she left most weekends and came back on Mondays. They all wondered if she was real.

"Fed up with the missionary position, was she Ray?" Adam asked. Jaz and even Josie sniggered. Ray scowled and went back to sorting letters.

"How about you, Josie?"

"I spent the weekend down the pub."

"Oh, nice to do something different for a change."

Jazz laughed. Josie was always in the pub. Her innards were pickled by alcohol.

After exchanging pleasantries with Jaz, Adam picked up his delivery bags and hauling them over one shoulder, he made his way into the common room. The radio was on in there.

To confirm the latest developments in this ongoing breaking news story, President Regan has been killed. Further to the earlier deaths of the Prime Minister and President Chernenko, it has been revealed that in this assassination too, an armed masked man appeared from nowhere. This time, the assailant appears to have bitten out the President's neck. Whilst White House security details took care of the assailant, it seems the President bled to death in short order – such were his wounds. Whilst there were earlier fears that the deaths would provoke a nuclear war, it seems that there is a consensus that this series of murders may be linked to an independent terrorist organisation..."

"Hurst- have ye not gone yet? Time is money." Moira loomed in front of him, like a part rusted battleship in her grey suit. Adam wished he had a bottle of champagne to launch her with.

"You are on your final warning, remember. If you fall foul of me today, sunshine, I will march you into the Postmaster's office."

So off he went, Moira's Glaswegian tones amplifying his tinnitus like a sonic cat-o-nine-tails.

His delivery round went well, considering the weather. He managed to offload the majority of his two mailbags, with just a couple of parcels he couldn't fit through letterboxes or were wrongly labelled.

He'd had time to pop and see Celia, one of his favourite customers: not too much between the ears, but beautiful. She would always open the door in her nighty and gown and he would savour his job for those few seconds or minutes before he would go on his way, until the next time he would have the joy of delivering to 45 Featherstone Road. He sighed as he walked from her house. He would love a nerdy girlfriend with who he could discuss the current state of science fiction and fantasy books and shows; someone who might be able to utter a few sentences of Klingon and would know all the names of the characters from Blake's 7. However, he would be a lifelong bachelor unless he lowered his expectations, or some intelligent and beautiful woman felt sorry for him and took him under her wing. *In your dreams, mate.*

As he made his way down Bordesley Green to the depot, he noticed more of the green flashes in the sky. Walking by the empty parking bays, he wondered why more of the guys weren't back. Okay, it had snowed some more, but the roads had been gritted and shouldn't have delayed anyone. Where were they all?

There was a flash overhead and a bolt of green thunder arced from of the sky, hitting the ground in the distance. He waited for the resulting boom- but there was no further sound. Had the strike hit the ground, or not?

Suddenly there was a scream from the direction of the sorting rooms. Josie emerged, running, her face covered in blood, one hand clutched to her neck. Behind her, gaining fast, was what could only be described as a monster.

It was humanoid in shape; he knew the word from the various Asimov or Clarke books he had read. It was heavily armoured, but the small areas of skin visible were a dark green hue and its teeth were fang-like; its hair resembled that of a punk rocker – a Mohican, they used to call it.

Adam watched transfixed, horrified, as Josie ran towards him, hoping for help or protection and as inevitably the creature caught up with her. It raised a fiery sword it had pulled from its back and it took Josie apart, cutting her to pieces.

Adam had two choices: puke, or run. This wasn't what the heroes did in the books or VHS videos he watched and read. Was it an invasion?

Dropping his mailbags, he started to run towards across the slippery car park towards the sorting rooms, figuring he would be better off locked in the stacks, rather than vulnerable out in open space. He made the mistake of looking back; the creature was feeding on Josie. A nimbus surrounding the creature had attached to her, using some sort of force to suck the life out of her. Adam decided not to look back again and took off, fast.

Once inside, he headed to the common room; then dashed through the sorting room, he noticed a husk of a man that looked like it might once have been Ray. Next to him, nearer the common room, lay Jaz, obviously dead. Dear God, not Jaz.

He reached the common room and flew through the doorway. There was another of the creatures there. Thomas, McKenzie, Taylor, and Rudford were already dead; it was feeding on the Postmaster, Mr Archer.

As Adam screamed involuntarily, the creature dropped the wizened corpse of Mr Archer and tracked toward him, a loud, insect-like clicking noise emanating from its throat.

"Hello human. Have you come to my dinner party?" the creature asked, in a voice like collected whispers. It resembled the first creature, but its hair was different. Why was he focussing on hairstyles and not on the fact all his colleagues were being eaten?

Adam about-turned and ran back through the doors- straight into Moira Lech. Moira was a ruin of blood and gore and was clicking, like the other creature.

"I've always wanted to rip your head off, Hurst," Moira rasped. "And now I have the chance."

Moira hadn't got a proper hold of him, so with an almighty shove, Adam took off again. In a blind panic he ran, heading towards what Moira knew was a dead end. She ambled after him as he hit the brick wall at the back of the yard. They both knew he could go no further. As Adam watched Moira slowly approach him, he realised she was changing. Getting thinner, taller, greener.

Suddenly, a door opened in front of him. Well, not a door exactly- a hole in the air, purple and sparking with electricity. Was this a wormhole? A woman stepped through, accompanied by a man who looked like he had been cured in salt.

"Adam- catch!" the woman cried. He instinctively held his hand out and caught – *a sword?*

Two things happened. One- he took in the latest young woman to enter his life. Petite, light brown-skinned, her facial features looked a cross between Caucasian and Chinese, no, Korean. Two- he felt an awareness in his mind fill him with the knowledge of not only how to hold the sword, but how to bloody use it.

"You take their heads off. It's the only way. Not traditional Vampires, but Whampyri. Essence Vampires – they steal your physical power. One-touch is all it takes."

He watched as Lucy rounded upon Moira, as the Haggis approached and deftly took her head off. Moira's head bounced, came to rest, and snarled.

"Crumb, are you recharged yet?" Lucy asked her strange companion, who looked like he had been freeze-dried and then baked. There was no moisture in him whatsoever.

"Mistress Lucy- stick pins in my eyes. I fear I am spent." Nathanial Crumb replied.

As Adam watched, the other two creatures approached from the left and right.

"You are from a different past. What are you doing here? Only the Whampyri know of Roaming between the dimensions." This was the one with the Mohican, which reminded Adam of Tharg from 2000AD.

"Adam. You don't know us, but we know you. You will need to fight one of them. I can only manage one and Nathanial is ready to fall apart. Take the one with the Mohican." Lucy smiled at him. "Has the download reached your muscle memory yet?"

He looked from her to the creatures and nodded. He did know how to engage the creature and how he might defeat it, but he also knew his chances of dying. The information was there as if it had always been. In one moment, he had been a postman, now he had the knowledge and approach of a warrior.

Lucy screamed a charge and engaged the broader of the two creatures, as the Mohican advanced upon Adam.

"Come on Adam. We will have to defeat others. Humanity is doomed on this version of the planet. If we do not get you to the nexus, then visiting this apocalypse will be in vain."

This version of the planet? He didn't get chance to ask.

He watched as the little woman pulled a large sword from somewhere behind her and struck out at the creature twice her height. It looked like it could kill her with its little finger, not needing its blade, nor its ability to suck out her life force.

He had watched too long.

"Master, a Pire approaches. Pour acid on my toes," the desiccated man cried.

Adam felt himself alter his stance, moving into a position he had never adopted in his life. Then he felt the concussion and vibration of fiery blade upon steel blade. The ring was deafening. Blocking the first blow, he then twirled away from the wall, slightly to the left of the creature. He gripped the sword in both hands and brought it down in an arc, cutting the air with a whoosh of speed-displaced air molecules. A breeze of an attack, aiming for the Mohican shorn head, ready to split it in two.

The creature laughed as it darted, lightning-fast, out of Adam's way, rounding on him again, but as he did, Adam realised that not only was he considering how he could improve his last move, but he was also planning the details of how to execute his next three.

Preventing a sweeping blow to his left flank, Adam came back at the creature. Blow and parry. Blow and parry. He noticed a chink in the creature's stance and went for the obvious thrust, but at the last moment feinted and let the creature step inside and open, just through his stance. As the creature raised its arm a little more slowly it should, Adam lopped it off at the shoulder.

The Whampyri creature screamed at first, then laughed. Adam watched as the bloody stump that had been its shoulder regenerated and grew back. The creature reached behind its head and drew the sword of flame again. As it did so, Adam danced inside and took its head. An old trick, his mind seemed to reassure him. A mind that had only considered swordplay in the context of Dungeons and Dragons, or in a Shannara book. Until today.

The creature burst into green flame; Adam drew his sword back into a defensive position and turned to face Lucy, who had also dispatched her creature.

"Well done, my Lord," she said.

"Liquidise my entrails in a blender," the corpse man added.

Lucy Avery and Nathanial Crumb were not allowed to say where they were from, or who employed them. It was all a bit MI5 with monsters. It had taken more than an hour to navigate back to Adam's house and they had seen off three more of the creatures.

Adam had seen more dead mutilated humans than he cared to think about. In order to go through a portal, they apparently needed the mummy man to recharge, before he could open a windows in the air through which they could escape.

"I'm a human and he's a Chronombie," Lucy offered, after he had made them a cup of tea.

"Eternal time creatures who, contrary to popular opinion, are not dead, just not alive yet. Created at the end of time to help some of us rescue some of you; they work backwards repairing causality loops. It's all I can say. I need to get you to the nexus. Then we go. You, however, have a lifetime of importance at the other end of the Universe."

"Why is he washing up?" Adam asked, as the mummy-man dried dishes that had been unwashed for a week or so.

"Whoever created them, some people say a god with a bizarre sense of humour, made them hard-working to the point of obsession, eternally loyal to their masters, not to mention thoroughly masochistic, as a defence mechanism! You can't bully or humiliate a Chronombie more effectively than they do themselves."

"Plough a furrow down my spine, young master. Any more jobs you require doing?"

"After half an hour with Nathanial, you wouldn't want to do anything to him that he hasn't already asked you to do. He's kind of indestructible, in a way."

There was a huge splash, quickly followed by a clunk.

"What was that?" Adam asked. Lucy tutted loudly, as if she already knew what had happened.

"Sorry, my Lord. My left eye just dropped in the washing up bowl and broke a plate. I'll go and find a kiln and some clay, fire you a new one. Rupture my spleen with a mace."

Lucy shook her head.

"Their life force might be indestructible, but they're like a shit box of Lego, where all the bobbles have shrunk and worn and won't fit tightly into the bases anymore."

"Why are you here? Why can I now wield a sword like an expert? What are those creatures?"

Lucy sighed; she had a habit of swinging her head to get her long fringe out of her eyes. She really was quite something and, in other circumstances, he might have tried to chat her up; however, the time-travelling sword wielding thing was messing with his head, along with a lot of other things he'd seen that day.

"Your world will not last much longer than a year. The Whampyri will harvest all the life force and then step sideways into another, parallel version of Earth."

That took a lot of processing. Earth ending, destroyed by energy vampires? She patted his arm like he was a child whose first long division sum had been a disaster.

"It's a lot to take in, I know. My colleagues are from an Earthbound agency, trying to shore up the Whampyri invasions at this end of the Universe, whatever the timeline or version of this planet. The Whampyri have managed to crack through Earth's defences- while we were fixing that breach, a whole host of them have come through and invaded three different versions of Earth. We have tied the breaches in this version, they cannot go sideward from here – they will cease to exist in this reality, or rather cease to be an issue. Planet-busters will reduce this world to dust in just over a decade. It's the only way to destroy them. We will let them starve for a bit first."

"And of all the people on this planet, why save me?"

He thought of his friends: the lovely Celia, dear God – if there was one – they would all die. Jazz. No, he was already dead.

"You are destined to be one the final bastions of hope in the Universe's fight against evil. However, you will do it millions of light-years away- on a planet that is cut off from the rest of our universes. A so-called theurgical world"

"What does that even mean?"

"Magic. It will go down on record that you invented the Whampyri name. It will be so because you will never speak of this conversation."

"A magic world?"

"Yeah, sounds shit, but it's not. Don't mention that either. It's meant to be a shock."

Adam looked from the beautiful young woman to the mummy-man and wondered for a moment if he had lost the plot. Was this actually happening? It felt real enough. He had seen Moira change and then be destroyed. He had seen his work colleagues slaughtered. He had seen the Whampyri rage with pure hatred and hunger. He remembered killing some of them. Was it a dream? Lucy broke his reverie.

"It is not a dream, my Lord."

Adam frowned as he made his "what the fuck did you just say?" face.

"Liberate my sinus fluid with a crochet hook, Madam, you have done it now."

Adam looked back from Nathanial to Lucy. "Why did you call me "my Lord" again?"

"Slip of the tongue," Lucy stuttered, her words belied by her "what the fuck did I just say?" face.

"Use my eyes for a conker fight, you have told him too much already. Large Pockets will be angry. I am ready to take us to the nexus. Adam- are you ready?"

Adam looked at Lucy, who nodded.

"Can we save my Earth?"

Lucy shook her head sadly.

"No. But one day you will try."

"So, it's not the end."

"It's not this world you will try to save. You will choose the wrong one. Even though you think you are right."

For some reason, preternaturally, he knew she was correct. He knew she told the truth; he knew he would try to save his world. He now knew he might fail. He locked that away.

"Let's go, then." If his world was doomed and he was going to be the only survivor, he may as well have an adventure.

Lucy and Nathanial took one of his hands each. Her hand was soft and smooth and lovely, Nathanial's was like holding a loofah. He felt- rather than saw- the portal open and he stepped through with his new companions...

...but when he arrived on the other, side thingy and whatsit were gone. What were their names, the old woman, and the young man? Had he been practising his swordplay too much? Killing Pires?

"Adam. Welcome."

A handsome man with very dark skin approached Adam. He was holding a black cat. It was strange- Adam hadn't realised where he was until the man had spoken, as if his appearance had somehow thrown off a mask on his senses. He was on what looked like a viewing platform. In space. Overlooking a massive spaceship-The *Skyflier,* its name emblazoned on the side of the ship, alongside the name of the company who had obviously built or sponsored it.

"My name is Bartholomew Gordon. I'm the owner of Bargo, construction company and maker of the ships that will rescue humanity.

Adam sighed. Was his day going to get any stranger?

ANGUS

"When Queen Victoria was assassinated in 1840 by Edward Oxford, the whole of the world shook. Such a promising monarch, cut off in her prime. Then, Parliament voted to raise Prince Albert to the Throne. It was named as *The Act of Stability.* Albert reigned well with Queen Constance for twenty years, until his death at Osbourne House on the Isle of Wight. You all know, however, that Constance murdered Albert after he had negotiated her succession: a fact which did not come to light for twelve years. The monarchy did not stand a chance after that point. The Russian invasion and subsequent three Baltic Wars almost threw Europe into another Dark Ages. The final treaty of St Petersburg was signed in 1899; by then, England had been a republic for twelve or so years. This great city may have been named Alberta after our last real king, but the name was the last vestige of monarchy in the country.

A bell rang. Angus Tavenor sat back on his desk as his seminar group packed away their bags and headed for their homes. Homes that would not exist in a year's time.

A figure stepped from the shadows.

Angus remembered looking at him head-on; a beautiful, blond, long-haired man, well over six feet tall and built like a steam engine.

If you knew how to look at him properly, as Angus had later, he looked like a blue furry monster.

The main hall of the University of Alberta in London was a work of art. Designed by Wren himself, after a fire destroyed London twice during the years 1666-1672. Its domes were as spectacular as New St Pauls and its layout as special as New Hampton Court, where the Royal Family had lived from the early 1700s until the fall of Queen Constance, the traitor, in 1872.

"Perfume Factory Large Pockets. LP, you said you would come today." Two other figures stepped from the portal behind the big man, who had now resolved into his actual shape. Arthur Poke and Ezekiel Crumb were LP's agents in London these days.

"Gus." Arthur clasped him in a bear hug. The boy was strong now. He had grown up well.

"I fear if I shake your hand, Master Angus, I will leave mine in it, so I'll just blow a kiss and wave. Crack my knees with a toffee hammer." Ezekiel still looked like he had been dead a thousand years, albeit immaculately turned out. He was a dandy still, just as he had been when Angus had studied under LP twenty years before. His fashion sense was perfect, like his brother Nathanial's legendary tidiness.

"It's today it starts, then?"

"Yes," LP replied, using the Zenobarts' olfactory system to communicate. He had a special machine that deciphered the myriad smells the monster diffused and translated them into most languages – often with mistranslations, however.

"And no one is saved?"

"Other than you, no. You know we are only visitors to your realm. Lucy, Abel, Andrew, and young Arthur here are all agents of mine, under the ancient sacred orders of Alfred the Great. To watch over the nexus and to protect as many of the side and artefact worlds as we can. The Earth-Zenobart Treaty is an ancient one. Unfortunately, under its components Earth One is always protected; where danger approaches via any of its parallels, then that parallel is forfeit."

It was a long speech for LP and Angus could smell aromas that harked back to his childhood. Aromas which conjured up melancholy, that made him think of his parents and his lovely husband Charles, who had died only two years before. He had wanted to die himself as he watched them lower Charles – or what was left of him- into the ground. He would never be with Charles again and Charles' remains would be destroyed, along with the billion inhabitants of his planet, purely because it was Earth 234 removed twice, not Earth One.

The essence of Earth 234 was lodged within an audio recording on a wax disk, that in turn lived within a version of the Earth, described in the pages of a living book. Hence twice removed. A world within a world within a world. Not the original: just a recording of a recording. LP and his friends protected those worlds with the Legion of Our Faltering Hearts. Named after the arrhythmia you would suffer if you didn't ground yourself at your natural birthplace once a year. It could be fatal if unchecked; walking between parallel worlds could give you heart failure.

"The Pires will be appearing soon." Arthur's tone was quiet, respectful. He reached behind his back and pulled out a thought sword, which he switched around and held pommel first to Angus.

"What about the Gold Lord?" he asked, taking the sword. He was already imbued with the knowledge of how to use it well, despite only having carried one for a short time.

"That abomination cannot leave this place. He is a fiction of this world and does not exist in any other." The smells were angry like burning rubber or bloody earth. LP was furious in his silence.

"We defeated him before."

"And look at what happened. We lost you. Our most promising agent."

"Yet I am of this world too!"

"No. You have a Faltering Heart. You were born on Earth One; you are true. Your parents brought you here to survive. You are one of the Chosen."

"And that's why all my birthdays happened at my parents' house back on Earth-One until they died and at Charles' Earth One home after that. They knew. Even Charles."

"He was almost as clever as me." Arthur piped up. Angus chuckled; the boy was a genius. He could smell a humorous response from LP.

Angus' reminiscences were shattered by a large explosion somewhere near enough to shake the building, but far enough away to not cause great damage. The dust of ages cascaded down from the ceiling, creating shining motes that danced in the colourful light cascading through the stained-glass windows of his seminar room.

"The Pires approach. They will be seeking you out, Angus. We must go. If the Gold Lord suspects what is happening and does make a play, then we need to destroy him. The Gold Lord cannot escape this reality again."

"Ezekiel. Take us to my house. It will be defended." LP ordered the ancient man.

Angus knew the drill. He grabbed Arthur's proffered hand and LP's furry one and they, in turn, grasped the Chrononbie's...

...Only Angus appeared at the other end. Where were LP and the others?

"Well, that was a piece of cake." A voice cackled. Humphrey Mortimer, the Gold Lord.

Angus reached behind his back and drew his sword. He muttered a few words; the sword danced with ethereal blue fire.

Humphrey cackled again. As unhinged as ever. The Gold Lord took the body of a new host every time he wore the last one out. Angus had watched with Andrew Poke when the Gold Lord had rejuvenated. It was horrible. Like a snake shedding its skin and invading another host through his or her mouth.

"Missing Charlie?"

Don't listen.

"Ironic that original Humphrey, when he was alive, was Charles' bit on the side."

"You do not deserve to sully my husband's name."

"He did it with women too. Did you know? On the evening of the Act of Sexual Liberation being passed, young Charlie Boy did it with Bertha, your maid. She with the bosoms like the Malvern Hills."

"You lie, Gold Lord. I will not be turned by thee."

The Gold Lord laughed.

"By thee? Then I was right; you are a Chosen."

"What do you mean?"

"You are talking prophecy. You live- we all die. This world dies. The sky will fall on our heads as the oceans boil. Yet you survive. Why?"

The Gold Lord neared him. Angus brandished his sword, but it leapt out of his grasp and flew swiftly across the room, landing with a clatter somewhere. A hand caught Angus by the throat and lifted him, choking, into the air.

Angus couldn't speak, unable to breathe. It couldn't end like this. Summoning all of his remaining strength, he gouged his fingers deep into the Gold Lord's eyes. Humphrey screeched in shock and pain, involuntarily releasing Angus, who dropped and rolled away, retrieving his sword, stowing it quickly away on his back. He made a beeline for the stable door, which he opened with surprising ease and made his way out into the yard.

LP's was a small farmstead. Yet it was deceptive. In one part of the large barn was a portal back to the University of Worlds on Earth One. Angus knew he couldn't go that way and unleash the Gold Lord on the World of Origin.

Instead, he headed for LP's library, housed in a tower, which stood incongruously to the left side of the farmhouse. The tower door swung open for Angus as he approached, slamming shut as soon as he had raced through, preventing Humphrey's entrance. Angus pelted up the well-worn steps two at a time, the dimensions of the place opening up like a sun-blessed flower, the scent of old books, of paper and ink, filling his screaming lungs. From within the dusty stacks of books- some as sentient as the people of this world, a handful of them quite evil- sparkled a bright, almost lyrical voice.

"Angus- you are here!"

Lady Anna Percival, young Arthur's fiancée, stepped out from behind the shelves, smiling a radiant, yet wistful smile. The Percivals had been agents for LP for generations, all Earth One descendants too. Anna was an English Rose: strawberry blonde hair, green eyes, and alabaster skin, as pale as Angus was dark.

"Anna!"

He strode over to her and wrapped her in a bear hug, as much to steady his nerves than to show his love.

"It's been too long."

"It *has*. Art and I have had quite a time of it, I tell you. Since Grandmamma died and I took on a full-time role at the University of Worlds." She kissed him on his left cheek.

"Still as handsome as ever," she smiled, blinking back tears. He knew where she was heading. "You could have anyone you wanted."

"I'm not ready for anyone else, Percy." Everyone called her Percy- even her family.

"Why didn't you come to the University?"

"I wanted to stay as long as possible with Charles I'd heard the prophecy that it was doomed- I just didn't want to believe it. Charles ordered me to keep his remains on this Earth, whatever happened. He was a child of this world, despite originating on Earth One. I am not destined to remain, it seems."

There was a thumping on the doors.

"It's Humphrey." Angus spat. Getting up, he reached over his shoulder and drew the thought blade.

"He can't get in here."

At which point, the door Angus had entered through exploded inwards.

"Bugger," Percy said, without humour, pulling out her own thought blade.

It wasn't Humphrey, but a group of his Lantern Heads. His own sick invention, a cross between Peeler policemen and lamp posts. They were the Gold Lord's henchmen, vicious, vile creatures. Created by an earlier incarnation who experimented on human cadavers, mobilising them with clockwork energy.

"I thought I'd seen the last of these things," Angus shouted.

Percy rushed towards the creatures, swiftly followed by Angus. The Lantern Heads had pulled their own blades: huge, glittering broadswords that looked like they could cleave a man or woman from shoulder to hip. Many of their victims were dead as soon as the reflections caught them – captivated by the light dancing upon that deadly steel.

Angus was nearly lost in his first engagement, barely parrying a sweeping horizontal blow. The thought blade absorbed some, but not all, of the kinetic energy, his wrists shaking as his shoulders absorbed the vibration. The Lantern Head had put all its momentum into a stroke; as Angus stepped back, he was able to make the space and bring his sword down on its neck. The head formed, like the gas lanterns of old and clunked, smashing on the floor, the creature winking out of existence, as was always the case when you ended one.

Angus had no time to draw breath from this encounter before the next Lantern Head attacked, with the rattling, haunting representation of laughter that a creature without face or mouth could conjure up: like the staccato rhythm the mantle made before enough gas was provided to ignite the flame. The monster pulled a second blade. This would be a double hander, it seemed.

Angus risked a look to his left, where Percy had dispatched another Lantern Head and was engaging a third. It was at this moment that Angus' opponent charged him, one blade raised in a 'sun in the sky' pose, the other, guarding his body in a 'protection of the land' stance. Angus extended his thought blade to the length of the Lantern Head's two swords, imbuing it with his will, making it burn with increasing strength.

By now, the Lantern Head's rattle was insane; the light behind its four glass panels glowing brightly, with confidence or glee. But Angus had something potentially even more powerful at his disposal; the knowledge that he could pull from the depths of the law of the library. Millions of pages at his beck and call-in moments.

Swordmaster Alberto Lucci, late of Queen Mary's court, had been a master at his trade. He had lasted well into his eighties and had taught generations of swordsmen. Walsingham had dubbed Lucci "Little Hummingbird", due to his lightning speed and diminutive stature.

The knowledge in his grasp, Angus dropped and skidded under the two swords brandished by the Lantern Head. He turned off his thought blade, but as he passed under the reach of the thing, he switched it back on, severing both creature's legs at the knees. *Thanks, Alberto Lucci*, he thought, as he rolled before the creature could fall upon him. It would still be dangerous without legs.

He stood, quickly dispatching the creature; it dissipated with a shower of sparks.

Percy was panting; she had destroyed her two opponents.

"I am not sure where LP or Arthur are, but we need to go. I need to get us to the nexus."

"You are coming too?"

"I have to, it seems. Despite Arthur's protestations, I am Chosen too."

"Chosen to do what?"

"To help humanity prosper. Eventually, all parallels to Earth One will be destroyed, or at least their human populations. It might take thousands of years, but it will happen. The Pires will succeed one day. There will be a point where it is probable rather than possible."

"The nexus."

Percy nodded.

"Come on. I'll tell you more on the way. We will need to go down the passages and out of the other entrance. The Tower has sealed the doors again, so Humphrey will have to blow them in a second time. If he has enough energy left."

The passages were accessed between Flora and Fauna and Archaeology. A hidden switch popped one of the stacks forward, revealing a dusty, cobwebbed corridor of stone, along which the pair made their way.

"The nexus point focuses on a version of Earth where it and The Whampyri are engaged in a great battle for dominance of Earth Two. The Skyflier company has developed a fleet of ships to take humanity to another planet. We are uncertain where this planet is located exactly, but it's likely it to be contained within a bubble universe, affording it greater protection from sideward intervention from the creatures. The future projections suggest that if we reach that world, the Whampyri will be defeated."

Angus frowned.

"The Earth Two population will need a watertight plan. The Whampyri aren't as easy targets as traditional vampires."

"Intensive light kills them, as well as decapitation. Earth Two humans will detonate the sun as they leave."

"What about the parallel worlds?"

"The Whampyri are the result of longevity experiments on Earth One, many years ago. The Cordivae Group - who were to blame for the emergence of the Whampyri- evolved into the Skyfliers Corporation in the late twenty-seventh century. They cut a deal with LP to ensure that once Earth Two died, only artefacts clear of the Whampyri would remain. The rest will be destroyed. Therefore, there will be none of the creatures in existence on Earth, in any of the parallel worlds and certainly not on the new one."

"Those versions of Earth die to protect the original," Angus sighed.

Percy held up a hand for him to stop, the light from the thought sword illuminating her angular face.

"It's here. Are you ready to run?"

He nodded. She sprung the mechanism, then looked back at him.

"Here we go."

Out they raced, emerging in the grounds of LP's enclosed residence. Suddenly, a portal appeared. Angus reached for his thought sword, but Percy laid a hand on his arm.

"It's Ezekiel's signature."

The portal opened and vomited out LP and Ezekiel, running at a pace. The portal closed behind them.

"Percy, Angus. I am so glad you are okay. Do I smell Humphrey on the breeze? Lantern Heads?"

"Yes, LP, we have just dispatched four of them. This young man has not lost any of his skills. Where is Arthur?"

"We lost him in the melee. He will find his way to you. Let us get you to the nexus point. We can do it from here, so we don't have to use the hardwired portal. Ezekiel, are you ready?"

"Indubitably, Master Large Pockets, rip my entrails out with a fish slice."

"Where am I going?" asked Angus.

"We." Percy replied, a tinge of sadness in her voice.

Whatever Angus's next adventure, it would be good to have her with him, but he realised this meant she would have to part from Arthur. They had been together for years, not in a linear fashion, but in the roundabout time travelling way of the League of Our Faltering Hearts. She wasn't Charles- but she was a good friend.

Another portal winked into existence. Arthur popped through, accompanied by his father, Andrew. Andrew Poke was an enigma. A legendary Agent: the one they all looked up to. Genius, but as clumsy as cricketer with no hands. Andrew had once led the battle against invaders from space for the British government, until they wiped him from history by accident. He had been invited to a hearing to give evidence against a man with a similar name and the stupid hearing officer had passed judgement on Andrew. His family and friends no longer knew who he was. His compensation, provided by LP, was a place with the University of Worlds and the most dangerous League job there was, alongside his wife Lucy.

"Angus!" Andrew cried, holding out his hands, then tripping on a clump of grass, landing in Angus' arms. Andrew's dyspraxia was as challenging as ever, it seemed.

Arthur sighed, embarrassed by his father's clumsiness, which was exacerbated in anxious situations.

"Whoops, sorry Gus," he whooped, in comedic fashion, standing upright and dusting himself down, as if he had fallen into a flour mill, then turning to Percy.

"Anna. I am so sorry you have been Chosen."

Percy's lip quivered almost imperceptibly. She wasn't going to break in front of them.

"Angus, I need to introduce you to Bartholomew. He will take you to your new world. I will not be able to stay too long; I'm not breaking the laws of reality, just bending them a little. Let us leave Arthur and Percy to say their goodbyes. It is a wretched time for them." LP nodded to the couple.

Angus shook Andrew's hand, waved at Ezekiel- in case something fell off- and followed the blue, furry creature through the coruscating portal...

...Onto a spaceship?

As Angus turned to give a final wave, something hit him palpably in his chest- not violently enough knock him over, but painful, all the same. He looked down at himself, but there was no sign of injury. Maybe it was something to do with the time displacement; he made a note to ask LP later.

Angus never did ask LP.

PART THREE

Dafydd, Vanessa and Fay

Dafydd Edwards made sure his twin nieces had dispatched the Pire, before breathing a sigh of relief. Van had skewered the creature, then Fay, the more insane of the two teenagers, had taken its head- accompanied by a "you bastard." He'd have to have a word about her swearing; although given the creatures had killed their parents a few weeks ago, a little colourful language was the least of his worries.

Dafydd had been as surprised as anyone to discover his nieces were Chosen. LP had given him the bad news that he was a few weeks earlier, in a particularly tense meeting at the University of Worlds. It is not often you are told your world is ending. He'd been an Agent working for LP since 1240, Earth One timeline, when he had helped foil an assassination attempt on Henry Plantagenet, third of his name. Aside from a couple of centuries in stasis to recharge his batteries, he had lived a long and prosperous life. He had lost count of how many nieces and nephews he'd had.

They were standing on Steep Hill in Lindum, which he knew as Lincoln. His adopted brother Linus and Heather, his wife, had lived there when the Pires broke through. As the main agent for the last hundred years on this version of Earth, he would be sad to leave. It was a negative planet; the significant rewrites to its timelines had caused it to have advancements Earth One would not have for a while - or might never have.

He looked at his Apple Body Net and noticed his vitals had calmed, his blood pressure back at 130 over 80. They had dispatched a whole nest of Pires in Lincoln and were just mopping up. The girls had done a lot of the work- their fighting skills were legendary. He knew they had fought in the National Gladiatorial Rings and had been richly rewarded for their defeat of Antonius Maximus, the emperor Malachi Caesar's favourite. Dafydd had kept a low profile at that point; Malachi was a bastard to deal with.

They were situated just down from the fort and the temple of Athena, a grand thing that had caused a huge outcry because of the frivolous use of tax-payers' money. The minority Christians had chained themselves to railings, like the martyrs they were. The legionnaires had merely cut the railings off, pressure group still chained to them, and dumped them into the Brayford.

Dafydd and the girls just needed to get to the nexus point and seal off this world.

As the girls moved towards him, laughing about their most recent dispatch, he checked his watch. Nearly time to make contact. He assumed Andrew was coming here- he might or might not have Lucy with him. It had been a while since he had seen Lucy, or her twin brother, Abel. Abel often dropped off the radar, as was his way, but Lucy was a good friend. Dafydd had studied with her when they had been working towards a joint mission, supporting Earth 731 from an invasion of partial robotic lizards- the Kallienthi.

His wrist set beeped with an incoming signal, Chronombie signature. The portal opened in front of him- out stepped Andrew and his son, Arthur.

"Dave!" Andrew bellowed, offering his left hand to Daffyd's right, then having to swap at the last minute. Dafydd shook his head and wrapped his friend in a bear hug.

"Two Pokes. I am honoured." He shook a miserable-looking Arthur's hand. It was bad news that Arthur was losing Percy; they were a legendary couple. At least he and the girls no longer had any ties with this world. He smiled at Arthur, hoping it conveyed a supportive sympathy. Arthur imperceptibly nodded; no young man wanted his emotions out on show, however much of a genius he was.

"Uncle!" Van hugged Andrew, followed by a shake of the hand from her tomboy sister, Fay.

"Hi girls. Want to tell me about your latest kills?" Arthur asked. Good lad- Art knew Andrew and Dafydd needed to talk.

Dafydd took Andrew through the threshold into the temple of Athena. If anything, it would be calm in there.

"I can't believe we are losing you too, Dave," Andrew was the only person who Dafydd allowed to anglicise his name; he never had got the hang of pronouncing the Welsh.

"I've known for a while. Ever since the Child of Cymru kept coming up in the prophetic algorithms in Arthur's machine."

"All the worlds will die eventually."

"You will have to cement your link with Earth One, Andrew. Or sail to the stars, like the girls and me."

The Temple of Athena was lit in pastel shades, all space, and columns. They were in the main atrium, where the gloomy light almost-shone down on Athena herself, part of the Most Worshipful Pantheon.

As a Christian brought up in a time when Christianity meant something or you got burned, Dafydd had never taken religion on this world seriously. Earth – 42 was accessed via an ancient Amphora, deep on the seabed of the Mediterranean, just off the coast of Corsica. It was an artefact world, where causality had spun off and anchored itself to an object back on Earth One. There weren't many where the Romans had prospered, but this was one of them and although he had enjoyed his time there, it was a bonkers world. They still crucified people for treason and terrorism, particularly the fundamental Christian terrorists.

"The place you are going to is the endgame for the Whampyri. We are hoping they won't get through, but if they do, the planet is quite special. It will defend itself- once Earth is locked down."

"The Whampyri won't get beyond those versions of Earth that will be destroyed?"

Andrew shook his head.

"There's no projected timeline that suggests they do. We have prioritised containment wherever possible."

"And where will you guys go when Earth Two dies?"

Andrew winked. "Back to Earth One. It is never attacked by the Whampyri, so stays sealed- as much as we know from the timeline modelling. It is as near to Earth Two as damn-it. Abel is there, sowing the seeds of the transference."

"Good old Abel. How's Alasdair?"

"They are married now. Abel is still sporting the scatty inventor personality. It prevents his darkness manifesting- as long as he stays in character."

Dafydd laughed, he had shared many a drunken evening with Abel and Alasdair when he had to pop back and ground himself on Earth One. Those visits, generally on people's birthdays, were cause for great celebration. Not to mention great prevention of heart attacks.

Suddenly there was a scream from outside the temple. It was one of the girls. Dafydd was out first, Andrew following, attempting not to fall over.

Dafydd hit the streets after a rapid descent down the temple steps- they were not steep, but awkward, designed for walking, not running. He rounded into Temple Square to discover his nieces and Arthur engaged with a Whampyri queen.

The queens were the best fighters: sleeker and more sinewy than their male counterparts, pink skin reflecting the light, giving them the appearance of someone who had been under a sunlamp for most of their existence. Arthur and the girls had all drawn their thought swords, but Van had been injured, one arm hanging limply by her side. While the girls engaged the queen, Arthur was dealing with a couple of her soldiers; he was the best of them at close quarters and no doubt Andrew would help him.

"Girls, away!" Dafydd yelled, drawing his dual swords. The twins danced away acrobatically, even Van with her injuries, brave girl.

The evil queen hissed. Dafydd and his friends were a potential energy source to the Pires, who were hunters who relished a chase. Gourmet meals always involved a good long hunt or a fight as an appetiser for the Whampyri.

The key was not to let them touch you. Pires were strong in their natural form- additional haemoglobin supplied to their muscles was the key to their strength. Whilst nominally dead, they still possessed a heartbeat, which pumped blood efficiently around their bodies. Brains did not work without blood supply, either. Supernatural Vampires lived off death magic and didn't need to breathe or have blood flow around their bodies. Whampyri were evolutionary developments; the next stage of humanity from the future of a spin off-world, intelligent enough to have mastered the ability to travel between parallel realities.

Dafydd attacked the Queen, while Andrew joined Arthur in taking on the soldiers, his thought blade overriding his conditions, transforming him into a deadly-looking swordsman- who just happened to look like your favourite uncle.

It took a while to finish them. Then Arthur shouted,

"Ezekiel is here!"

"Girls!" Dafydd called. They knew what to do. Fay was helping Vanessa, who despite her injuries, was still fearsomely strong. The Avery girls would be legendary.

A wormhole opened before them. Then another queen attacked and Andrew was taken down.

"Get through to the nexus." Arthur shouted. "I'll help Dad. Ezekiel, help them."

Dafydd had his arms around both the girls and as he threw a backward glance towards his friends engaging the Whampyri queen, they stepped through the void and promptly forgot all about their previous lives.

SKYFLIER ONE

ANGUS

Angus felt strange; not because he had forgotten his past life, nor because he had been Chosen as the last bastion of humanity. It was because of the voice in his head.

Ever since he had woken on that very first morning after his arrival, he had heard Charles's voice.

Angus sat eating breakfast in the mess. He shared a table with a lovely boy called Adam, who was a bit lonesome and emotional, but exceptionally handsome; a Welshman called Dafydd who was rugged but a little old fashioned in his views and two beautiful young women called Fay and Van.

"It's short for Vanessa," she had said.

"Just Fay" added the other girl, bluntly. Van's sister was a lot more serious.

The girls could remember they were sisters and that Dafydd was their uncle- but nothing else. Bart had assured them all that their memories would return.

Adam sat quietly, eating bacon and egg sandwiches. He seemed as thoughtful as Gus.

"You will want to kill him one day," Charles said about Adam. Gus ignored Charles, but it wasn't the first time he said this about the handsome young man.

Bart had asked Angus if he would take up a position as schoolmaster for the children on board Skyflier One, which seemed to suggest Bart knew about his past profession. There were seventeen of the young "Chosen" on board and apparently, they all needed to be schooled. Angus was more than happy to oblige; he began to discuss with the crew what those lessons might be.

Dafydd, it seemed, had also been given a job. Bart had asked him to train the "Chosen"- both young and old- in self-defence techniques and swordplay. Although they seemed to be able to wield their thought blades competently, they needed to be taught the art of warfare.

Adam was to be their communicator, linking the displaced "Chosen" with members of the crew. He was to receive training in the Skyflier systems, particularly those that dealt with information and communication. The journey was going to take seven years. The thought of it just made him itch. It seemed an inordinately long time; they were aboard a ship that did not utilise faster than light technology, but instead could punch a hole in the fabric of reality into a bubble universe. However, the point they needed to punch through was not only seven years away, but was in a region of space where black holes were rife. In such a location, time and other dimensions were bending and if they were to punch into a bubble universe, then a super black hole was the place to do it – apparently.

"We will conquer that world," Charles said in Angus's head, as he was trying to get off to sleep that evening. "It is ripe. Imagine our power on a thaumaturgical world. It would be endless."

"I have no wish to create miracles," Angus replied, "unless it was to bring you back, Charles. Although you would have put no stock in such beliefs."

Wait. How did he now know who Charles had been?

Then the grief hit him.

"I protected your memories when you came through, but I've unlocked some now. I might share more of them with you- if you do as I say," Charles said.

That sounded a little like blackmail.

"You would not have demanded such things, Charles; you would have given me anything I desired, if you could have done so. I am sure of it."

The voice that wasn't really his late husband laughed.

"You need to get used to listening to me; you see, you are about to change, my dear," Charles began. "You have been bitten. Bitten by a pire."

Angus sat up, horrified. He was imbued with the knowledge of what a pire was once more.

"Then I must tell them; they will need to kill me. Are you the disease inside my head? The vicious immortality? Lucifer's curse?"

"Our curse is of human making, Angus. We are not children of fallen angels- we were grown. On the original Earth- Earth One-magic exists in small pockets, although it tends only to be linked to the dead. A witch called Isabelle created the magic that led to the Pires. It was a curse that became perverted over time. Scientists used her curse to fuel their science. She trapped some of them and they did her bidding. She is the true mother of our kind."

"Then she is evil," Angus replied.

"Is it evil to want to survive? Make yourself anew? Have children, build a strong family? Aren't they values too, Angus?"

Angus considered for a while. Those values were the reason he had accepted the role of teacher for all the "Chosen" children without a second thought.

"I was your husband, Angus. The humans killed me because I was turning into a Pire. They immolated me, after decapitating me. I felt it all, Angus. I should not have died."

Angus was confused. He now remembered being married, to a man named Charles. He had loved Charles very much. What if they *had* killed him?

"No, you died in a dirigible accident. That voice is not you, Charles."

"What if I said I could come back? What could you find me a host? I could be your husband again."

Angus was muddled. This Charles was so convincing. Part of him could feel there was something of his husband in this voice.

In that moment, his defences came down; the Gold Lord had him. The Gold Lord laughed.

"I knew you would be easy. Always target one who has lost the most."

Angus didn't hear Humphrey Mortimer, the Gold Lord. He continued to hear Charles, whispering in his thoughts. His darling Charles, the love of his life.

"I want the one known as Adam Hurst to be my new host. Such a fine young body. That will last me some time."

Angus nodded. "Whatever you want, Charles."

Vanessa

Van kept dreaming of a man called Aeflynn Valkslander. She found the name hard to pronounce, let alone spell. He called himself Flynn and asked her to do so too. The dreams seemed more than dreams, however.

She was dressed in a red velvet gown and she looked like she was in her late twenties, but she knew she was older in this dream. Ancient, in fact.

"I dream all the time, Van. Sometimes the events in them are real, other times they are imaginings of my life with different endings, or beginnings, or middles too. In those dreams I find clues."

They were sitting on a balcony; she was sipping wine. Van had never had wine before; it was cool, sharp like sour apples, but very refreshing. Flynn smiled at her. He was so handsome. Later, she would not really be able to recall him, but in the dream, she saw him so clearly. He was tall, strong, muscular; he *was* in his early twenties, younger than her, younger than her by thousands of years.

"Fay is going to be bitten soon Van, and it will cause the destruction of millions of people on the new world. The Pires will be ruled by her. She will be their queen. She will let someone called the Gold Lord through – he is the Pire essence, born of a spell. I have dreamed it so."

Van nearly choked on her wine.

"Fay hates the Pires. Wait. How do I remember that?"

"I'm helping you remember. One day, you will get all your memories back. You will remember this. I will probably be long gone by then, but you will remember."

"You are not making any sense."

"I'm breaking the rules, Van. I have learned to travel through time. I want to destroy the Gold Lord and the Pire King and Queen before they even reach our world. You would not approve. The *you* that's lying beside me in my bed, the future you, would be so angry right now, if you knew what I was doing."

"You're saying we get married?"

"We might. Unless what I do means timelines change and we never meet; or I don't get called."

"Then you wouldn't be able to do this. Talk to me, presumably. It's done by magic, isn't it? I can feel it."

"You could be right. Paradox. You are clever."

"I heard Bartholomew talking about causality and the wormhole we will have to punch into the bubble universe. It's not without its risks, apparently. We could rupture time, cause ourselves to be caught in a paradox. We could end up in a universe where the Pires are dominant. So many possibilities."

"Does Bargo have a cat in your time?"

"Bargo is a company, not a person."

Part of her knew that this was more than just a dream; here she was, conversing with this beautiful boy, who had just said that one day they would-be lying-in bed next to each other as man and wife. It was a thrill. She didn't want it to end.

"Fay could kill me, Van. It's as simple as that. If the Gold Lord takes her and she comes to my world, then it is doomed. The Pires have terrorised the world for seven ages. We have all but wiped them out many times, but Gustav returns from his grave every time, ready to come and get me. I am meant to defeat him one day. Do you know who he is? Gustav?"

"There is no one called Gustav on this ship."

"He may have another name. You need to keep your eyes and ears peeled. He may not even be Gustav yet. The Skyfliers do not recall when he changed."

"Wait. Flynn, there is an Angus Tavenor. He is the teacher on the ship. He has been teaching the little ones for three or four years. Fay used to help him out with the reading lessons, but now she's too busy training in military combat with the security forces. So, I do it."

Flynn went pale. "That would make sense. You have been known as Vanvear for thousands of years. Vanessa Avery. It's a derivation."

"I have been alive for thousands of years? Will be alive? I am confused. I suppose dreams are confusing, though."

The boy called Flynn smiled. "You are a powerful sorcerer. One of the Chosen."

"The Chosen is what we call the survivors of Earth. We are the people upon the Skyflier."

"We call the magic users of our world - the Chosen. Once they are called to their magic."

It was all too much for Van to take in. He took hold of her hands; leaning forward, she could smell him. A masculine, musky scent, intoxicating.

"I may have to kill your sister."

"No."

"I love Fay as much as you, but she will be responsible for the deaths of millions over thousands of years. She may bring forth the Gold Lord."

"She wouldn't do that."

"She will become the greatest of Gustav's queens."

"Angus is gay, he had a husband."

"It's a figure of speech."

She felt stupid then and pulled her hands away. She was so very tired.

"Van, you are fading. You are falling into a deep sleep. I am using so much power doing this. I may have to come for Fay. If I do, I am sorry. I don't want to kill her, but it might be the only way."

Van yawned.

"What threat could my fifteen-year-old sister be to your world? She wouldn't harm any of you and neither would I. We...

Van fell asleep.

ADAM

"Dear Chosen. The time has come." He played the little fanfare soundbite through the comm.

"I am glad to be announcing that we are about to punch right into the pocket universe. I'll save the science for Bargo to explain, but you really shouldn't feel a thing. Adam Hurst out."

Adam dropped the comms unit and sat down heavily. Bartholomew looked over at him and smiled.

"It really will be okay."

"Have you ever done this before?"

"No."

Van walked over to Adam and put her arm through his. Seven years after their departure and she was a beautiful young woman now. From the other side of the bridge, Fay glowered- a permanent fixture of the security detail, Bartholomew's personal guard.

Adam had grown to look on them both like his nieces, treated them as such. Van had called him Uncle Adam for a few years now and it felt right. He had started to read passages from Earth's holy books to them; he had discovered he could hold an audience in the palm of his hand, whether he was reading from a holy book or one from Terry Brook's Shannara series. Dafydd called him the priest- and it had stuck. The name didn't sit right with Adam at first, but then he had warmed to it. He had started to compose sermons. Postman-turned-priest in seven years. Now he would be finding out what was on the other side of the bubble, he was nervous- for himself and for them all. His flock.

Dafydd now led the security team on the Skyflier, while still supporting the girls as a father figure. Adam had caught up with Dafydd earlier about the stasis notices, but the Welshman was distracted, nervous about what might happen to them all after the punch.

"Dear Chosen," Bartholomew began. "We start a new chapter. As you know, we have identified the planet in the bubble universe that can sustain us, thanks to advance research by Andrew, Arthur, and Lucy Poke. Anna Percival has already gone through with the vanguard and waits for us there as our anchor, our beacon."

Adam watched Bartholomew pause for breath. You didn't build a company if you were an introvert and he really was a good orator. Adam had the utmost respect for him; he always said he wasn't a leader, but a guide, repeatedly insisting to Adam and Dafydd that they would be the leaders when they reached Nova-Gaia, the name they had all decided to give the planet. An ancient name for their old planet, whatever dimension they came from.

"The punch will not be without its risks. You all know that; we have never kept it a secret. Many of our number have gone into stasis; the booths will support them through the intermediate journey through the dimensional rift. This is not like another parallel Earth, this is another universe entirely. A younger universe and Gaia sits at the far reaches of it, one of the first planets to be born in the bubble.

"Gaia is still billions of years old and we know that there were once life forms upon its surface- very advanced beings, albeit now extinct for millions of years. Gaia has many similarities with Earth, give or take a few degrees of axial tilt: its two moons, much smaller than ours, impact upon it in a similar way. We have calculated our landing point geographically once we have punched through and reached the planet's upper atmosphere. We will advise as soon as we have entered orbit.

"What we do not know is how long it will take us to get through the barrier into the bubble universe. Our theoretical physicists do not concur. It could be instantaneous, or it could take years. If it is the latter, then we will all enter stasis. So, make yourself safe. Listen carefully to my messages from now on- and have a safe journey."

Bartholomew sighed as Adam cut the link. Van smiled at him and at Bartholomew. Even Fay had a brief smile upon her lips.

"Engineer. Please ready us for the punch. Can we all take our seats for further briefings from the medical officers?"

The door to the bridge opened and Angus entered. Whilst it was not unprecedented for the teacher to visit the bridge, it was uncommon, especially at such a pivotal moment.

"Mr Tavenor, you should be safely strapped into your bunk."

Angus did not look well. Adam sensed some movement out of the corner of his eye. It was Fay. He realised with shock that she had pulled her thought sword.

"Pire," she spat.

Adam looked at his friend in fear. Not Gus, not after all this time, not now. How many more of them had he infected in the last seven years? They thought they were free from the disease of the Pires and now, if they did not deal with it, it would follow them to Gaia. They would doom another world.

There was a glow about Angus, golden, like the corona of a sun. He wheeled round towards Adam and launched himself at him. Adam pushed Van out of the way as Gus approached.

Fay leapt into action, propelling herself towards Gus, but as she sprang forward, blade drawn, Gus reached out and took Adam's neck in one exceptionally strong hand. Gus had been the gentle teacher, a wise and helpful soul. How had he hidden the Whampyri virus for the seven years of their journey?

As Gus' fingers tightened, Adam heard a voice fill his head.

"At long last. My new body. Hello Adam, my name is Humphrey Mortimer and I am the Gold Lord."

Then, all hell broke loose.

FAY

Fay didn't hesitate to scythe the teacher down. He was a Pire. Van screamed "no", but Fay put that to the back of her mind. She had a job to do. First, she needed to wipe the creature out, then they needed to check everyone for the virus.

As Angus fell to the ground with a guttural squeal, Adam put up a hand and a bolt of bright light shot from his palm, narrowly missing Fay, enveloping Gus.

"What the fuck? Adam?"

That was when a hole opened on the bridge and the tall handsome boy appeared.

VANESSA

It was Aeflynn. Flynn, from her dreams. He looked over at her and such a warm smile crashed across his face, replacing the anger that had been there moments before.

"Bargo. My name is Flynn. I am from the far future. You are moving though the barrier between universes and this was the most opportune time for me to intervene. The timelines are wrong upon my world. The Gold Lord should never have come here. Neither should the Whampyri. I am here to destroy them."

Adam turned to the boy and laughed. Angus growled.

"Gustav. You were one of our greatest forbears. The Teacher. You do not bring evil to Gaia. Not in the real timelines." Flynn shot out a bar of energy towards Angus and it hit him squarely in the torso.

Van watched on as Angus changed. She seemed to shift to somewhere else. She could see things. Lines of power, cords, between people. Some healthy looking, some dark and diseased. A dark cord wrapped around the teacher- linked to his heart. She looked at the others on the bridge. All free of the diseased cords.

He is the Gold Lord. A great evil. In one timeline he came to New Gaia and wreaked evil upon this world. Stopped it from developing as it should.

"Who are you? Why do the others look like ghosts?"

I am taking advantage of the power that is flowing through Flynn. I am Vanvear. I am what you will become in the future. In my timeline, the disease of these two creatures came through. The Gold Lord has killed Flynn in other versions of our world and we cannot have that. Flynn is the Saviour. He will bring us back to Earth One. He must live.

"How far in the future are you?"

Vanessa, it seems you will live until the end of time.

That's nonsense, she thought.

You will have time later, between the third and fourth age, to contemplate that. For now, we need to act. When I bring you back to the present, the Gold Lord will have jumped to your sister. You need to send my power at her and don't stop. Are you ready?

Well, it wasn't the most crazy thing she had heard or done in her life.

"I suppose so."

Okay. Now.

Van was back in the room. The power was flowing from the boy called Flynn to what used to be Angus, but looked like a Pire now, screaming, all fangs and claws.

Adam had fallen and was unconscious.

Quickly. Vanvear urged in the back of her mind. Her future self, for God's sake.

Vanessa felt the power growing in her; she pointed it at her sister, who looked across and laughed.

"I am the Gold Lord. You cannot defeat me. My power is as old as time itself."

"And so is ours." Flynn shouted. "Now. Van, Bargo!"

And she unleashed the power that was in her, the power her future self would unleash time and again in defence of New Gaia and its people. The power hit her sister, and she knew that if this worked Fay would be safe. *No, Van.* Her sister screamed. It was awful.

Power shot from Bargo and then Flynn, as he redirected his power away from the teacher, who had moments before been a Pire. Angus lay upon the floor- human again.

Our husband has cured him. The curse ends. No one else on the ship is infected. Now to Fay. We must cure our sister. I do not want to kill her again.

"Gold Lord, you are hereby banished to the place between universes. May you rot for all the horror you have brought to our worlds."

There was a guttural, yearning scream from her sister. It was wrenching at her heart. *Stay strong young one.* A gasp of "mother," came from Fay's lips, then her voice deepened and she fell to the floor.

The power was pulled towards Flynn and out through the coruscating hole that wobbled behind him.

The power faded from the three of them. Flynn blew Van a kiss and bowed to Bargo, then he stepped through another hole that winked out of existence, seconds after the other that had consumed the Gold Lord closed.

PART FOUR: SHE *IS* THE HERO

PETAL THE ASSASSIN

Petal the Assassin was enjoying being in her new body. The rejuvenation process had worked and for the first time in years she felt fit and healthy again.

The constant in-the-field guerrilla operations she had carried out, the hand-to-hand combat and the use of weapons at close quarters had taken its toll. So, with a heavy heart, she had decided to change her body.

It had been a costly process. Her paymasters had bound her to another contract that would see her killing hundreds more in payment - not that she had expected otherwise and not that she cared.

Petal lived for one thing and one thing only: the thrill of the kill. She needed the optimum body- a new, youthful form, lean and fit, so she could carry out her orders to the best of her ability. Petal had always wanted, from an early age, to be the best.

Sarah-Jane adjusted her belt a little. Her suit could do with the attention of a proper tailor to re-size it, but it was not surprising it was loose- it had been made with another physical shape in mind. The weight she had lost recently, for her new role, had meant her wardrobe needed a few tweaks throughout.

She put on her overcoat in the darkness of the alley, as the rain pattered noisily and removed her glasses. They were no longer any use to her.

Sarah-Jane's car was parked around the corner, down an alley and she quickly moved toward it, trying to dodge an inevitable soaking from the incessant rain. "Falling from heaven like the tears of a million bereaved mothers". That had been a good line from what she'd been reading earlier.

Sarah did not want to be recognised. If she were seen in this location, at this time of night they– the press - would put two and two together. They would probably know who she had become.

She bleeped the boot on approach; it lifted and she stowed her bag carefully. Once in the car, she slipped the key card into the slot, pressed the button, and listened as it growled to life. The wipers sprang on automatically having detected the rain, the AI sensor well-ahead of human reaction. The swish-swash wiping motion sang the slow, reassuring rhythm that would guide her way home. She said "music" but then "stop"; she didn't want to be too wired when she got back, but still awake enough to celebrate. She had another early start again tomorrow, the second day of her new, important job.

The first kill in Petal's new body had been a doctor, one Jessop Winthorpe, a scientist, who had been carrying out research into particularly nasty forms of a biological agent the government were planning to use against further targets in the Middle East. Thousands had died in the attacks so far, including many young children and if Petal was going to enjoy any part of her job, it was the killing of those who hurt innocents.   Petal had her code. Yes, she would kill anyone if commanded, but not without sound reason. On more than one occasion, she had been offered a generous payment for a random killing but had refused on ethical grounds.

The motorway was stop-start. So annoying; if Sarah didn't get there soon, her plan would not work out. She needed to get to the children first, she couldn't let their father see her. It would be all over then and her stealth would be in vain. Pondering the length of the queues and the bad weather, she pulled into the superstore and parked up. She had about an hour to get there; the journey was about fifteen miles. She would be able to go and get what she wanted and still make it on time.

Petal needed a new knife. The superstore had an outward-bound section that sold survival knives. Something heavy-duty and durable-a stiletto would not be strong enough and a bowie knife would be too large. A very sharp cooking knife might suffice, but the handles were usually plastic and therefore difficult to grip, if one's hand was slick with blood. She spoke with the department assistant and showed him her licence for carrying a knife. It was, after all, part of her cover. By day, Petal worked freelance for the Forestry Service; by night, she killed unsavoury and unethical people, making the world a safer place- or at least her part of the world.

She stored her new addition, a wooden-handled hunting knife, in the boot of her car and drove away. The rain had slowed, thankfully, but she was still a little early for her plan to work outright, so she pulled over and ate a sandwich and a packet of crisps she had purchased as she left the store. It was then her phone rang with the tones of ACDC's Highway to Hell. Petal's signature tune.

"Hi," the voice said over the hands-free, "I need you to carry out another quick job for me."

Petal sighed. "Tonight? Haven't I done enough for you today already? I've got somewhere else to be too, remember!"

"An associate of the good doctor you assassinated earlier. She's in on the financial management of the biological research organisation. In fact, she's the DOF, Director of Finance. Only appointed today."

"Control, I am not stupid. I know what a DOF is."

"If you get to her quickly, you can intercept her before she gets home. She has two young kids, both girls - not that it matters - her husband looks after them all day. If you get to her in time, you can deal with her before she gets home. If not, you are going to have to kill her in the house."

"That's risky and I'm not killing the husband and kids."

"You need to intercept her then, Petal. I've sent the coordinates to your sat nav. Catch up with her, deal with her. You get a hundred thousand in bonuses."

"Hundred grand? You must really want her dead."

"If you knew their full plans, you wouldn't hesitate."

"Try me."

"Above your paygrade. Control out."

Sarah-Jane was getting nowhere. The traffic was ridiculous- she was not going to get back until the girls were in bed. Dave would be spitting again. How many times this week had she missed reading the bedtime story as she had prepped for her new job in secret? She looked in the mirror. Had that car been behind her all the way from work? Sixty odd miles. Surely not? She was always spooking herself with the things she had to read recently. She *wasn't* being followed.

She couldn't change her route, could she? "Rose, give me an alternative route." What a thrill, she thought, sarcastically. A creature of habit, she followed the same way home every day. Dave said it was part of her nature.

Suddenly the phone rang and it made her jump.

"Hi, Dave." She said. "You okay?"

"You going to be long, love? I've ordered a Chinese."

"Hopefully not too much longer. The traffic's really bad. Must be this weather."

"You will be back to read the girls their story and... you know...?" There it was- the undertone. She couldn't fail today, of all days.

"Sure-thing, baby. Got to go. Police driving past."

She clicked the end call button on her steering wheel. Damn. Must be an accident up ahead.

Petal had pushed the lorry off the road. Her car was still driveable but probably a write off; Control could pay for that. The lorry had hit the embankment and had toppled over, blocking a lane. That had then enabled her to reroute and get behind her next victim, who sat in the traffic right in front of her now. Blocking one lane would slow the DOF's route home. Like all accountants, this woman was a creature of habit. Same route, every day.

The traffic eventually made its way through the diversion and Petal trailed her target through the streets again. They were probably four miles or so from her destination. She noticed the woman's car was very well driven; hopefully, she *was* just a DOF and nothing else more difficult to kill, like a special forces agent, or a special branch police officer. It would be just Petal's luck. She remembered that woman who'd looked like a skinny college girl, but had been a Russian agent. The bitch had broken Petal's left wrist- her leading hand- while she attempted to garrotte her, holding her down with her knees. She'd had to get one end of the garrotte in her teeth. She had killed Christina Mikhailovich in the end, but at a cost – her radius, two teeth and a good few nails.

Finally, Sarah made it home. She parked the car and grabbed her bag from the boot. As she beeped the car fob, she decided she wasn't going to go in the front way. She was late, but the girls would be still up waiting for her. She needed to enlist their help in surprising their daddy. It was his birthday after all- and what a surprise she had. She had kept the secret about her new job for so long, waiting for this moment. She hoped he'd be pleased. Although he hadn't wanted to her to go back into the industry, now their financial security would be assured.

Petal, out front, noticed to her annoyance that her soon-to-be victim had moved around the back. She had hoped to take her on the approach to the house. The job was starting to get complicated. She checked her weapon. The new knife would make enough of a mess of this woman to ensure any other people linked to work on biological agents would reconsider their employment. Climbing the fence, she scaled the downpipe.

Sarah-Jane was lucky they could afford their big house. Her most recent jobs had been lucrative, if less secure than her new one. The team around her had mostly been welcoming, considering she was in the lead role and so many of them had to defer to her, the new girl. No- one had been rude or unfriendly, which was fabulous.

Sarah-Jane thought back to all those damn jobs and assignments she had carried out as a new graduate. She had been unemployed for a time unemployed and it had worried Dave, but now she had landed on her feet. Dave couldn't work because of his arthritis, so she was the clear breadwinner.

Quietly opening the door to the back stairs, she headed up to surprise the birthday boy, clutching his presents in her arms.

Petal put her finger to her lips. She had taped the two girls mouths up, but they were still making the devil's own noise. She threatened to kill them and they quietened a bit. She wouldn't kill children of course, even as part of a clear up, but she would threaten all sorts of terrors and hells to shush them. She heard a noise at the bottom of the stairs and settled into position again, a tiger ready to pounce.

David heard two cars pull up, but then nothing. Where was his wife? The girls were meant to be in bed waiting for her, but they were making a hell of a noise. He began to make his way up the stairs.

Damn. Petal did not want to have to kill the girls' father, but she would if she needed to. Orphaning the girls would go against her code somewhat, but needs must. She had locked the children in the bathroom and waited. If it was their mum, then she could do her duty and get out quickly. She could hear footsteps on the stairs; this house had two sets, one of them linked to the granny flat across the hall.

Had Sarah-Jane made too much noise?

Would Dave get upstairs before her and ruin the surprise? She couldn't hear the girls- normally they would be playing on the PlayStation 8, or watching YouTube, or fighting. She grasped the handle of the door to the girls' room. She had texted her eldest, Nadine, to say she was coming and to be ready. She opened the door- no sign of the girls. If they had followed her instructions, they'd be hiding in their wardrobe. In she went.

Dave turned the handle of the girls' room and went inside.

Petal waited inside the girls' bedroom, knife raised, like a big cat poised for the kill. With a faint creaking noise, the door opened and as soon as she saw who it was, she pounced. The thrill of the kill.

"Cut!" came the shout from behind her.

"Well done, Sarah-J. That's in the can."

"Surprise, Daddy!"

The girls and Sarah-Jane shouted at the top of their voices as she flicked on the light switch. She had put her new mask on and was in the full outfit. Dave's face it was a picture.

"Guess who I am?" Sarah-Jane whipped the mask off and Nadine and Ella screamed with excitement.

"You are the new Petal. The new Assassin?"

"Now, girls," she said. They all shouted Petal's catchphrase. "The thrill of the kill."

Dave grabbed her and gave her a big kiss.

"Happy Birthday, lovely. Sorry I kept this a secret. I had to sign a publicity agreement. I've got a press conference early in the morning at the BBC. I have brought my first script home for you, babe; we've all signed it. "The Case of The Biological Engine". It'll be out this time next year. The director knows you've been a fan for years and has said you can come to see it being filmed soon."

"Oh, you beauty!" Dave cried and hugged her, his wife Sarah-Jane, and for at least three seasons, the shape changing Petal - the Assassin.

TRANSLATION

"Luntargh, this is Howellas."

Vane Howellas was sick of shouting over the noise. He didn't feel at all well and wiped his brow with one battle-dirty forearm, his com grasped in the other, gun slung across his back.

The noise of conflict from years of civil unrest made his ears ring, the burning smell of plasma blasts and human filth tinged the air and made him choke. Listening and speaking in this godsforsaken atmosphere would be difficult.

"I have news of Parl, he's on Vest's private platform, but I think his wife is still on the Presidential Barge. Any sign of Parl's Feds?"

Aben Luntargh, sitting in security control halfway across the planet, shrouded in the comfort of an anonymous environment, depressed the *talk* button. The re-route buffers hid his precise location from the planets NET. He coughed; his stomach cramps were getting worse.

"No, H. I'm keeping an eye on him for Control. His God-forsaken brother has just been taken out, a stem bomb malfunction. We got him on the Equator Platform just as he was about to execute thousands in the Sun district and we've locked the whole area down. The Intel suggests Parl's other cronies released a contagion in the Eastern District an hour ago. There's nothing left but a shit load of problems; there were twenty thousand civilians scooped up as a precaution. Even with a buffer seal and viral distillation, many will not re-transport- they will have to be reported as dead- and Vethos was included in those figures.

"Shit." Luntargh ran one large, calloused hand through his hair. The deputy leader of the rebellion dead, too?

"It could kill billions, Lun. Data suggests the contagion must be pandemic, an ancient retro-analysed colony origin disease, perhaps. But it's been changed, re-engineered, and has a near-one hundred percent hit rate. Most of the twenty thousand would have been dead in minutes. Not sure there is anywhere safe enough to send them to. Global Health has allegedly introduced a vaccination into the air on Parl's orders, but it's not working. Evidence suggests the disease was stolen from government labs. It's a set up."

"We have similar Intel. H, we've had further outbreak reports from your area. It's spreading. Get out while you can."

"I will, but not before I've found the girls. Dear Gods. When this started, I didn't expect our families would die."

There was no response, other than a pause- then a scream.

Elli Sampson stepped into the survey ship's translation booth and set the familiar program controls. As the translation engine began its hum, she adjusted her suit. It wouldn't be good if it failed. She double checked again.

Please be ready for your translation, attach your helmet and breathing apparatus now.

"Thanks," at least her semi-sentient suit was calm,.

Elli was looking forward with trepidation to another angst-ridden day, watching the hours of data visualisation the translation engine had for her. Her specialism was finding information relating to ancient or lost civilizations, or their long-lost traces. Her recent data-digging involved researching the end of Praxian society and the retrieval of lost or untranslated event data. To piece together her paper's narrative, she needed to re-live the death of a civilisation. Her thesis was currently entitled *The Fall of the Golden World*. What a fall it had been.

Her methodology- one she had spent many months postulating based on early evidence retrieved from Praxia- was to prove or disprove the various theories that had rattled the halls of the great history houses of Oxford Major and the Vellums of Gha.

Her theory was that Praxian citizens managed to survive the great switch off, the failure of the solar lamps. She was convinced they escaped to the stars as their sun failed. There was more to her argument, however. It involved the sad, but inevitable, discovery of untranslated souls in ancient transporter buffers. They were trying to transport somewhere.

Debate had raged for centuries concerning the souls who were trapped galaxy-wide in translation systems. Ethically, there was an argument to leave the stored beings be. Thousands of years in a transportation buffer was quite dead, some said. An alternative-and mostly religious- ethical view was that these were souls in need of rescue.

A chance encounter with Edene Mar, a friend of her History professor, Christopher Dyer, had led her to Praxia. Dyer had introduced her to Edene, the leading data archaeologist this side of the Long Galaxy, at an end of year awards ceremony. Professor Mar was looking for data that could enrich Oxford Major in the Arch Principal Battle for Truth, primarily to get one over the Reading Warriors of Gha. They were all looking for creator truths: proof of the existence of their god, goddess, gods, or ancestors. Edene was leading the vanguard and making a tidy sum doing so. *Depending upon the value it held for the buyer, of course.* They had remained incognito, however.

Edene had hired Elli as a research student following that one conversation. They had talked about her thesis work, which had focused on the emerging field of immersive history. Immersive history was the recreation of actual events, from the ghost data left behind in a quantum state, by civilizations who had advanced to level 5 or beyond. The data essentially stored in memoriam as a series of zeros and ones, could be read with the right technology, even though the servers or computers that once housed them had turned to dust. All worlds at this stage of development generally used some form of quantum data storage, whether that be for the secure collation of library back-ups, or the information that allowed translation engines to break a person down into a digital signal and reconstitute them at another place.

Edene had suggested Praxia as a place for Elli to hone her research skills, as it had been relatively unstudied. The ancient Praxian data buffers, according to quantum data projection tools, had information dating back to the fall of the Praxian system over two hundred thousand years before. It was all in ghost quantum data stacks.

Her job was to translate the information and try to save those lost souls who had been effectively imprisoned for two thousand centuries, trapped as data.

Section Leader Edsil Lough picked up the buzzing com-set and put it to his ear. It was his Field Commander, Jessuck Tathe. A gnarled old campaigner.

"Have you got the signals analysed? Can we get the plague out of the victims by doing a transportation purge?"

"It's feasible; it's just there's no time. I've got Government forces at my door. We are being battered out here. I think we might lose this stack. The best I can do is cue the data to come online when the main system is up and running. If government forces get here, they will pull the switch and everyone including the transporter engineering teams will die. Myself included."

"I wish we had got Parl out of the game before now. He'll kill millions of common folk. Only the elite will survive. My kids were at school in the plague zone. I'd sure as hell like to see them again. You get that don't you? I understand the sacrifice you will have to make, but ensure as many of you as possible transport into the buffers at the back of the queue. When this is all over, I will make sure you get out."

The hum of the translation machine reached a crescendo and Elli felt a momentary wave of peace as her body was reduced to data, then shot through time-space in an atom-sized stream through a pre-determined pin wormhole.

Simultaneously, she stepped out of the translation booth platform onto the surface of Praxia 3, at the entrance to the ancient stone ruins. The ruins were a set of old underground buildings that afforded her all the shelter and protection she and her equipment needed, as she set about proving her hypothesis in situ.

She surveyed her surroundings, as instructed by the safety manual, to avoid any disorientation following translation. The 360-degree view showed a battered, rusty-green terrain. The land had been parched by the bombardment of solar radiation that had sloughed off the remaining thin atmosphere, long after most of it had escaped to the void, as the sun shrank towards infinity.

She looked up at the red dwarf; the sun, as always, looked back like a sad, waning storm-candle in a soot-coated casing. Often, she was mesmerised, caught like an insect in amber, soaking up that weak, orange-tinged light. You could never look directly at a young sun, but there was something beautiful, albeit sad, about looking at a waning one; an ancient matriarch seen through the eyes of one of her dead children.

There was nothing living as far as one could see, just the startling landscape that dwarfed the mountain ranges of her home on New Earth 3. No flora or fauna, only gigantic geological features: the pistachio green mountains rich in copper ore that reached high into the pink streaked sky, the ancient valleys, originally carved by the long dried-up river systems that riddled the planet. If you looked from orbit- and she had done so many times- the geography looked like the efforts of a child on a beach who had built sandcastle defences too far from the sea; irregular and parched, many parts breached by landslides, as the earthquakes set about the frost-dried land.

Apart from the ghosts of its civilization stored in its stacks, Praxia did not exist. She needed to restore its legacy. And the more she recalled the vignettes that she had witnessed on the visualizer day after day, the more determined she became.

Jevis screamed as a blast just missed his head. He jumped over the wall and sped towards the trees at the back of the estate. His father was dead, shot minutes ago in front of him. Janta Preel had gone to work as usual that morning and had come home to tell his son how much things would get better- and real soon.

Jevis's mother had died in a traffic accident the previous year and since then, Jevis had returned home from school and waited patiently for the three hours until his father's return. Jevis would be lost without him. They were more than father and son; they were best friends. No longer. His father a rebel? An anti-government spy? He had allegedly stolen a thought-blade and would not give it up, even though he knew they would shoot him. Why would he risk his life for such stupid politics? Like his mother, Jevis could not bear the fractionalisation of society. Yes, the World President was a stupid, wig-wearing, gold make-up adorned fool. Yet, he was finding a way they could get off the planet, wasn't he? How could his father have jeopardised that for his own selfish gain? He spat. His life was likely at risk. When the President purged, he purged good. If he could get to the woods, he could find the old sewer drains and escape.

Jevis was eighteen cycles old. Another two and he would be a man. He never imagined he would be entering manhood without his parents. In fact, he would never enter manhood. The arc bolt hit him between the shoulders on the scrubland before he had reached the first tree. He felt the hum of a death transporter and knew he would become data streams, left to rot in a virtual computerised prison. The fate of traitors and their families on Praxia was a place in the Eternity Prison.

Elli's makeshift work area was just how she liked things: sparsely furnished with a desk and comfortable chair, lit with minimal bio-luminous cells. The large square of the data machine and the portable translator engine hummed quietly to her left, a constant calming dirge behind the loud music she played to keep away the loneliness. Too reminiscent of the Eternity Prison she had heard a lot about in recent info-dumps.

She sat down, took her data pad out of its protective case, opened to the virtual pages of her most relevant notes, and began reviewing the story of the end of Praxian civilisation. She was currently looking at incidents leading up to and including the civil wars that had hampered the Praxian world government, in its attempts to evacuate the planet.

There was a ping and she noticed another set of data had translated into an event clip by the wonderful prediction and event resolution algorithms. Should she watch them now? They would be harrowing- but no time like the present. She switched on her suit's immersive phones and watched, like a powerless goddess, as the heady and violent events unfolded.

Peatrim Fus holstered his gun. As Presidential guard, he had had truly little to do in his forty-year career, but now he was protecting the little gaggle of children that belonged to the President and his wife with ice in his blood.

The President might be a bastard, but he was a good employer. His family had wanted for nought. Peatrim had realised, even before the President's wife Jella had spat her final order at him, that his family's lives depended upon his ability to them off the ship. The ship that was heading for the planet, with one of its engines fucked.

As he replaced his gun, the first tears flowed. His family would be killed for this. Can Yoleh, the bitch wife of the rebel leader, stood before him with a thought blade fizzing in the air. The children were petrified. Their mother would be distraught.

Then he realised who was next to Yoleh, bound and broken: the President's wife herself.

"Your honoured service is over, Fus. There will be no need for a Presidential guard after this afternoon."

She raised her gun and he knew it was futile. Maybe his children would survive if the President and his wife did not. There were still presidential cronies littered about, however.

His last thought as Yoleh shot him was of his three daughters, Canna, Jebin and Lei, chasing their speelsnape in the gardens of their home.

She gasped and shut down the suit's headphones, tears welling in her eyes. She allowed them to sting for a while, a small sufferance compared to those billions that had died in horror. Despite the somewhat erratic syntax of the translation caused by her language algorithms, the overall meanings were loud and clear, the visuals self-evident. Some of the secondary historical accounts she had read recently suggested there had been wide-spread political unrest on Praxia 3 during its last years. Proof of civil war was more than she could have wished for, however harrowing. The clips she had experienced certainly backed this up.

She had a drink and calmed herself, but she had to make the most of her time, so she continued to pull in data. The clips that started to come through were littered with accounts of terrorist activity, including a major attack on the Eastern district that government opposition thought they had contained.

The Praxian government's attempts at constructing the massive solar Satellite lamps in the atmosphere had kept the planet warm for a time, upwards of a hundred and twenty years before Parl's assassination. Unfortunately, they had exhaustively mined the planet and its near dead relatives during that time. You couldn't heat a planet cheaply. They had also been battling rising sea levels for thousands of years; the solar lamps had been slowly drying Praxia out as a result. The after-effects of centuries of mining had caused tectonic activity to increase ten-fold.

With sub-light expeditions bringing back no news of alternative Praxianoid-supporting planets, building the long-distance arks was a race against time. Or possibly just pissing in the wind. Working late into the dark, pistachio evening, Elli started to data mine a search about the arks themselves. She found a translation buffer store associated with the early project developing the massive colony ships, which were also meant to hold the feared Eternity Prison, but there was no quantum data within. Moreover, it appeared that only one fully functioning ark had been produced in the end. A set of minutes she had come across from the Stratoconstruct board meetings suggested that the money from the government's allies had dried up.

Shortly after she had finished her lunch, there was a ping, suggesting another data thread or factual reconstruction was ready. This one was also fit enough to be visualised, including real-time image recordings and the feelings and thoughts of those recorded. The summary suggested this was the assassination event that ended the war. She had read about it in documents and had set the data miner off the day before with hashtags and reference keys to collect as much as it could.

Moudrim Vest glanced with undisguised contempt at the man opposite him. Smelling of the smoke of battle, the World President had arrived earlier that day to try and impress on him how he and his family should have the best cabins and stasis arrangements on the first ark on its journey off-world. A cowardly and self-indulgent action from a leader with only self-interest at heart.

Parl stood just over five feet, dressed in gold, the gold make-up plastered over his blue skin matching his golden hair. Revive treatments and political machinations had meant he had been President for nearly one hundred years. A century of tyranny.

Vest, the CEO of Stratoconstruct nervously brushed back his prematurely blue-white hair. He was elegantly dressed in sombre colours, as befitted his station. He and his organisation had planned for the end of the world. They had delivered a means of escape. The president was here, as usual, to commandeer his ideas and take the glory.

What Parl did not realise was that the well-placed ark-ship-producing Stratoconstruct Board had rebelled secretly against their President and had made an alliance with the coup. The continued purges of government officials, so called sexual deviants, artists and learned people at the hands of Parl's wicked sons, had led to widespread hatred and fear.

In response, the rebels had ingratiated a security officer into the inner circle of the President. The officer had become the President's only real friend. But Spev Burty would also be his President's end.

Spev stood next to Parl, no emotion on his stoic face. He was a mountain of a man, a handsome but strategically shaved gruntle-bear. Vest knew that Spev would be sacrificing his life, as he would be too, if the President was fitted with anti-assassination devices, as was rumoured, hence the carefully chosen nature of the assassination. Just that morning, the rebels had killed Parl's eldest son; the brain stem bomb taking out half a district. You needed to take the head off just below the chin, but above the brain stem device, then cap with a suppressor. Spev had been through his plan with Vest across a secret communication link and had practised his timings.

"Security to Mr Vest. Sorry to disturb you and the Honourable President, but we have a security breach."

Honourable, how ironic. For the time-being, Vest would act the dutiful subject of the Head of State. No giving it away- not until the final set of dice were rolled.

"Sir, may I respond?"

Parl inclined his head. He acted more like an ancient emperor than a democratically elected president.

"Report." Spev ordered, playing his duplicitous role with aplomb.

"Dupree's rebels are on board the Barge. They took the President's wife and children on deck and shot them. There's been a video cast. It seems Dupree is heading this way. The Presidential barge has been compromised and is spiralling toward the planet."

Vest looked at the slimy gold man who was beginning to realise his Presidency was coming to an end. The surprise on the face of a dictator knowing his crimes were coming back to haunt him were not lost on Vest. As ever though, despite word of his wife and children's alleged murders, Parl was thinking about himself.

"Contact my Barge staff, I need safe passage." Parl screeched. "Spev? Find out if the bastards have actually killed her."

"Your honour, comms has been deactivated- trying to re-establish a signal." Spev went through the motion of contacting the barge through his wrist-patch.

There were sounds of screaming and the broadcast abruptly cut off.

"Get it back online." Parl knew the sound of a deliberately cut signal.

"I don't think so, Mr President. It seems the Barge has exploded." Spev looked at Vest, trying to keep the lie from telling on his face. Spev was good, Vest would give him that.

Parl was better at interpreting situations though; he reached for his blaster. Spev shot a look at Vest, who nodded.

Spev reached over his shoulder and pulled the biggest thought-blade Parl had ever seen. In one sweep, Spev took the President's head off, splattering them both in a fine, bloody mist before Parl could even raise his gun. Spev grabbed the body before it fell to the floor and capped it with a blocking device he had pulled from his pocket.

Vest exhaled suddenly holding his breath for so long, then noticed a pain shooting through his left foot. Decapitated heads were heavy.

Elli was sitting in her quarters, watching the data spew from the engine. The visualizer events she had watched in the last week had showed the end to the World Presidency. More and more breakouts of engineered microbiological events had killed hundreds of millions in the towns and cities of this once wonderful planet.

Forty-seven billion had died. A sobering thought. The Elite had caused the downfall of their old world. The Gold had fallen.

Her data pad pinged again. This information was sure to be as interesting as the rest. None of the freedom fighters who had discovered the source of the microbiological attack, save Yoleh, had survived the coup- or the disease.

President Yoleh, wife and sister-in-law of the freedom fighters Dupree and Vethos, was celebrating her tenth Anniversary as the leader of the free people of a doomed Praxia. An equal curse and blessing. The coup upon the Presidential Barge, in which the first Lady of the President of the World had been killed, along with her family and despised retinue, still held legendary status. Some elitists believed they were still alive and would return. Yoleh had shot them herself, so she knew they would not. Even the little golden children. It was one of her deepest regrets, depending on how she was feeling at the time.

Yoleh still occasionally wiped away a tear at the thought of those massive losses, but even more so for the loss of her love, Dupree.

Many of her remaining citizens were in stasis or held in buffers, ready for the long journey to the nearest life-supporting planet. Only a few thousand surviving children, who would be most affected by cryo-stasis, remained whole and un-translated, as well as the civil servants needed to close-down the planet and the military, who would remain functional until the end.

"Madam President," Vest announced, knocking on her open door.

"Ah my love, welcome back." She looked up at her second husband of eight years as he bent down to kiss her. "Have you solved the data link?"

He smiled that wonderful smile. "Any transported citizens will be copied back to the Goliath, should they fail. A back-up, as it were, then we can re-translate on board and try again before we leave the system for good."

She sighed with relief. Once they began to translate the senior staff into stasis, they should not face the casualties they had with other cohorts. If they were to move onto the children, she could not bear to think one of those little ones spending eternity as a data set - never translated.

"There is one other thing. We have picked up that the planet is becoming increasingly erratic on the western quarter. There's volcanic activity in response to the strange gravity- huge tectonic movement. We hope the transporter buffers will survive. You must give the order to begin soon. I know it's early, but belt and braces, my love?"

"I'll speak to the Council of Souls; we do things democratically now."

Elli had found the data set from the ark-ship *Goliath* – well, that was the nearest translation that she could assign to it. She began an intensive data search that led her down a cold and barren Praxian path. She had travelled to the Western Continent on one of the shuttles to view a buffer stack, but it had not been sealed; there wasn't enough quantum data to process. If there were untranslated souls left in the shadows of the ghost-cloud, then they could not be reconstituted. So sad.

Although barely a mile away from her working base, the Eastern buffer was showing signs of untranslated life- lots of it.

For the next six Praxian cycles, Elli gathered and catalogued the raw data. She had found a third residual buffer and had submitted the ethical applications to her University to re-translate people; she was waiting for the response.

On an unusually, if somewhat weak, sunny day (which meant high solar ray bombardment), she sat at her desk, tying up the translation routes into orbit. A rescue ship would be waiting, filled with an experienced team of staff who would be able to deal with the Praxians as they re-translated. The support staff would consist of scientists, medics, and psychologists. They would see people into their own future with as much support as possible.

Elli was just about to submit the pathway logs, when an alarm suddenly went off on the data regulator. That wasn't good. She dashed over to see what was going on. Her flight colleague Moe's voice came over the suit link.

"Elli, we are picking up some ridiculous solar flare activity. You are going to be stranded down there for the foreseeable. Can't translate in this."

Sometimes, when the sun threw out particularly nasty solar flares, the subsequent radioactivity could affect the mechanisms. It wasn't the first time. Just meant a few more hours down on the surface.

Then the engine buzzed, and an alert sounded.

Elli. It seems the translation engine has linked with the data buffers. It is drawing translated souls to it.

She checked her data pad; the number of souls was quickly counting upwards. She checked the data again. It was connecting elsewhere. There was another buffer on the planet. A fourth? A further back-up? *Shit.* It was squirting more data into the system.

A thin high-pitched whistle, like tinnitus magnified, sounded until the noise leveller on the suit phones kicked in and amended it. It was familiar, like the re-materialisation of an incoming body whilst being reconstituted. Numbers counting down plus noise equals people about to appear.

"Urchah." The translation cut in. "Help." It was a young, thin, croaking voice. A boy of about thirteen had materialised behind her, his arms were outstretched, his face pleading. His lips were already dark blue and soon he was on his knees, retching. He was dying.

Warning, life signs in distress in your immediate vicinity.

She wanted to switch off her suit regulator and give the helmet to him, but how could she help if she could not breathe herself? The boy's face was purple now, he would not survive. Her suit pumped her adrenalin at the point she started to get teary.

She tried to move towards him, but she was held fast; some force was exerting itself upon her. A circular, glittering void opened behind her; she was only able to look back over her shoulder at it. She could not turn around- she was stuck, as if in plasticrete.

More and more people were translating in front of her, appearing out of thin air, then falling to their knees. Most were viable translations, some were abominations due to ancient virus riddled, or incomplete data- all would die. The screams were terrifying and heart-breaking in equal measure.

She looked back at the coruscation. "Moe, are you picking this up?" No response. "Moe."

As she watched in paralysis, Praxian children continued to appear and die. The image at the end of the wormhole was solidifying.

She was no tech, but she knew she must isolate the re-materialisation circuit, if there was one. "Suit, initiate pause on the translation process."

"This process cannot be reversed. Warning- three hundred and fifteen souls are dying and the number is increasing. I will struggle to prevent further materialisations."

"Can you identify the problem at this end causing the translations?"

"Affirmative. The system is picking up a retrieval signal; postulating that it may be linked to the original translations onto the ark via the opened wormhole."

"Is the time code for the other end of the wormhole consistent with the data I last viewed? Is this a past event link?" She was making it up on the spot.

"Searching. Positive. Theory. We are being pulled back in time."

"Shit."

Yoleh switched of the media link and looked at her husband. His face grew more lined each day. He carried this burden for her and their people. The Transporters were not working at all well; over one hundred thousand souls were trapped in the buffers from the original cohort of transmat engines- including their own thirteen-year-old son, Yelleth.

They had to forge ahead. Once the majority were transported, they would retrieve the buffer and take the data with them so they could rematerialize them at the other end of their journey.

What the people did not know couldn't hurt them. The needs of the many, and all that. Dear Gods, poor Yelleth. Not that he would know what was happening.

"Have we found anything out? Anything at all about the hundred thousand in the buffers?"

Vest shook his head; he was drinking lug fruit spirits and it wasn't even noon. She could not criticise- she was, too. It took the edge off.

"We should have manually entered stasis."

"That would have taken years, my love."

"But not twenty."

"That I can agree. With hindsight, I suppose we could have done some of it manually. "Twenty million people?" Flying in limited shuttles, a thousand people a day would have taken us fifty-five years. We didn't have the resources to build more shuttles. It would have limited the size of the ark. Wait twenty odd years, or let thousands die?

"Suit, the wormhole is solidifying. I am presuming I am interacting with a historical event. Patch me through to Tech Leader Hussein."

"Moe here."

"Hi Moe. I'm trapped in what looks like a link to the past. Is that possible?"

There was a pause; he was probably downloading data into his mind-ware.

"Cambridge have only managed to link wormholes back a couple of years, due to the Time Laws. Interfering in our own past etc. However, the science is there. You just re-jig the translation beam and slow the frequency so it loops slower, bigger the ark etcetera. In theory, it would be instantaneous, if it were legal. "

"I'm not going to be able to get out of it. The pull on me is tremendous. I have a vanishing point for fuck's sake. I'm being translated down a wormhole at the speed of snail. I'm not breaking the Time Laws; they are breaking me. Dear Goddess."

Focus. Deep Breath. Trying to belay her panic, she looked at the poor souls translating around her still. All of them children. She caught a massive sob. The dream of the night before was coming back to haunt her. The suit had already warned her about her blood pressure- it shot her a relaxant.

"Override safety parameters six seven three zero one. Senior Data Archaeologist override Elli Chambers. I need to translate into the past, or I'll die. Record and send."

That action is still potentially illegal, however safety parameters for threat or loss of life have been initiated.

"Elli, what the fuck are you doing?" Moe shouted, almost screamed. Oh god Elli. There is no fixed end to the wormhole, you..."

"Love you, Moe. See you la..."

She held her breath for what seemed like thousands of years.

Yoleh, readying herself for departure, was momentarily distracted from her thoughts by the noise of the safety alert system. Then, simultaneously, something appeared in front of her. A sparkling whirl of orange and blue light. An image within blurred, then solidified.

It was a very shapely humanoid woman in a very fitted suit, which covered everything but her face; a handsome, kind face, not beautiful, but attractive, light brown skin, all freckles and green eyes, the suggestion of a lock of bright orange hair.

"Suit, translate to common and vice versa." the woman said. Yoleh didn't understand her at first, then the suit spoke in Praxian common.

Translating.

"Hi, my name is Elli and I do not have much time. I am a data archaeologist from many thousands of years in your future. I have found the hidden data buffer for the one hundred thousand souls you think you have lost. Many have died being re-translated, sorry transported, in the future; more are dying. Madam, I don't have long. Maybe seconds. I can't explain the wormhole; it seems it's linked to solar flares my end. Please, start a manual transfer of the rest of your people to stasis. Something is going wrong and you will all die. Do not go ahead. Repeat. Do not go ahead."

Retrieval begun. Wormhole stability breaking up. There is no anchor in this timeline.

"How do I know this is not a trick by the elitists?" Yoleh shouted above the noise the wormhole was making.

"You don't, but I will spend the rest of my life trapped in my past for doing this. I know you need to leave the system as soon as possible. Please heed my warning. The first translation was a boy, about thirteen-years-old- he asphyxiated in front of me. Then there were other children. Hundreds of children."

"But..."

"I am being pulled in another direction. Suit. Suit respond. Stop the translations- turn the tech off until, you are sure."

Then the shapely woman called Elli in the skin-hugging suit was gone as the hole winked out.

Yoleh looked at her data screen and made the most important decision of her life in a split second.

"Security. Code one. Stop transporting. I repeat, stop transporting." She couldn't have Yelleth dying thousands of years in the future. He needed to live in his own time.

It felt like hours before Elli could see again. She couldn't believe what had happened. Was this what she had been worried about all this time? The sense of impending disaster? She had realised in a moment that she could prevent the loss of those children's lives. She had acted out of desperation. She hoped it had worked. The dream could not be allowed to come true.

She had suddenly re-appeared in the translation engine chamber. Her equipment was no longer there. She wasn't surprised, she was probably thousands of years in her past. She looked around trying to get her bearings.

"Suit. Report."

Atmosphere Earth normal plus or minus 1% oxygen levels and seven percent...

She looked out towards the steps from this ancient underground place. Was that greenery? In sunlight? Hang on, that head stone was not there before. She moved over to it, took off her helmet and mask. There was an inscription, but she could not translate it.

"Suit. Can you read it?"

This suit is currently updating. There are over forty million update events to consider. Translating. "To commemorate the deliverer, Elchamber. This monument is testament to her ascendancy and delivery of over one hundred thousand souls. All saved from the Torture of the Eternity Prison. In addition, many Children of the Lost were re-acquainted with their descended families."

Elchamber. Too familiar for her liking or coincidence.

"Suit, establish time."

From local records and the location of stars in the sky, I calculate you have re-materialised thirty-seven thousand years in your future.

"Fuck."

"And we have been waiting for you ever since, Elchamber."

A blue skinned man materialised from nowhere, possibly translated, but he had done so stealthily. He was very tall, not handsome but fit and muscular. He wore a toga of sorts, but little else.

"For thirty-seven thousand years?"

"Yoleh escaped the system with all her surviving people, even most of the children. On Praxia 4, you now happen to be more than just a saint. My name is Marl, by the way. I am an envoy from Praxia 4, our new homeworld and a direct descendant of the Saviour Yoleh, may she be blessed. You are also mentioned in the teachings of Yelleth the prophet, the first to be retranslated."

"Nice to meet you Marl. I am not going to jail, then?"

"We don't jail our gods we revere them in the Diamond Chambers."

Elli smiled for the first time that day.

"Oh, good I really need a beer. I'm parched." Then she passed out.

The End of Impossible Fruit -
Impossible Fruit Too will be available early 2023